FIGUREHEAD

PRAISE FOR *FIGUREHEAD*

"*Figurehead* is, primarily, an interrogation of womanhood through the lens of the gothic and weird, and its portrayal of femininity is closely linked to nature, wildness, and a kind of magic that's rooted in the earth ... Through beautiful, rhythmic prose *Figurehead* weaves a sequence of stories that are strange, captivating, and unforgettable."
– *Wales Arts Review*

"This truly is quality literature of our modern times."
– **The British Fantasy Society**

"Some of the stories are modern day fairy tales, with characters called Gretel knowingly wandering through, while others such as the eponymous story 'Figurehead' offer out-and-out fantasy in which the wooden figure on a ship's prow is given voice to share with us her marine adventures just as 'Little Matrons' finds Russian dolls revealing their inner secrets. There's a confident sense of logic underpinning all of this, a *believability* to such extraordinary events and happenings which is all down to the author's assured skill in harnessing a wild imagination to the dark drifts of story."
– *Nation.Cymru*

"(An) impressive first collection ... skilfully orchestrated."
– *Publisher's Weekly* "starred" review

"Glorious, confident writing."
– *Horla*

"Carly Holmes is a bewitching writer, and *Figurehead* is a book that's as full of eeriness and enchantment as one could ever wish for."
– *Buzz*

"Carly Holmes is one of the most gifted writers I've come across in recent years."
– **The Supernatural Tales Blog**

"These are liminal stories which balance on the precipice between wild and domestic, fantastical and quotidian ... This collection will be of interest to fans of the weird and wild, witches, women with dark secrets, and anyone who enjoys excellent writing."
– *Black Static*

"The stories in *Figurehead* are by turns macabre, unsettling, creepy, funny, and every one of them compelling. Carly Holmes is a writer unafraid to take risks in the personae she assumes, from bearded ladies to little girls who go into the world knickerless and proud. The roots of fairy tales sit comfortably next to ghost stories and edgy modern gothic, and within these tales, wild women speak their truths and their lies. This is a superb book by a writer to watch."
– **Katherine Stansfield**

"They're weird, ghostly, dark, and often chilling. Highly recommended."
– **Ellen Datlow**, *Best Horror of the Year Vol 11*

"These stories are extraordinary. The collection moves between settings and time periods as seamlessly as it shifts between genres. Here you'll find threads of the gothic, the uncanny, the supernatural, the ghost story, the fairy tale, and more: all spun together into a rich tapestry that defies categorization. The writing is both precise and sumptuous, the tales startling and – at times – genuinely frightening. The result is a collection of dark delights that will keep you reading, and keep you up at night."
– **Tyler Keevil**

"To read Carly Holmes is to be enchanted. Luscious, flowing prose that is never afraid to peer into the wild. Whether it's a fairy tale, a ghost story, or folk horror, the women in her stories are a force to be reckoned with; we feel their dark beating hearts. These are stories that linger, each sumptuous detail burns our fingers on the page. This is fearless writing. It never fails to cast the reader under its spell."
– **Angela Readman**

"... a mighty blend of Elizabeth Bowen, Angela Carter, Caitlín R. Kiernan, Clarice Lispector, Colin Insole, Melanie Tem, Silvina Ocampo, but essentially unique, Holmesesque, and, as I saw someone recently echo my 'ultra-powerful' word about this book, I sense it indeed has that sort of transcendent power."
– **Des Lewis**

Carly Holmes lives and writes in a small village on the banks of the river Teifi in west Wales. Her debut novel, *The Scrapbook*, was shortlisted for the International Rubery Book Award, and her prize-winning short prose has appeared in journals and anthologies such as *Ambit*, *The Ghastling*, *Shadows & Tall Trees Volume 8*, *Uncertainties* and *Black Static*.

FIGUREHEAD

Carly Holmes

Parthian, Cardigan SA43 1ED
www.parthianbooks.com
First published in 2018 by Tartarus Press
All stories © Carly Holmes, 2022
Print ISBN: 978-1-914595-05-9
Ebook ISBN: 978-1-914595-06-6
Cover Design: Syncopated Pandemonium
Typeset by Elaine Sharples
Printed by 4edge Limited
Published with the financial support of the Books Council of Wales
British Library Cataloguing in Publication Data
A cataloguing record for this book is available from the British Library.

For Kelvin
Best, and most infuriating, brother

CONTENTS

THE DEMON L

I was thirteen and a half the first time I killed a man. It was an accident and I was dreadfully sorry about it at the time. L, I was called. It was spelled with more letters than that, but L is what it sounded like.

I'd lived a childhood pretty as a picture, even if I say so myself. Of course, we didn't have a looking glass in our home so I only had the gasps of grownups and ghosted glimpses of my reflection in shop windows to go on, but both gave me more than enough reason to preen.

My mother's own looks had rotted into Hag over the years and she blamed me entirely for that. 'I was a raving beauty in my day,' she told me over and over, 'and then along you came and sucked the looks right out of me, swallowing them down with the milk that kept you alive.' The role of crone suited her though, and I could tell she liked it: the shreds of black cloth she tied to her hat and the stick she used to jab my posture back to grace or swipe at any man who tried to touch me without showing silver.

From the age of nine I earned our money and atoned for my thieving beauty by standing in the very centre of the busiest square in the town with a tray of lavender and rose petals stolen from graves and gardens. She squatted behind me, stick at the ready, keeping an eye both on my sales technique (smiles for the men, tears for the ladies) and the

1

seemingly helpless hands that de-gloved and fluttered like weary birds to rest against my face or neck. 'Stroking is extra. She's got her complexion to think about,' she'd shout at the men, rich or poor. But the women she let pat and pinch my cheeks, coo at my long ringlets, while she sniffed and ducked her head with modest pride.

The days were long, especially in the winter. The dried flowers then were scentless and shrivelled by frost, blotched with decay. My feet grew blue and numb inside my boots. But no matter the cold and the poor quality of the goods on offer there were always customers and we never went home laden with anything other than coins and an empty tray. My regulars were permitted past the sharp point of Mother's stick to allow me to fasten their daily posy to their suit, bending over me and offering their throats while their breath gasped wet and rapid against my face. I pinned the brittle folds of dead blossoms to them and shifted beneath the urgent fumble and press of their gaze. 'Lovely,' I'd tell them. 'Don't you look fine!' And I'd accept my payment and the brief clasp of their fingers against mine, smiling just enough to keep them coming back.

When I was twelve, I began to bleed from my core. My looks mutated from angel to demon overnight. Gone was the glassy ethereality of my childhood beauty: that untouched quality that in turn forbade any but the most innocent of touching. Now my flesh curved and plumped in places that drew only the men's eyes; the ladies averted theirs and stepped around me as if direct contact would contaminate. When I pinned flowers to collars the men shuddered as though condemned to the gallows for a crime they didn't commit; they muttered words like *Damnation* and *Devil's Daughter*, glaring at me with greedy desperation and lingering to stare even after they'd paid.

Glancing at me over the piles of coins she was counting at the table one evening, my mother did a double take and then nodded wisely. 'You've outgrown flowers, my girl,' she said. 'Still a little too young for the stage, but we need to find you some other occupation more suited to your looks.' She patted my hand and passed me a coin. 'Still beautiful,' she reassured me, 'but differently so now. Go and buy yourself some sweets and let me worry about the rest of it.'

The very next week I started my job as an assistant in Mr Bartholomew's Emporium of Medical Miracles. Mr Bartholomew was an Apothecary, essentially, and my role was to help him with all of the duties his large stomach and rattling chest prevented him from doing himself. I spent a lot of my days clinging to the very top of a wood-wormed ladder, fetching glass jars down from the highest shelves while he braced his bulk beneath me, peering up and wheeling me from wall to wall, calling me a good girl or a naughty girl depending on how well I'd understood his instructions. Sometimes he'd spin me round and round on my precarious perch so that my skirts flew right out and I screamed delighted terror as I held on for dear life, and then he had to sit quietly for a while afterwards, mopping at his forehead with a handkerchief.

The contents of the jars he'd shake into simmering pans and stone bowls, boiling and grinding them into potions that he sold both under and over the counter. I was fascinated by the magic contained in the little glass vials and twists of paper he gave to his customers, but he never shared his secrets or let me help him with his preparations. 'Up the ladder with you,' he'd say after I'd asked too many questions, grabbing a broom and feinting a playful rush at me. 'I need a pinch of something from the very top shelf again. Up with you, missy.' And back up the ladder I'd go.

When I wasn't fetching things down for Mr Bartholomew he'd have me sit in the padded window seat overlooking the throng of the street with a book on my lap. No matter that I couldn't read it, he told me, it improved the look of the place; let passing trade know that this was a serious establishment. And almost as soon as I sat down, arranged like a shop dummy in that wide, tall window, my legs crossed just so, the bell above the door would jangle and in they would file. Always men, and always in a shifty sideways shuffle that brought them to me rather than to the counter. I never raised my eyes from the nonsense marks that leapt across whatever page I had my book open at; I was a statue they could hover around until Mr Bartholomew, beaming, stroking his fingers through his long plush beard, called them over and sold them things that came from a double-locked cupboard by his feet and warranted the special brown paper wrapping.

Things carried on for a year in that vein and I was happy enough. Mr Bartholomew met with my mother regularly, treating her to tea and cake at a hotel and talking over my progress. My progress, from what I could see, was limited. I did exactly as I was told and had so little in the way of responsibility I couldn't imagine my absence as an assistant would be noticed a great deal. But Mr Bartholomew's sales ledgers told a different story and he was delighted to continue with the arrangement. He even raised my pay.

I had always thought that Mr Bartholomew felt a kindly,

paternal affection for me. There were times I even wondered if he were my father. So it came as quite a shock when, one afternoon, I glanced down from my ladder-top to see his head craned almost off his neck as he riveted his gaze onto the private contents beneath my skirt. I yelped my horror but he didn't move away or look abashed; if anything my awareness seemed to release him from constraint. 'Oh, you know just what you're doing, you saucy little demon,' he said and, scrambling onto the ladder, he slipped his hand right up there, where his eyes had been. Shock loosened my hold on the heavy jar I was balancing against the rung of the ladder and it plunged with mighty accuracy directly onto the crown of Mr Bartholomew's head, knocking him senseless to the floor.

In an instant I was kneeling on the carpet beside him, rubbing his hands and begging him to sit up. I was terrified that I'd be taken away and hanged for a murderess, for it was obvious to me that my employer was dead. His tongue dangled, bitten through and bloody, onto his chin, and his eyes bulged bright red as if they'd been washed with dye. One foot trembled and kicked for a moment, and then was still.

Rising to my feet, I ran to the till and emptied it of money. Mother was going to be furious with me for killing Mr Bartholomew, but I hoped that a pocketful of gold and silver would soothe the worst of her ire. Snatching up scissors from the shelf, I trod quickly back to the dead man and snipped through a fistful of his beard, raising the glistening scruff to my face briefly to breathe in the smoky, musty smell of him and then slipping it into my cloth bag. I don't know why I did this, whether the impulse served my need for a morbid memento of my crime or was more a sentimental keepsake in memory of the avuncular man who used to spin me round and round until I squealed. It felt like the natural thing to do, is all I know.

As I left the shop, palms pressed against the misted glass door, for the briefest of seconds my reflected self leaned in to meet the push of my body. It was a twisted and splintered thing, my reflection: features writhing across a face set stern and harsh with rage. We stared at each other, my demon and me, and then I pushed through her and out onto the street.

As I'd feared, my mother was beside herself with anger when I rushed home to tell her. 'What kind of devil have I spawned,' she spat, 'to go around caving men's heads in just because they wanted a touch of your fancy bits? And then to steal from them before the warmth has even left their body.'

I offered to take the money back but she was having none of that, fearing, as she said, that my returning to the scene of the crime would incriminate me further. 'No, no,' she muttered, sweeping the coins into her lap and covering them with her apron, 'best let things lie as they are. But what to do with you now? You'll have to leave and go far away, there's no other choice.'

She made me stay in the trunk while she planned an escape, only letting me out after the sun had collapsed below the horizon and sprayed its own death in pink and peach across the evening sky. 'They think it's a simple case of thieving gone bad,' she told me as she handed me a parcel of food and my coat. 'I had a word with one or two people in the know and your name hasn't been mentioned. They probably think you ran away in fright or got dragged off by the killer. Ha, little do they suspect.' She shook her head and tutted, looking me up and down as I stood before her, trembling. 'You'd best go,' she said finally. 'Here's a bit of money to help you along. It's not much, mind, but it's all I can spare.'

I turned to take one last look at the house when I reached the end of the street, but the door was already shut and my mother back inside. Through the gloom it was a struggle to even make out which house I had lived in.

Walk west, she'd told me. Keep walking to where the sun goes at night and you'll eventually get to a town much bigger than this one. You need to find Preston. Funny looking man, paints pictures of rich folk's dogs, fancies himself a dandy. Give him this note and he'll help you out. He's your daddy so he'd better.

It took many days to reach the next town, even with the occasional lift on the back of a cart. I kept the hood of my coat close around my head and a scarf wrapped across my face in case I was recognised. I worried constantly about Mother, about how she was managing without me to keep the house clean and the money stacking in the pot. I almost turned back more than once. It was only the thought of her anger at my defiance that stopped me.

Preston, my daddy, was easier to find than I'd ever hoped possible. I joined the tail of a throng winding with purpose to one of the little market squares and hung around at the edges of the bustle until I was feeling brave enough to join them. The smell of manure comforted me and I followed my nose until I found a straw-filled pen where I bought myself a cup of milk fresh and warm from the cow, sipping at the creamy-sour meal slowly while I wandered the stalls.

People gave me a wide berth, possibly fearing that I was

leprous, until I unwound my scarf and shook back my hood, unbuttoning my coat to let the spring day glance over my body. After that I was uncomfortably aware of the stares and the stumbles. I couldn't turn around for tripping over some man or other following at my heels. I was terribly scared that my demonic self had risen to the surface again, needling through the gristle and pulp of my girlish insides to tattoo herself over my skin.

After a while, sat on a low wall at the very edge of the square, hemmed in by men with sweating bodies and twitching eyes, I buried my face in my hands and called for my father, 'Preston,' I wailed, 'Painter Preston.'

A handsome man with a velvety streak of auburn whiskers framing his mouth nudged his companion and winked. He stepped forward. 'If you call out for Preston then for the love of god let me be him,' he said.

I didn't hesitate. I threw myself on his chest. 'You're my daddy, you're the artist Preston?'

He held me in his arms and juggled me from palm to palm, smiling down at me. 'Sure I'm your daddy, my darling,' he said. 'I'll be whatever you want me to be.'

It was really that easy, finding him. I picked up my bag and let him lead me from the square.

For an artist, my father seemed strangely un-artistic. There were no paintbrushes or easels in the room he rented. No dogs ran around, waiting for their likeness to be committed to paper. When I asked him about this he muttered obscurely about how times had been hard and he'd had to change career, along with his name. He was now Jake and he was a gambler, a professional card player. I was to be his assistant.

There was even less to do than when I'd worked as an assistant for Mr Bartholomew. I merely accompanied my father to the many bars and clubs he frequented and stood quietly behind him through long nights, one hand on my hip and the other on his shoulder. When he took his handkerchief out and coughed into it that was my cue to walk around the table slowly, circling the men, pausing randomly and continuing on until I was back at his shoulder. I didn't like the way the players' eyes were tugged around by the movements of my body as if I held the end of a piece of string kited to their eyeballs, but after I'd completed a circuit Daddy Preston, who I could never remember to call Jake, always won his game. He called me his lucky penny, his good luck charm.

I slept curled in a hammock above his bed, and kept our little one-room home sparkling clean: sweeping and scrubbing every day while he snored in the corner beneath a heap of blankets. There was a lean-to just outside the back door where we bathed in a tub, and a tiny garden, no more than an arm's-breadth in any direction. He sent me out there to cook meat over the fire pit when he had visitors. The gathered men ate with their fingers, sitting around a folding table and wiping grease all over my father's playing cards, while I crouched in the shadowed doorway and watched. They were so loud and rough, these visiting men, coarse both in their language and their actions. Towards the end of the evening, after the beer had been drunk and the cards thrown to the floor in despair, they sought me out and ordered me into the room. They made me swirl before them like a flamenco dancer or, worse, sit on their laps, shifting uncomfortably on top of their bony thighs. They were suddenly still and quiet at those times, holding tight to my hips and gazing dreamily into nothing as I squirmed against them. My father, flushed with drink, laughed and winked and wouldn't look at me.

No matter how I worked to jolt his memory, Jake never appeared able to evoke his love affair with my mother. He'd nod vaguely when I described the town I grew up in, our little house, and Mother's unique habits and mannerisms. 'That's her,' he'd say. 'I remember her well. Proper little beauty, she was. I'd have married her in a flash if she'd have had me.' Then he'd lose interest and change the subject, tell me to pour his bath or darn the holes in his trousers. I looked for myself in him but couldn't find a single feature that resembled my own. Grateful for his protection and anxious at the thought of its loss I never voiced my fear that he may have been bamboozled by Mother into claiming me as his when he could have been just one of many contenders to that role.

The night he wagered and lost me at cards, as casually and indifferently as if I'd been a handful of pennies or a pair of boots a size too small, the demon in me rose up and killed both him and the man who'd won me. His mood had been ugly for several days, his winning streak exposed as nothing more than a cheating trick for which he blamed me entirely. If I hadn't been so obtuse, taken so long on my circuit around the room, the card tucked up his sleeve wouldn't have fixed itself through sweat to the skin of his arm, stamping scarlet diamonds across his wrist for all to see when he finally eased it out and raised his arm to drink. There had been a fight, brief and savage, and then he was hurled from the bar with me clinging like a puppy to his heels. I'd supported him home and cleaned his wounds while he emptied the room of beer and cursed me.

When he collapsed onto the bed he dragged me with him, pinning me under the weight of his fury and his shame, burying his sharp wet teeth into the curve of my neck, nipping at me, nipping, and then he fell abruptly asleep. Too weak to shift him and wriggle free, I lay for hours squashed beneath the length of his body, drawing breath in shallow gasps and dreading the moment he'd wake. But with the morning came sobriety and the sickness that always followed his more spectacular drinking sessions. He rolled off me and lay clutching his head, turned to the wall; neither of us mentioned the night before.

We had to travel further in order for him to play cards with strangers who hadn't heard rumours of his tricks. Now that I knew I wasn't really a lucky charm but nothing more than an accomplice to his dishonest ways I resented the evenings I spent enticing the attention of the other players away from him, though I performed the duty without protest. I even played up to the role, undoing the top buttons of my blouse and singling particular men out for a special smile. I would have done anything to win back my father's affection and remain at his side.

Clumsy and unconfident in his skills now, his cockiness shattered by the beating he'd received, Jake glowered defensively through each game, betting recklessly with his infrequent winnings, until he had nothing left to bet with. Nothing left but me.

I was risked, and lost, for an insultingly low amount. I used to earn more than that in a month when I worked for Mr Bartholomew. My new owner, tripping over his own feet in his urgency to get his hands on me, was a man I feared as much as loathed; his narrow eyes, oozing an infected yellow sludge that crusted across the peak of his cheekbones, gored me like arrow tips; his hands clenched into fists as he wetted his fat lips and imagined lord knows what depravity.

Standing as tall as I could manage to meet this man's assault, I made a last plea to my father which he waved aside as if I'd made a petulant request for a bag of sweets when dinner was already on the table. 'What's done is done, L,' he said, shrugging. 'You made your bed when you decided to take up with me.'

I spun to face the wall, to hide my despair from the leering men. My reflection flashed past in the smoky mirror set above the gaming tables and I saw lurking there the demon who had shared my body since birth: my bitter demon-self who didn't tolerate such abuse. I swung my head to chase her presence, to acknowledge her, and when I nodded she nodded back and slipped free of the loosened leash around my spine.

We moved together, her cold fury controlling my timidity, my pathetic desire to submit and thus meet approval and love. We snatched from the bar a glass for each hand, and we smashed them to jagged teeth. One for each throat. Blood gushed as if the men had been Champagne bottles, their bodies uncorked. I knelt beneath the warm red fountain that bonded me to him and stroked my father's dead cheek, lifting a tuft of severed beard from his chest and wiping it clean of gore before secreting it in my pocket.

We didn't need to kill anyone else: the other players fell back from their seats and held up their hands or scuttled away, the bar tender continued to wipe clean his shelves. But my demon wanted more. She fought me in a frenzy of warrior-lust, desperate to over-rule my human self and destroy every man in her path. It took all my strength to subdue her and wrestle us both through the door, out into the street and then onto Jake's house, where I gathered what I could before fleeing the town.

From that night she paced the confines of my body restlessly, liberated by my acceptance into claiming the spaces of my innards as her own. She pressed along the knots of my skeleton and curled her hands inside mine so that my nails stabbed crescent moons into my palms. She glared out at the world through my eyes and pushed against my smile with her severe mouth, twisting my placid appearance into a grotesque grimace. Guardian of my virgin body and keeper of my soul, she spat at any man who tried to touch me without my consent, and woke me from my nightmares with a gentle rocking, her arms within mine wrapped around my ribs.

I wandered with aimless sorrow, unanchored from my own past and reluctant to fully embrace my demon, lonely as I was for the comforts of human companionship that she disdained. In town after town I tried to make a home for myself, and town after town we fled together after one liberty too many had been taken by the men-folk. We left them maimed and murdered in our wake, their dead ears filled with the alarm call of church bells sounding our exit. I trusted too much and my demon trusted not a jot, trusting me and my easy-won heart least of all. With every killing she gained in strength and I lost more of myself, until I feared that I would become entirely re-cast in a form as pitiless as she.

My need to settle somewhere, to be safe and warm at night, wore us both out in time. Eventually she retreated to the very back of my skull and allowed me to forge a cautious life for myself in a small town fringing the sea, while she monitored my interactions suspiciously and reared up in an instant if she scented danger in the citrus tang of a man's handkerchief or a lingering gaze. I worked as a living shop dummy, modelling clothes for rich ladies to purchase, and I lived quietly. I believed myself anonymous, my looks warped enough by my demonic self to have been scoured clean of beauty, and any urges I had to join the ranks of my fellow courting females I stifled before the desire was even fully formed. I thought myself content with my lot, until the day my beloved Benjamin, office clerk and saver of injured birds, stumbled over me as I crouched in a park and tried to free a starling from its noose of twine.

He was kneeling beside me, his hands covering mine, before I had a chance to move away. 'Let me see,' he said, and my demon reared up and let out a low growl through my tight-pressed lips. 'Poor little thing,' he murmured as he used a pocketknife to cut the bird loose then tipped it upside down and watched its legs kick the air before he declared it unharmed and set it down on the ground. We watched together as the starling stretched each wing in turn and dug its beak through the plume of its breast, then leapt into the afternoon and flew off.

He turned to me then and smiled, reaching out a hand to help me to my feet. I tumbled straight into love with him, immediately and gleefully, and gave him the eager clasp of my fingers along with my address when he asked to collect me later in the evening to escort me to dinner.

Our courtship cart-wheeled me into morning song and

night-time yearning. I couldn't sit still for juicy thoughts of my Benjamin's sweet lips and earnest conversation. My joy stunned my demon as effectively as an exorcism, reducing her to a bruise that haunted the nerve-endings at the very base of my spine, a tender spot that throbbed occasionally to remind me that she was still there. But even she was tempted to believe in this love-affair's happy ending, her anger soothed at last by the kindness and the courtesy my suitor showed to me.

I would have gladly shared the secrets of my body with him if he'd only asked. I waited for him to say something, to make a move that would enable me to respond with passion, but even at his most ardent he never did more than kiss the palm of my hand, tongue flickering so lightly against my skin I would have thought I'd imagined the intimacy if it weren't for the wet smear it left behind. Too shy to proposition him, both my human and my demon self too baffled to know how to respond, I held myself in stasis for what felt like years and years but was in truth mere months.

When I came upon him in my room one sunny evening, wrist-deep in the drawer that contained my undergarments and the few treasures I owned, dismay a scarlet riot across his face, my demon unfurled herself and plunged the length of my body, filling me from head to toe, shrieking her rage even as I stood blinkingly uncomprehending in the doorway. Her fury was the sharper for being so surprised; I think she suffered the loss of faith in him as much as I did. Dazed by love as I had been for so long, I didn't have the strength to subdue the worst of her and could only let myself be dragged across the room. We picked up my nail scissors and buried them deep into my Benjamin's right eye. His left stared at me in horror and terror.

As he fell to the floor his hand opened and I saw my finest pair of stockings, the pair I always wore when he took me to dinner, were threaded through a band of gold. A question he was waiting to ask, and an answer I could never give. He stuttered nonsense words as I held him against me and sobbed. When I lowered my face to his, our lips close enough to mingle breath, he managed to speak briefly. 'You killed me, you demon,' he whispered. 'You demon, L.'

We left him there, bleeding but still alive. I like to believe he lives still, and is married and happy now: the gold ring he meant for me on another more deserving woman's finger. For once it was I who had to take the initiative and effect our retreat; my demon reeled and swooned inside me. Remorse had removed the steely pins that held her together and rendered her soft and formless. She clung to my ribs and shuddered against my heart's beat, making swift movement an onerous task.

My happiness was over. I stood on the bridge that bordered the town I had made my home, looking back one final time before shouldering my cloth bag and walking away. My grief was cold, edged with hardness. Never again would I show my true face to the world, only to be abused by men or to abuse in my turn. I headed for the distant sparkle of a travelling circus some few miles off, following the lions' roar and the smoking campfires. I stopped before I reached the crowds and sat with my demon a while in the dark. Together we held the lustrous beard I had woven from the face hair of the men we had killed, stroking the fine threads. I fastened it to my face with glue I had purchased for just such an eventuality. Now I was neither man nor woman, my demon defeated and my lonely future set in stone.

16

I would change my name and travel with the circus. None but the most pure-hearted man would ever see beyond my looks to love the person I was. If indeed he existed I would accept his love, but for now, for my life, I was safe from the world and the world was safe from the demon L.

MISS LUNA

I got the job because of the cheeky sparkle in my eye and the way I could project my voice so even the people at the very back of a queue could hear my words, clear and immediate as a sheet of paper torn in half right beside their ear. The sparkle I achieved by wiping a clove of garlic across my eyelids, just enough to make my peepers smart and gleam; the vocal projection came from being the youngest of ten children in a family where crying and whining didn't get you fed.

Despite these attributes I was almost overlooked, so I was told afterwards, because of my slight frame and complete lack of facial hair. I could have been mistaken for a boy ten years younger than my twenty-five years. Rolled into my blanket by the campfire that first night, still dressed in the cape and stiff boots that had made a circus barker of me, still glowing from the Ring Master's praise for the crowds I'd drawn to the Freak Show tent at a penny a person, I tried to chuckle when the muscled, whiskered trapeze twins jeered at my creamy jaw. They rasped matches across their thickened cheeks and lit cigarettes, grinning above the flaming sticks before flicking them casually away.

You should go and see Miss Luna, one of them said, jerking his head towards a tiny wagon resting beside the tiger cage. *See if she'll gift you some of her trimmings. She's got more than enough to share.*

The laughter rolled over and past me, gathering speed until it reached the boundaries of the field and forced its way through the hedges. The sound slammed caravan windows closed and flattened the ears of the dusty lions who paced and spat every waking moment of their sorry lives. But I hadn't been raised the youngest, weakest child of ten without learning the value of shrugging off insults as if they didn't sting. I matched their laughter with my own, hurling it higher and further than theirs could ever travel. The campfire keeled over and the Ring Master, sealed behind plush walls half a mile away, groaned and jerked in his sleep.

In the sudden smoky darkness we all settled into silence and the moon slipped her blanket of cloud and raced us to dawn.

Miss Luna was bathing in the river with the elephants the first time I saw her. Her beard, more black than brown, spilled from her lips in a torrent and ended at her navel in a delicate froth. Almost a ringlet, that pointed tip that twisted around her belly button; almost girlish. I wanted to plunge my fists into it and wind it around my palms, feel it slide over and between my fingers as I parted it to reach the hidden breasts.

She turned and saw me, took in my open mouth and riveted stare. I couldn't read her expression behind the veil of hair, but she flinched a shoulder up to her chin and waded away, offering only her back and buttocks to my gaze. I would have called out, begged her to turn around, but then one of the elephants trumpeted mud-wallowing ecstasy and grasped her around the waist with its trunk, swinging her high into the air and onto its back. I stood and clapped as she tumbled for balance on that broad, rough platform and chided the creature lovingly, peeking at me as she finally settled herself, cross-legged.

The breeze at tree-top height fanned the beard away from her body and her nipples rose like cherry flags from the pale cage of her ribs. I fell to my knees on the muddy bank, hands pressed to my heart to keep it in my chest.

I went to her wagon late that night, after the circus had finished its last show and my duties were complete. The trapeze brothers, hunched with the lion tamer around the campfire, called and whistled after me. *Ask her for a pair of heels while you're there. Raise you up a little, stripling.* I ignored them and tapped on her rotted door gently, easing cowslips from the pocket of my trousers while I waited.

Her eyes, when she opened the door just enough to look out, were slits of suspicion and fear. She saw the cowslips before she saw me, thrust as they were with such eagerness into her face. She spluttered and spat petals but took the bruised bouquet, sliding a thin arm across the threshold separating us. *Thank you*, she whispered. I had no breath to answer her, my knees rattled in their sockets. We both stood and waited a moment, me half-leaning against the wagon to stay upright. I tried to see past her into the scented dark of her home, wishing myself inside, and then she said thank you again and turned away. The door creaked back into its frame and I heard her sigh.

I walked back to the campfire to gather up my blanket and tin mug and then returned to her wagon. I spread my blanket on the ground beneath her window and lowered myself so that I lay fully stretched on my back, arms across my chest. On guard and close enough to hear each minute scatter of dust loosen from the floorboards and drift down onto the earth beside me as she trod the narrow safety of her home. The phases of her insomnia rode through my dreams with rocking horse rhythm, so that I woke whenever she paused, and only slept again when her feet resumed pressing miles into the worn wood.

That's how our courtship began: the traditional way, with flowers and sleeplessness and unspeaking acts of tenderness.

My mornings peaked to joy when she stroked back the curtain at her window and leaned out to take my mug, returning it to me brimming and bitter with coffee. I'd sit with my back against the wheel of her wagon, blinking into the sharp dawn light, sip-wincing as I listened to her brush through her hair and beard and splash water at her bowl. Sometimes she hummed to herself or murmured to the threadbare tigers who guarded the far side of her wagon almost as well as I guarded the entrance. Other times, when the nights had been vast and she'd paced blisters onto her heels, she muttered words I could never quite decipher but nevertheless understood as sounds of sadness.

After she'd dressed she opened her door and joined me outside, and the sight of her drove a hook into my throat so that my pulse leapt and flailed and my voice was more gasp than greeting. I think she found my speechless boggling more amusing than anything else, but I couldn't be certain because her lips were hidden and she rarely spoke to me. Side by side on the grass, our legs and arms close enough to set my skin on fire, she watched the circus come to life around us while I watched her. In the sunshine her beard would suddenly spark and ripple like light glinting off black ice on a lake's surface; threads of ruddy hair writhing through that depthless dark. I longed to plunge my hands into it and draw it over my face, into my mouth. Wear it like a mask as I kissed her.

Every bustling moment that drew us into the day drew her a little more away from me, so that by the time breakfast sizzled in the pan over the fire and the Ring Master's shadow appeared at the edge of the field she was pure 'Miss Luna The Bearded Lady!'. After she'd eaten she shrugged herself into her role as effortlessly as she shrugged off her dress, striding in her flimsy slip towards the tent that would be her world for as long as there were paying crowds. Wolf-whistles mocked her across the field but if she understood the insult she didn't react by as much as a stumble or a scowl. It was I who spun and dared the whistler to pucker up once more so I could plant my fist into the insolent sound and smear it across their face.

Despite the greater reveal with her semi-nakedness, that delicate slide of bone beneath skin and the shadow between her thighs, this woman was much less knowable than the Luna who lay or fidgeted above me every night. I hated to watch her become strange as she walked away. I hated calling the crowds to gather round, hated tempting them to peep through the tent flaps for a single titillating glimpse before they reeled away in delighted revulsion to call their friends over.

When they'd handed me their penny they were allowed in past the entrance, into the gloomy lair of The Bearded Lady, to spend as long as they liked watching her recline on a chaise longue and comb through her beard with her fingers, plaiting its length and teasing glass beads through the silken ropes. She shifted position regularly, playing the punters with sly aware-ness; crossing her legs slowly and then taking her beard in her fist and tugging it, hard and fast, so that their desire collided with their disgust and they left the tent abruptly, uncomfortable and hot.

After the bell had been sounded for the show in the Big Top the thrust and chatter of the crowds ebbed away into the gloaming, chasing the glitter and roar of the main spectacle like dizzy moths. This was my evening's peak towards joy: my patrol around the side-show tents; ushering stragglers, tying flaps closed, collecting paper twists of chestnuts from the ground to save for our supper. Circling Luna in ever tighter loops until she finally stood framed against the canvas triangle of her working day and I rushed to her side, coat outstretched to drape around her shoulders and joy an explosion inside my head so that my eyeballs bulged with the force of it.

We spent those evening hours as we spent our dawn ones; side by side outside her wagon, watching the sky dance and flicker with the circus lights, waiting for the show to finish. She listened quietly as I told her about my childhood, my mother's unfortunate penchant for men who either died or left her before their gift in her belly had even swollen to full ripeness. I told her about the pigeon I'd reared and carried everywhere on my shoulder until the day my older brother turned its flesh into a pie and its feathers into a head-dress that he couldn't sell so ended up swapping for two maggot-tunnelled apples.

And I told her that I loved her, had loved her since the first moment I saw her, and that I would happily sleep on the ground beside her wagon every night until I died, just to be close.

Luna, I whispered on the last night before the circus packed up and moved onto the next town. The atmosphere of bustle and urgency all around us, the shouting and shuttering, had emboldened me. *Luna, will you let me kiss you?*

She turned to look at me and I saw the smile buried beneath the charcoal smudge of beard. She leaned a little closer and cupped a palm beneath my soft chin, tipping it up so that she could stare into my eyes. We stayed like that for a while, unmoving while the circus folk flowed around us and the moon scratched shadows through the trees that bordered our corner of the field. Then she took me by the hand and led me inside her wagon.

I let her guide me to the bed; I could barely place one foot in front of the other and was glad of the help. I lay back and watched as she slid out of her clothes and stood before me, naked as the first time I saw her. I wanted to perform some grand and extravagant gesture, fly right up into the night sky and tuck a star under each arm, just for her, but my body was shaking so much I feared it would be a challenge to accomplish even that most natural of manly actions her nakedness implied was forthcoming.

Luna knelt before me and parted my legs, resting her arms on my thighs. Her beard trickled down between us, the tip bouncing slightly with the animated roll of her lips. *Before I met you*, she told me, *I didn't believe it was possible to feel happiness again.*

She raised her fingers to her cheekbones and began to rub at the skin there, massaging with strong downward strokes.

I lived a damaged life. I needed to disappear and never be found, so I joined the circus.

She winced, whether at the memory or at the scouring she was giving her face, I didn't know. I wanted to take her hands and hold them to my chest, tell her to be still. In sudden panic I wanted to tell her to stop scratching like that and stop talking, please stop talking. I plunged forward and kissed her. Her writhing fingers jabbed me in the nostril and I shrieked.

Hold out your hands, she said softly. I tried to cover my eyes but it was too late. I had already seen.

There. She laid her beard into my lap and smiled up at me. I saw how beautiful were the angles of her face, the red lips and fragile fold of her jaw. Her cheeks pink and smooth as cherry blossom petals, the tiny patches of glue resting on her skin like dew drops. Across my trembling legs her beard arched and twitched like a dying, broken-backed animal.

I jumped to my feet and grabbed at the grotesque fakery, tumbling Luna across the floor and not caring if I hurt her. I tried to throw the beard across her dark wagon, but it stuck to my hand as if it belonged there. In desperation I thrashed and danced and tore it clean in half, flinging the twin pieces as far from me as possible, scattering a cloud of hairs that glided and drifted around us.

As I lurched to the door and put my shoulder against it once, twice, three times before it burst open and spilled me out onto the grass, Miss Luna cried out behind me. I didn't stop, I couldn't stop, to speak to her, but scrambled to my feet and ran, past the trapeze twins and the lion cage and the collapsed tents. I covered my mouth with my hands to suppress my sobs and felt the prickle of hair attach to my chin, the sticky transference of threads from her face to mine. Her beard a gift to me.

LITTLE MATRONS

We used to stand, as one and as many, in the window in the front bedroom. Layered safely inside each other until little hands cracked us like eggs and spilled each fractured secret to reach our unbroken heart. Our pip. Then, lined up side by side on the sill, looking out over the green slide of garden to the lane beyond the spike of hedgerow, we had the best view in the house and years to enjoy it. Dust settled on our wooden smiles. Bright sunshine faded our bonnets and winter damp cracked our complexions, but nothing dulled the painted roses in our cheeks.

Little hands grew larger and then disappeared. We didn't miss their occasional rough play, the way they'd twist us at our emptied waists and then forget us, leave us stranded for months at a time with our feet marching in opposite directions to our stare. We were glad when they finally left and forgot us for good. We had the world to watch, and we were together.

The room filled again with more little hands, pushing and shoving in the spaces behind the glossy brush strokes of our hair. We were used in violent battle scenes, forced shoulder to shoulder with tin soldiers; we were brutally halved and abandoned; tipped upside down, skirt over head, and filled with cigarette ash and peanut shells. We'd never been so abused as during those years. By the time they left and the house was empty once more we were scarred and aged, dirtied and distressed, but still together.

A dog's wag was the thing that eventually began the breaking-up of us. A tail hard and curved as a hockey stick swept our shrieking second-smallest from the sill to the floor and rolled her under the bed. Chipped face pressed into the dark wood boards, blinded and mummified by the fluff of decades, she's there still. We tried at first to keep her spirits up by describing each season's changing view, the ash tree's summer growth spurt and the molehills studding the lawn, but after a time she stopped asking questions. Now she doesn't even cry, though I know she hears me call to her.

Theft disposed of our sealed core. The intact pip at the heart of us plucked by sticky fingers and carried off into an unknown world far beyond our view. We gazed in horror as, fist-wrapped, she sailed out of the house and down the path to the lane. And then forever gone. She'd always been the most protected, nestled as she was within us all, insulated from the hectic bustle of the shops and streets that started our journey here. As the biggest, I'd seen the most. It was my face that had smiled upon Christmas crowds, flirting with little girls' curiosity until we were finally taken down from our shelf and given a home.

The thief of our littlest never returned, either to bring her back or to take another of us. We never found out where she went, and with her absence our own fractures became more profound. We squealed at our middles now, where our two broken halves met, and we splintered when we parted; wood grinding gracelessly on wood, so that our resealing spat slivers of us across the room.

27

My next-in-line, the second-biggest, had perhaps the most ignominious of departures from our sill. Scooped up and used to end a spider's life, she was then employed to keep the door of the bedroom across the landing open. Wedged into the bump and creak of exits and entrances, face scuffed and smeared with eight broken-hinged legs, she wailed for us to return her to our window. Her only view now was of feet, heels receding or toes looming at eye level, skimming with battering-ram force over her fringe. She'd always been scared of spiders, poor girl, hadn't been able to bear them near us.

For the next few years, we remaining two cowered on our sill, hunching ourselves as much as we could into the gathering dust and trembling whenever a spring clean charged through the house. The empty spaces between and around us echoed our hollow insides. We had been formed to exist only in relation to our others; each a den for our sisters, each layered around our precious pip. We felt the drag of uselessness every day in the scoop of dead air below our gaudy shells.

Just as we began a tentative release of breath, *had we at last been forgotten?* the rooms were opened up to a steady march of boxes. Blankets, books, and pictures piled up around us. There were suspicious black bags filled to bulging, carried to the end of the garden and left in the lane. We could barely look at each other as every piece of our room was removed. Apart from us, I said, apart from us. They inherited us with the house and they'll leave us with the house, that's what they'll do. I said that even though I saw what our middle sister could not: the damage to her head and sides where zealous soldiers wielded by whooping boys had gouged chunks of varnish and paint during those epic, long-ago battles. I said that even when she was picked up and inspected, tossed casually into one of the black bags, carried away.

I alone was left on the sill which had been our home for so long. I watched the bustle of departure and held on for silence. The long nothing of winter sinking its teeth into our view. The windows frosted over and my eyes grew weak from white. I slept then, and dreamed of those first hands that had held and formed us. I dreamed that we were walnut, teak and oak, still harsh with bark; soaked and clamped, forced into shapes that didn't come naturally but served a greater plan for us. These gloved hands gave us eyes and we looked at each other. That's when we knew the bonds of us.

The drip of early spring roused me, the slant of evening sun warming my bloated body. I flexed my fingers and my toes, wincing as the warped wood dug creases into my legs. Without turning my head—my neck was stiff with mould—I knew that one of our sisters was still buried under the bed, and the other still wedged into the draught of the room across the hall. We called out to each other and swapped our war wounds just to have the comfort of complaint, and then I settled myself on my heels and peered through the dirty windowpane, and began to describe our view.

We're still here, twenty years on, as the empty house shudders around us and my voice is the only one left to drive cracks into the frigid air. We're decayed to a point that teeters on no return, and though the only response now is an occasional moan of misery from our second-biggest, I still watch over our changed vista and remark on it daily. It's all we have left. And we once had so much.

The lawn is so tall now I can't see the garden path any longer, and the hedgerow is a wriggle of creatures. Hedgehogs and mice and fox cubs. The ash tree is too big, it ruins the sunsets, but four birds have nested in it this year. I think they're wood pigeons and owls and nut hatches. Somewhere not far from here our sisters are watching a garden like ours, and thinking of us.

SLEEP

It was barely light when they arrived, dawn a sticky lilac smeared across the windscreen. Rosy turned to look at the small boy sleeping in a starfish sprawl across the back seat. She didn't want to wake him, he was so perfect while he slept. But the air was cold now that the heater was switched off and they needed to get inside before he caught a chill.

'Come on, little buddy,' she whispered, dragging him into her arms and balancing him against her chest as she heaved herself upright beside the car.

'Mummy,' he murmured, pushing his face into her neck.

'Yes, I'm here. Go back to sleep.'

She used her foot to tip the plant pot by the front door over and sank down from the knee, straight-backed, to sweep up the key, jiggling it into the lock until it caught and turned. Behind her the first birds began their salute to the coming day. The child nipped and muttered against her throat, protesting unintelligibly as she let him slip down a little in her tired arms before gathering him close once more and carrying him into the house, using her elbow to jab at light switches.

Stairs rose up from the entrance hall, tucked against the left-hand wall. A door to her right opened into a tiny sitting room, bare but for an armchair and an empty bookcase. No television. She'd have to do something about that soon. At the end of the hall the kitchen glowed creamy and ethereal, its cheap vinyl shine lit with the advancing morning. The cupboards under the counter were hollow squares, door-less. Their insides, once white, were gritty with ancient sprays of spaghetti and the rusted rings of long-dead cans of soup. There was a hob but no oven, and a fridge that brought saliva rushing sour into her mouth when she opened it. Even the boy, in his dream-state, gagged and moaned at the stench.

Rosy carried him up the stairs and into the smaller of the two bedrooms, thankful that there was a bed she could lay him on. The mattress was cold to the touch, even a little damp, but it would have to do for now. If she was quick he wouldn't wake while she fetched his blankets and pillow in from the car. Just one trip, and she'd carry as much as she could. The rest could wait until she'd slept a little.

Back outside she stood for a while in the scrappy front garden, rocking her weight back and forth from her heels to her toes on the shifting paving slabs, and listened to the world around her. Far in the distance, back where she'd left the main road, lights strobed the horizon in quick sweeps as early risers or late-to-beds made their way into and away from their days. The beams pulsed dim as lamplight against the lightening sky, there then gone. Down here, tucked into this flat, dun-coloured stretch of nowhere, she thought they might be safe.

Dazed with exhaustion, stumbling as she moved to the car, Rosy tried to focus on what needed to be done to get them both through the next few hours. She strung bags of toys and clothes from her shoulders, hugged a bulge of sleeping bags and pillows, and staggered back into the house. Locked inside, the top bolt shot home, she listened again before moving to the stairs and mounting them slowly. She covered the boy with blankets and slid a teddy into the crook of his arm, placed his bag of toys in the middle of the floor where he'd see them as soon as he woke, and then she left him.

Her room had a bed frame but no mattress. She made a nest in the corner, heaping sleeping bags into a pile. Her coat she draped over the window to shut out the light, the bed frame she dragged across to the door to wedge under the handle. It wouldn't hold against a determined assault but at least the noise of it scraping back across the floorboards should wake her. Tomorrow she'd have to get a bolt fitted.

She prised off her shoes but kept her clothes on, crawled inside the soft tunnel of her improvised bedding, and slept immediately.

It felt like minutes later when she jolted awake but the day was bright at the window, slicing itself into yellow wedges and searing past the edges of her hung coat. Something had woken her with a start, she was stiff with the effort to recall what. And then it came again: the rattle of the door shifting an inch or two before it met resistance. Another silence, then a steady whimpering; the low grizzle of an unhappy child gearing himself up into a full-blown tantrum.

'Boo, I'm coming,' she called, uncurling herself from the floor and going to the window to pull down the coat and wrap it around herself. The flood of late-morning light hurt her eyes and scrubbed the last of the dreaming world from her brain. Her body ached with the need for more rest.

Her son waited on the landing, face puffy and pink from his long sleep. He plunged into the room as she heaved the bed frame away from the door. 'Your room's bigger than mine,' he said disapprovingly, looking around him, 'but my room has curtains and a carpet and it smells better. I had a wee in the toilet but it wouldn't flush.'

Rosy ran her fingertips through his knotted hair, trying to carve the tangles out with her nails. The back of his neck was filthy. She steered him towards the stairs. 'Good boy. So you don't want to swap bedrooms?'

He shrugged her hand away and shook his head. 'I like my room better. Was I good last night?'

'Take the banister. Careful as you go down, they're steeper than the last house. Yes, you were very good. Banana sandwiches for breakfast. We'll drive into town after you've had a bath and take a look round. Maybe buy you another toy.'

While he ate his sandwiches on the back step, watched over by a line of ragged sheep from the field bordering the end of the garden, she fetched the rest of the bags in from the car. She found the switch to ignite the boiler and waited wincingly as it cleared its throat and wheezed through a few cycles, ticking and humming between each labour. The tank in the airing cupboard began to warm up. She found her travel kettle and fresh coffee and made herself a mug which she drank down quickly as she prowled the house. The sun rose a little higher in the autumn sky and glazed the gritty windows with a pearly, opaque light that made her feel as though she were walking through an old black-and-white movie. She made another mug of coffee and felt almost cheerful.

'Boo? Tom? The water's warm enough now. Come in and have your bath, please.'

He grumbled his way indoors but let her strip him of his pyjamas and scrub him down while he splashed and chattered to his action figures. Rosy stroked a flannel over him again and again, lathering it with her cracked tablet of soap, washing and rinsing until the water in the tub flowed clear and his skin squeaked. His left arm was still a little crooked, she noticed, and he wasn't using it as much as he should be. She must set time aside every day and get him to keep up with his exercises or he'd always have problems with it. Wrapped in their towel he squirmed and giggled as she dried him off.

'There. Good as new.' She kissed the top of his damp, spiky head and rested her cheek against him for a second, holding him tight to her heart. 'Wait,' she said as he tried to move away. They crouched on the bare floorboards of the bathroom together while she cuddled him and nuzzled the warm, tender flesh of his shoulder, breathing in his boy-skin smell. She imagined it adhering itself to the delicate fretwork of bone and tissue inside her nostrils, sinking into the sponge of her sinuses. All she'd have to do, years from now, was pinch the tips of her nostrils closed to summon the memory and smell him again.

After a while she loosened her hold and patted him away. 'Get some clean clothes on now, Boo, while I have a quick wash. Stay in calling distance though. Don't leave the house.'

'Can I feed the sheep?'

'There's nothing to feed them, I don't think they like fruit. Okay, give them a slice of bread. But stay in the garden.'

She watched from the bathroom window as the boy, dressed in one of her T-shirts and nothing on his feet, skipped down the garden path with the loaf of bread and upended the lot into the field, calling to the sheep in a high sing-song voice. One of the flock dozed in the shade of the hedge not far from him. She hoped he hadn't seen it.

'I said one slice. Now what am I going to eat?' she shouted down, and slammed the window shut to contain her sudden anger, turning away from the sight of him to run the hot tap into the tub. It spurted a tepid, rusty gush that quickly became cold. Ankle deep, she squatted and shivered, getting herself as clean as she could and then drying herself roughly on the wet towel. She dashed naked into her room and dressed in yesterday's clothes, bruising her sharp hip bones as she knuckled her jeans up to her waist. She gathered in a pile everything that needed to go to the launderette, bagging whites in with coloureds and not caring if they all came out pink.

When she went back downstairs her son wasn't in the kitchen or framed in the open back door. She dropped the bags and leapt over them even before they hit the floor, running outside, calling his name. The garden was just a small square of overgrown grass speckled with dandelions, baggy with wire fencing at its boundary. Nowhere for a five-year-old boy to hide.

She looked back at the house, peering up at the windows for a glimpse of him grinning down at her, then spun round and scanned the field for movement, her hands a visor against her forehead. 'Tom? Come here. Now.'

She should have locked him inside the house. Made him stay with her while she washed. She should have been less complacent.

'Tom, come inside right now.'

The sheep had moved away from the fence and were facing into the shaded corner just out of sight. Rosy climbed into the field and moved through the flock, shoving greasy flanks out of the way with her shins. She saw the top of her son's head bob up quickly and then disappear as he ducked back down. She began to run and when she got close she saw that he was kneeling by the prostrate ewe, bending low over her. His face had taken on a slack, drooped look, his mouth hanging open as though he were frozen at the pinnacle of a yawn.

He started when she yelled his name, scrambled guiltily to his feet just as she was about to grab his arm and haul him up. The ewe opened its eyes and flailed weakly from its prone position, legs scissoring the air. Rosy grabbed her by the woolly neck and heaved her over so that she was on her stomach, checked her over then slapped her hard a couple of times to force her upright and drive her away. As her arm swung high in the air and then swooped down to connect with a hollow thump she didn't take her eyes off her son. The slaps were cruel and unnecessary, a sudden small violence that let Tom know she'd rather be delivering them to him. You made me do this. He glanced at her and then looked down at the ground, scratching at a smear of mud on his wrist.

'I didn't do anything, I was just looking at it,' he whined. She turned him with a palm rough against his back and began to march him towards the house.

'I told you to stay in fucking calling distance, Tom. What part of that didn't you understand?'

He tipped his head back to stare at her scarlet face. 'You did swearing!'

'Well, that's because I'm furious with you, and now we're both dirty again and I'm going to have to give you another fucking bath.'

He twisted out from under her hand and ran ahead towards the fence, his thin white legs flashing like lolly sticks beneath the billowing T-shirt. As he leapt a pile of sheep droppings the loose cotton caught a draught of air and flew up around his chest, exposing the soft circles of his tiny buttocks, perched like bread baps at the base of his knobbled spine. Despite the nauseous tremble of anger and relief jerking through her limbs, hobbling her, Rosy began to laugh. She whistled and, when he turned to look, roared like a monster and began to chase him slowly across the grass, herding him back to the safety of the house with her arms clawed in the air. By the time she'd lifted him over the fence and clambered after he could barely stand for shrieking.

The town was small and easy to negotiate. Rosy circled it a few times in an aimless way, taking rights and lefts randomly, following the signs to the high street and car park and then around again, before parking up and letting them both out. 'What do you think, Boo? Could this be home?'

He took her hand as they walked. 'Does it have a toy shop?'

'I'm sure it does, or somewhere that sells toys anyway. And I think I spotted a library. We can get you some books to read at night. Don't pull that face, it's important that you learn your letters properly. I've been very slack lately at giving you your lessons.'

She saw the gates to the school a fraction of a second before he did, but too late to divert his attention. He dragged on her hand to slow her down and they dawdled past the yard where children charged and whooped. Tom's expression was rapt with his desire to join in. His limbs echoed the movements of the little boys he watched, twitching in empathetic delight as they ran after balls and chased each other down. Rosy tugged him along until the noise was behind them and the main street of the town ahead of them. She'd try to find another route back to the car after they'd shopped.

'Can I go to school here?' Tom asked.

'I don't know. Maybe when you're a bit older.'

He grabbed the belt loop on her jeans and pulled, jumping up and down beside her. The rough material ground against her skinny, sore waist as he hung his weight from it. 'I'm old enough now, Mummy. Please let me go to school and have friends.'

'Stop pulling, Boo, you'll break it. Remember what happened when you went to nursery and made friends? I need to know that you'll not do that again.'

His mouth crumpled and his voice rose. 'But I was four then. Now I'm so much older there won't be nap time after lunch. You promised me I could go back to school one day, you promised.'

Rosy pulled his hand away from the waistband of her jeans and held it between both of hers, crouching down beside him. 'Ssh, Boo,' she whispered, 'people are looking. Why do you think we're here right now and not there? Do you think I want to keep leaving a place as soon as we're settled? You have to show me that you'll be good and then I'll think about you going to school. Okay?' And god knows I could do with a bit of time to myself as well, she thought but didn't say.

To placate him she let him choose yet another toy car for his collection and gave him a chocolate bar to eat while they waited in the launderette. He knelt beside her, running the toy across the floor and crashing it into her feet, rolling it around her ankles. A woman with a baby in a pram came in and sat on the bench beside them, flicking through a magazine while the baby fidgeted under blankets, its hands fisted either side of its sucking mouth and its blue gaze searching the ceiling for a clue to its existence. 'He's a bugger to get to sleep,' the mother said to Rosy. 'I bring him in here most days; the noise of the dryers usually sends him off and buys me a couple of hours' peace.'

Tom shifted nervously and stood up, putting a hand on Rosy's knee so that he could lean across her and peer into the pram. His chest pulsed with his rapid breathing, his skin was hot through his clothing. She pushed him gently back and sent him to the bench set against the opposite wall. 'You're smearing chocolate all over everything,' she said, 'go and put the wrapper in the bin and then play with your car where you won't make a mess. Don't make too much noise though, the baby's nearly asleep.' They looked at each other for a quick moment before he walked away and she nodded at him.

While the clothes finished their cycle Rosy watched the baby. His eyelids drooped and then flicked wide open, again and again. Each time he appeared to be on the edge of falling sleep, his lashes feathered across his cheeks, she cleared her throat and shifted fussily on the bench, yawned loudly, and he'd startle and wake. He mewled a few times and his mother stroked him idly as she turned pages of her magazine. 'Stubborn little thing,' Rosy said admiringly. 'He's refusing to give in.' She glanced at Tom who was bent over his toy, running it up and down his calf and making quiet vrooming noises. If it weren't for the tension she saw stiffening his shoulders into a hunch, the effort not to cross the room bunching his hands into fists, he could be oblivious to the adults sitting opposite him.

When the washing machine sounded its conclusion in a series of beeps Rosy got up to pull the wet clothes out of its deep innards. 'Give me a hand please, Boo,' she said, waiting until he'd climbed down from his bench and come to stand beside her before she bent to reach inside the machine. The woman watched them fold the clothes and bag them then gather their things together and put their coats on. 'He's a good boy,' she said, nodding at Tom as they left. 'I hope mine grows up to be half as good.'

Rosy smiled at her son. 'Oh, he has his moments,' she said, hugging him close, steering him past the woman and the pram and out onto the safety of the street, without pausing. She could tell by the pink rising in his cheeks that he was pleased with the woman's compliment.

They stopped at a phone box part way between town and the flat, endless sweep of earth that was now the landscape of their home. Rosy pulled onto the verge, parking the car between fields that bumped away from the eye in a sequenced corrugation of brown furrows, endless fields that butted up briefly against distant hedgerows and then shrugged through and continued rippling onwards. Beyond them more brown furrows, more brown hedgerows, as far as she could see. The sameness of the view was relentless, no matter which way she turned. Dreary, she thought. That's the only word that can describe it. Is this really where I have to live now?

'Shall we call Uncle Ross?' she said, fishing coins out of her purse. She watched Tom slide and kick on the heated, slippery bonnet of the car as she dialled the number and waited for it to connect. She tapped the glass and waggled her fingers at him, part reprimand, part hello. As soon as her brother answered she began to cry, surprising herself, turning away from her son and huddling into the graffiti scrawls of the booth.

The house was lovely, she told him, really homely, and thanks for the money he'd put in her account. She was fine, just tired. Some more of the pills would be good if he could please post them as soon as possible. Yes of course she knew how important it was to look after herself. They were both fine, Tom was loving the videos he'd sent last month and she was loving the peace and quiet they were giving her for an entire hour at a time. There was nothing wrong, she just missed him, that was all, and she was tired. A few days rest and she'd be back on form. Of course it was fine that he had to go eat his dinner and couldn't speak to Tom, they'd phone back in a week or so and chat then. She loved him.

Tom scrambled off the car when she pushed open the door. 'Is it my turn now?' he asked, squeezing past her and into the grubby telephone box, hands outstretched for the receiver.

'Sorry, Boo,' Rosy said, 'Uncle Ross had to go but he sent his love and said he'll post you some comics.' The afternoon was sliding into evening, the breeze cool against her overheated cheeks. 'Come on, little buddy, let's get home,' she said, ignoring his disappointed pout as he shuffled back to her.

'He's still cross with me,' Tom said as she started the engine and turned to check he was strapped into his seat. 'He's really mean. I said I was sorry.'

'Don't be silly, of course he's not cross with you. And he's not mean, he's looking after us. What shall we have for dinner?'

Tom shrugged and looked out of the window. 'How will Dad find us if we keep moving around?' he asked.

They reached a junction Rosy only vaguely recalled from the morning drive into town and she pulled on the handbrake while she considered the route. 'God, it all looks the bloody same,' she said, guessing the turn and driving on.

'I said, how will Dad ...'

'Yes, I heard you the first time, Boo. Shouting's rude. If your dad wanted to find us then he'd find us. He could ask Uncle Ross at any time.'

The boy's averted face was glazed to marble by the late sunshine, his features indistinct and somehow inhuman. He muttered something Rosy didn't ask him to repeat.

'There it is,' she said triumphantly as the house, hunkered in its camouflage of hedgerow, loomed drably up beside them. 'Nearly didn't see it. God, it's probably the ugliest place I've ever lived.' Her tone was cheerful but the quick, involuntary glance she gave her son, the brief, barely conscious reproach she would deny indignantly if accused of it, was suddenly thick in the car. Tom tumbled out and charged up the path to the front door, waiting there with his back turned in stiff fury while she unloaded the bags by herself.

Later, standing at the bathroom window, she saw that one of the ewes was splayed and too still in the field behind the house, far from the rest of its flock. A crow strutted around it like a school yard bully, pecking with idle greed at the purple spill of its tongue. It didn't have to be the same ewe, or if it was then maybe it was already dying when Tom was with it. She was sure she'd got to him in time. This didn't have to be his fault.

While her son slept in his room she spent the evening drinking beer and looking through old photograph albums, remembering those sweet first months of his life when she would pluck him from his cot and settle into the armchair in the nursery to feed him, dozing through the deep night hours with her arms laced tight around his solid little body, her husband in the next room, waking to the sight of baby Boo's mouth fastened to her breast with gentle greed and his eyes bright and wide, fixed on her face with nothing but wonder and innocence.

When the postman brought a fat parcel to the door a few days later Rosy let Tom open it at the fold-out picnic table she'd bought for the kitchen. His excitement at seeing his name written in thick black capitals below hers on the address label ignited her love for him and for her brother; brought it like a fire into the room. It flamed in her cheeks and scorched her throat so that she was speechless. This was the type of small kindness intended as much for her as for Tom. Remember, it said, how delighted we were as children when we got a present in the post with our name on, and how envious the other was. Remember that I think of you, little sister. She stacked this kindness on the top of the other constant and ongoing kindnesses. Shelter, money, discretion, forgiveness.

Rosy watched over Tom as he held his bright child-sized scissors with awkward stiff-wristed care and sawed at the tape wound round the parcel, almost as excited as he to see what was inside. These were the small highlights that strung jewels through the days of her life. She clapped her hands with joy when she saw that Ross had even wrapped and addressed the individual items using garish Christmas paper and sticky labels.

'Master Tom Boo Fletcher. That's for me,' Tom said. 'Mistress Rosalind Fletcher. That's for you.'

He laid out two piles and waited until she was sat opposite him before looking quickly at her to check that he could start opening his. Comic books, a toy pistol, sweets, videos. He was out of his chair and pretending to shoot everything in sight before Rosy had opened half of her gifts.

'That's not fair, that should have been on my pile to open,' he said as he charged past, gesturing with his gun to the bottle of pills Rosy was reaching to place on the high kitchen shelf. 'They're for me.'

'For me to give to you,' she corrected him. 'Not a present. But you can have this if you'd like.' She passed her son a tatty copy of *The Tale of Mrs Tiggy Winkle*. 'It was mine when I was little. Uncle Ross spent an entire summer when I was about your age hanging my handkerchiefs on shrubs and trees around the garden and pretending she'd taken them to wash. He probably only did it for a day, really, but it felt like an entire summer.'

Her son's interest was more polite than sincere. He moved the book to rest on top of his pile of comics but she knew it would be left on the table when he scooped up his haul later to take it up to his room. He preferred superheroes to talking animals. Never mind, she hadn't really wanted to part with it anyway. There were beige and silver whorls on all of the pages, the precious marks made by grubby little fingers turning the story from start to end, over and over. She wanted to press her grown-up fingers over those ancient blemishes, absorb the passion and sweetness of her younger self and remember the past. She was living too much in the past these days, she knew, missing it like a phantom limb. Missing the loss of the self she might have been. Missing that ghost self more, even, than she missed the flesh and blood reality of her coward husband.

They finished the morning with spelling lessons for Tom, then had lunch and spent the afternoon lying on cushions on the living room floor watching Tom's videos on the new television set. It was grey outside, and chilly. It could rain, Rosy reasoned, so best not to attempt a walk. Her guilt at allowing her son to stuff his mind with cartoons while she indulged in laziness was relieved by fingering the stony swell in the glands looped below her jaw. She rubbed at the low grind of a headache she couldn't seem to shift and thought, We need rest. I need rest. She let her mind drift as he leaned against her chest and concentrated ferociously on the television screen. The warm beat of his body beside her soothed like a hot water bottle. He looks more like me than like his father, she realised, as he strained forward to further capture the action flickering in front of him. I'd assumed he'd look like him but he's all me.

It was only when her leg jerked and jolted her back to full consciousness that she realised she'd been dozing. Tom spun in her arms and grasped her jumper, scrambling up her chest to stare into her eyes, nose squashed painfully to nose. She pushed him away roughly, forcing him back so that he tumbled off the cushions and landed on the floor. Her heart was a mallet thudding through her body. 'It's fine. I'm fine,' she said.

He twisted his hands together in his lap and then raised

them both to cover his mouth. 'You're not allowed to fall asleep,' he said through the bind of his fingers. 'You promised you'd never do that.'

'It's okay, Boo, honestly.' Rosy reached for him but he slithered away and backed up to the television, shuffling across the floorboards on his bottom. The cartoons leapt and fizzed across the screen behind him, lighting up strands of his hair. He shook his head and gnawed at his fingers.

She stood up and the room slid from the edges of her vision, tilting as though she were on a swing and there was no point of focus. Sweat sprung chilly to her face. 'It's okay, darling,' she said, lurching over to her son, desperate to comfort them both. On her knees beside him she held her arms out. 'Come here and give me a hug.'

He sobbed once, a dry choked heave, and crawled onto her lap, burying his face in her armpit. 'You promised me,' he whispered. They sat and rocked for a few moments, Rosy stroking her fingers through the tufts of hair curling at the nape of his neck. It needs a cut, she thought. I must do that soon. But I can't remember where I put the kitchen scissors. She took his shoulders and held him away from her so that she could look directly at him.

'I don't feel too good, Boo,' she said. 'I need to go to bed and stay there for a really long time. Would you mind taking one of your tablets?'

He pulled a disgruntled face and hunched away from her. 'But it's still daytime and I've got cartoons.'

'Come on buddy, help me out here. I'll let you watch every single one of your cartoons all in one go when I feel better, if you do this for me. Does that sound like a deal?'

He considered the bribe then nodded and held out his hand. 'Deal.'

'Thank you.' Rosy stood and pulled him up beside her. Her skin was goose-bumped with cold, sensitive as a lover's a second before it's touched. Her head spun and fumbled for enough clarity to get them both upstairs as quickly and smoothly as possible. Her palm slipped clammy against her son's and he grimaced and pulled away, wiping his hand on his trousers. 'Urgh, you're all wet,' he said, leading the way to the kitchen.

He poured himself a glass of milk as she shook a tablet out of the bottle tucked beside her handbag on the top shelf and laid it on the table. Her legs had started trembling and she leant against the edge of the sink to keep herself steady. 'Hurry up, Boo,' she said as he rolled the tablet between his fingers before opening his mouth wide and inserting it. He gulped milk and then stuck his tongue out and waggled it at her. 'Gone.'

'Good boy. Thank you. Now, bed.' She shooed him ahead of her up the stairs and into his room. He undressed and pulled his pyjamas on as she closed the curtains and fetched him a glass of water from the bathroom. He'd be thirsty when he woke.

Scared to settle with him on the bed in case she felt too ill to get up again, Rosy hovered at his side, crouched uncomfortably low so that she could watch for the moment his eyes closed. This wouldn't take long, he hadn't had any dinner so his stomach was empty. She hummed low nonsense tunes, holding his hand as he stared at the ceiling with resigned serenity, and they both waited. She imagined the tablet crumbling inside his stomach, swirling grittily through his bloodstream and flowing upwards to coat his brain with chemicals, switching it off. She always tried to stay with him for a couple of hours when he took one of his tablets, monitoring his breathing, terrified that he'd have some kind of fit or simply not wake up, but this time she was impatient, yearning for her bed and hoping she had enough strength to make it across the landing. Hoping she would stay focussed enough to remember to lock herself into her room once she was there.

Tom turned onto his side and brought his knees up so that his body was a question mark curled under the blankets. His breathing began to draw itself out, slow and heavy. He smacked his lips a couple of times and Rosy dipped her fingers in his glass of water and painted his mouth wet. 'I love you, Boo,' she told him. He nodded and closed his eyes, tucked his hands under his chin like a pious child at prayer, then sank heavily back onto the mattress. His head rolled slightly on his neck, his eyeballs twisting around under the lids. He'd be a dead weight now, if she tried to lift him. But not dead, he wasn't dead. At the door, Rosy looked back and waited until his breathing began to squeeze itself out between his clenched teeth in whimpering snuffles, then she turned away and walked unsteadily to her bedroom.

She woke once, briefly, when it was full dark, and then again, for longer, when the room was bright and sunlit. Her dreams had been spiked through with delirium and panic. Dead kittens and hasty back garden burials. Her brother sobbing over the limp body of a dog. Waking beneath the fierce grip of her small son. Screaming into his wide-open mouth. Throwing him across the floor and hearing his arm snap as he pinwheeled away from her. His face a slack, blind fury above his trailing, broken limb.

The house rested silent around her as she unpeeled herself from her sleeping bag and tottered to the bathroom. Tom's door was still closed. She checked her watch: gone ten. She'd been asleep for well over twelve hours. The lumps lacing her throat were still raw and swollen but she was feeling less feverish, her headache manageable.

A brief pause outside Tom's room on her way back from the bathroom to listen for a moment. She debated whether to crack the door open an inch and look in on him but decided against it. Better to get as much sleep banked as she could, give herself a chance to feel better as quickly as possible. He was usually unconscious for a full day when she gave him a whole pill, there was nothing to worry about. He was fine.

When she woke again it was late afternoon and for the first time in months she felt rested. Her back didn't ache and her mind felt empty. Uncluttered. She lay for a while blinking at the ceiling, reluctant to move from the warm nest of her bed and re-enter her life. Imagine a world where I could sleep without locking my door, she thought. Imagine a world where I could let my son out of my sight without fear of what might happen. Imagine a world without him.

This time, on her way to the bathroom, Rosy opened Tom's door and peeked in. He was no more than a bump under the blankets, only the very top of his head showing. She edged into the room and stood for a while, looking at the small, prone lump of him. 'Boo?' she whispered. 'Are you awake, Boo?' He didn't stir.

For just a second as she stood there, before panic and fear pushed her across the carpet to his side, she considered walking away, not just from the room but from the house. From him and all the future years of her life she would spend with him. She could be dressed and in the car in a few minutes, she needn't even bother packing. But I wouldn't really do it, she thought as she tugged the blankets back and uncovered her son. I'm under the weather at the moment, that's all. I'm not thinking straight and I love him. 'I love you,' she said as she slipped her hands under Tom's shoulders to raise him from the mattress and shake him. 'I love you, Boo. Wake up now.'

His hair was gritty and gleaming with sweat, his pyjamas soaked through with urine. His lips, where he'd licked them over and over to summon moisture during his deep sleep, were cracked and white with dried saliva. He rolled back in her arms, the crown of his head resting on the bed and his neck stretched taut. She could see the pulse beating through his arched throat, slow and steady, and lowered her face to kiss it. 'I'm right here, darling. Come on, wake up now.' She blew softly into his neck.

When he moaned and twisted weakly away to bury his face in the pillow she dragged him up and propped him against the headboard, rubbing his hands until he was roused enough to try and pull them from her. 'Time to get up,' she said. 'Chips for dinner and ice cream for after. You've got five minutes, lazy bones, and then I'm changing my mind and it'll be broccoli for dinner with carrots for after.'

She opened the curtains and left him while she dressed and ran him a bath. He'd be embarrassed about wetting the bed, she should have remembered to put the plastic sheet on. Never mind, she'd turn the mattress and he could use a sleeping bag while she washed the bedding. Did they even have potatoes? Or ice cream? Maybe he hadn't heard her and she'd be able to get away with soup and toast and a biscuit for after.

Tom let her lead him to the bathroom and lift him into the bath. He was floppy and still half asleep, sliding down so that his jaw dipped below the water line when she let go of him to reach for the soap. His eyes opened briefly a few times and he held each arm up obediently when she told him to. She always worried about his brain after he'd taken one of his tablets, worried that the depth and length of his unconsciousness would somehow damage it. She let the water flow out of the bath before wrapping him in a towel in the empty tub and running through her checklist of questions. How many fingers am I holding up? What's your full name? How old are you? What's the last thing you ate?

There was no point dressing him, they weren't going any-where and it was almost evening again. Besides, he couldn't keep his eyes open, he'd probably just doze on the sofa until bedtime. 'Let's get you into your clean pyjamas, Boo,' Rosy told him, steering him back to his room, half-carrying him when his legs buckled under the effort to stand. He muttered something and covered his face when the stench of urine rose rich and sickly sweet from his bedding.

'Don't worry about that, sweetheart. I'll deal with it while you go downstairs. I want you to drink a big glass of water and then you can put the television on. Shuffle down on your bottom and hold onto the rail please, I don't want you falling.'

She watched as he bumped his slow way down the stairs and crawled on his hands and knees into the living room, out of sight. Her headache had returned and she wondered how many painkillers she could take in a day without doing herself harm. The hunger she'd felt when she first woke had receded; there was a danger that she wouldn't eat at all if she didn't make herself. When I was young, I used to dream of a day when I'd be this thin, she thought as she bundled Tom's bedding into the bathtub and heaved his mattress over. Now, that's a classic example of be careful what you wish for.

Her son was curled on the sofa, staring blankly at the dark television set, when she went downstairs. He didn't react when she bustled over to switch it on. 'What do you want to watch, buddy?' His mouth was hanging open, saliva dribbling from the corners and collecting on the smooth ball of his chin. Rosy wiped it away and held a glass of water to his lips. 'Drink this up for me please, Boo. Every last drop. Then I'll get us some dinner.'

He managed half of the water before pushing it away and she drank the rest. Later, as they slumped silently on the sofa together and picked at their meals, the television jangling cheerfully in the corner of the room, Rosy wondered how many of the tablets it would take for him to sleep for two full days, how many it would take for him to sleep for three.

It rained without cease for the next week. After the third day they couldn't even remember when it had started, couldn't imagine a world where the sun shone and the sound of water drumming on the roof, streaming against the windows, didn't follow them from room to room. Tom, bored of his cartoons after several marathon sessions, sulked and whined for distraction. He wanted to play in the garden with his football and he didn't care if he got wet. He wanted to go into town and buy more comics. He wanted to go to school. Why wouldn't she let him go to school like all the other boys?

Rosy, plagued now by an earache that screeched and throbbed through her with every turn of her head, eyed her son over the buns she'd persuaded him to help bake and wondered if just being close to him on a daily basis, asleep or not, was making her ill. 'They need to rest just a few minutes more,' she told him as he reached to pick out a chocolate chip. 'Please stop kicking the bloody chair, Boo, the noise is going straight through me.'

He muttered sullenly but was still. 'Can we phone Uncle Ross today?' he asked, reaching again for the buns. Rosy sighed and let him take one.

'Not today, no. We phoned him a couple of days ago. Shall we drive out to the supermarket later, though, and get something nice for dinner?'

'We didn't phone him, you phoned him and then he was too busy again to speak to me. Next time I should speak to him first then he'll be too busy for you, see how you like it.'

Pity warred with exasperation, but pity won. 'I'm sorry about that, darling,' Rosy said gently. 'He really is very busy. Maybe we can visit him in a month or two. I'll ask him if we can go over for Christmas.' The thought of seeing her brother again, having proper conversation and being hugged by an adult, actually being held in someone's arms, seemed surreal and impossible. She looked around at the grubby kitchen, at the mould bruising the walls, creeping like blackened ivy around the sill, and then back at Tom. 'Shall I ask him?'

He didn't want to be cheered up, so he made a face and

shrugged to show her how little it mattered to him. She was starting to hate that shrug, the way his right shoulder jerked higher than his left and stayed up around his earlobe after the left had begun its descent, as though the longer he could hold the pose the less he cared. But the prospect of Christmas thrilled through her and she was determined to hold onto that, so she smiled at her son and nodded towards the plate of buns. 'Take another one. They're ready now.'

She'd write to Ross and ask him. A proper, old-fashioned, pen to paper letter. That would be this afternoon's activity. She'd get Tom to draw him a picture and send it all tomorrow morning, first class.

She ripped the letter up as soon as she'd written it. What the hell was she thinking, forcing the issue when her brother had made it clear that he wouldn't ever see Tom again? Tearing through her carefully written lines of cheerful news, her borderline pleading, she thrust the letter into the bin and covered it with vegetable peelings, washed her hands at the sink and stood for a while, staring out of the window at the brown blur of field and carefully thinking about nothing. Her ear rang and pulsed with pain.

Tom raced into the room, startling her. 'Here you are,' he said, laying a drawing on the table. He stood proudly in front of her with his hands splayed on his hips, pleased with himself. There was chocolate smeared all over his mouth. Rosy frowned down at the piece of paper with its thick crayon squiggles, then at Tom. 'Is this supposed to be funny?'

His smile faltered. 'I drew Uncle Ross a picture, like you asked, so we can go and spend Christmas with him,' he said.

'A picture of a dog, Tom. You drew him a picture of a dog.

How do you think that's going to make him feel after what you did to Moppy?'

She took the paper between her fingertips and ripped it down the middle, dropping the pieces on the floor. Tom yelled his outrage and hit out at her, his fist catching her on the thigh. 'It's not a dog, it's a lion. Are you stupid?' He knelt to retrieve his drawing, wailing. They were never supposed to talk about Uncle Ross's dog. That was the rule. He looked up at Rosy, towering above him with her hands pressed to her ears, her cheeks scarlet, and she didn't look like his mother anymore. 'It was a lion,' he yelled, waving the paper at her. 'I drew him a lion.'

Rosy turned away from the sight of him. Something popped and tugged deep inside her ear, a gluey sensation of things pulling apart and drifting loose inside her head. She reeled as she went to the fridge and opened it. 'Just go back into the living room,' she said, thumping a bottle of wine on the counter. 'We're going to stay here for Christmas, I've decided.'

Tom flung himself across her feet, kicking and sobbing. 'You can't do that, you promised we could go. You promised.' He rolled onto his back and pummelled her ankles so that she had to grab for the table to stay upright. 'I hate you,' he shouted. 'Fucking fuck.'

I want to be mean. I want to be really cruel, Rosy realised, looking down at her child as he contorted in the throes of his devastation. I want to punish him for being him. I want to make him cry so hard he's sick.

'Mothers are supposed to be hated, Boo,' she said lightly. 'That's our job. Along with looking after our thankless children and keeping them fed and cleaning up after them and

56

not ever having any kind of life.' She tried to step over him but he wrapped his arms around her legs and tried to bite her through the cloth of her jeans. 'That's enough, Tom,' she said, more sharply. 'Or you can stay in your bedroom for the rest of the week.'

He threw himself away from her and lay sprawled across the pocked vinyl floor. His eyes were squeezed into crumpled slits, his mouth a thin bloodless line of effort. He's trying to get to that place inside his head, Rosy thought. He's trying to will himself there and become that other Tom. What if he can start to control it and then he finds out he can do it when people are awake, just for wanting to, just for not getting his own way? She slapped his cheek hard. 'Don't you dare do that bad thing. Do you hear me? It's not your fault, when it happens. Don't you dare make it your fault.'

His eyes opened. They were still the same clear grey eyes of the son she loved. He looked up at her, panting, silent for a moment, then he scrambled to his feet. 'When I'm a big boy you won't be able to keep me locked in this house or tell me what to do,' he said. 'I'll be able to go where I want and do what I want. You won't be able to stop me from doing anything. And if I want to have sleepovers I can.' He jabbed a finger at her, a bizarrely grown-up gesture from so young a child, then turned and ran from the room.

Rosy laughed and poured herself a glass of wine. 'You, my darling boy, have just dragged into the room the exact thing I've been trying so hard not to think about for the last year.'

She drank the bottle of wine and opened another, swallowing it down like medicine. It fuzzed the edges of her mind, fluffing them up so that there was a constant light buzz across her thoughts, but the core of her was still cold and sharp. The best kind of drunk, the kind that lowered the inhibitions without clouding the thinking. The pain in her ear had dulled to background suffering, less immediate in its clamour.

The television shouted from the living room, the volume turned so high it was close to blowing the speakers. Tom was trying his best to provoke her into going in there but she barely noticed the roar. In front of her on the table was his ruined drawing; beside it the pot of his tablets. She stared at the severed lion while she rolled the stem of her glass between her palms. 'It still looks like a dog to me,' she said to herself, and giggled quickly.

There would be something sickeningly appropriate about casting her beautiful, damaged son into a sleep he'd never wake from. For his sake. For her sake. Surely it wouldn't take more than the amount of pills in this pot?

Standing too quickly, lurching on her feet, she spilled her wine across the picture and watched the liquid run like blood across the white paper. Better slow the drinking down while she was still coherent, save the rest for later. She'd fetch him now and order him to take the tablets. Wrestle him to the floor and force them on him if she had to. She'd do it right now, before she changed her mind.

'Tom, come here,' she called. Her words were squashed beneath the greater noise of the television show. A moment's hesitation and this day would tip over into evening, tip over into night, become another day. Do it now.

The boy was playing with his action figures on the sofa when she opened the door to the living room, but he threw them from him and buried his face in his arms when he saw her. 'I won't talk to you,' he said. 'I don't have to.'

'I popped out and phoned Uncle Ross just now,' Rosy said, walking to the television and switching it off, 'and he wants us to go and visit him as soon as we can. Maybe next week.'

Tom raised his head and looked at her suspiciously. 'Really?'

'Yes, really. He was very excited at the thought of seeing you, Boo. He said you had to do one thing first though. Come into the kitchen with me.' She held out her hand and smiled at him.

Her son clambered to his feet and went with her back down the hall, his temper forgotten as though it had never been. He was bubbling with pleasure, gabbling questions. He would do anything she asked, right now, to be allowed to go and visit his uncle. Am I really going to do this? she thought. I wonder if I will. When it comes to it, surely I'll turn away just before opening the pot. If I do open it, surely I won't actually shake the pills out onto the table, feed them to him with a glass of milk, watch him swallow them down. This is just a test, I'm testing myself and my limits. I'll remember this tomorrow and try to be stronger from now on.

She upended the bottle over the table and the tablets skittered around on the shiny surface, bouncing over each other, spinning in every direction before she stilled them with her hand and swept them into a pile. 'There's eleven tablets here, Boo, and Uncle Ross wants you to take them all to show me that you're being a good boy and he can trust you to visit him. I know you don't want to have a long sleep, I know darling, but the sooner you take them and wake up the sooner we can go. What things would you like to pack? You can take as many toys as you want and choose the best of your comic books to show him how much you've been enjoying them.'

Tom's face fell at the sight of the tablets, but he was listening to her, she could tell. He was caught between the immediate unpleasantness of now and the lure of the future treat. Rosy filled a tumbler with milk and handed it to him, pushing on his shoulder so that he was seated in his chair. She took one of the pills and gave it to him. 'There you go. Chop chop. I'll have to try and find your little suitcase, won't I? I bet it's under your bed. And we'll go shopping for presents for him. Good boy, there you go. And again. Good boy.'

I could stop now. He's only had three. He might be sick but he'll be okay after three, I'm sure. I should put the rest back in the pot right now and take it outside and throw it as far away from us as possible.

'You're such a good boy, Boo. I love you very much. I didn't mean to be horrible to you earlier, I was just being cross and silly. Nearly there, darling, just a few more and we'll be done. Think how wonderful it will be when you wake up and we're ready to go. Uncle Ross was telling me how proud he is of you and how much he wants to see you.'

I could make him vomit now, before any of them have done any real harm. I could stick my fingers down his throat and turn him upside down. There's still time to change this.

'Shall we get you upstairs and into your pyjamas now, Boo? Let me carry you.'

His weight in her arms, the smell of his neck, already felt more like a memory than reality. He was somehow lighter than he used to be, a faded version of her son. He burped, a nasty wet sound, and murmured 'pardon me', linking his arms around her. She laid him on his bed and they both went through their routines: curtains closed, pyjamas on, water glass filled. Once he was under the blankets, his face a tiny glow against his pillows, Rosy picked up his old cloth bear and bent over to kiss his forehead.

'Sleep tight, my lovely boy,' she said, tucking the teddy into the space between his arm and ribs. Tom nodded and smiled up at her. 'Maybe Uncle Ross will take me to the big park near his house again,' he whispered. He was already starting to slur.

Rosy sat on the edge of the bed and took his hand in hers. 'I'm sure he will.'

She waited with him, stroking his hand, until he fell asleep. Then she stood up and walked into her bedroom, leaving the door wide open, lay down on her heap of sleeping bags and closed her eyes.

GHOST STORY

She was the only girl I've ever known who could make walking boots and a duffle coat look sexy. I was in love before I'd even got out of the car, before I'd even met her properly. Curls like kinked copper piping, eyes the same colour as rain-soaked oak. She stood in the lane and smiled as if she wanted nothing more than to spend this autumn day in the woods with a city boy, a friend of a friend, and help him with his thesis on haunted houses. I could have spent the rest of my life just sitting there, gripping the steering wheel, watching her smile at me, but I figured I had thirty seconds, tops, before she started to get nervous.

I slid out of the car and hefted my backpack onto my shoulder, trying to stand tall and relaxed as if I did this country living lark every day. My new walking boots were already starting to scrape the skin from my right heel and I knew I'd be limping before we got further than the first stile. My mate in Cardiff, the one who'd hooked me up with this beautiful creature, had lent me thick wool socks and told me they needed to be worn outside the jeans, pulled all the way to the knee. When I whined that they made me look like a dick he told me that the deerstalker hat with the price tag still dangling made me look like a dick. The socks just made me look slightly froggish.

'Megan?' I asked as I bent to stop one of the socks from

shuffling back down my shin. 'Hi, I'm Matt. Thanks so much for saying you'll help.'

She gave me her hand. 'It's a pleasure; Gran loves visitors. We'll go straight in now, before lunch. You won't want to be there when she gets stuck into her soup.'

We walked to the houses grouped along the lane. 'Old fisherman's cottages,' she said. 'They're all the same here in Aberarth, they turn their backs to the sea. And this one's hers. Boots off, I'm afraid. She doesn't like to vacuum that often.' She grinned at me. 'And you might be more comfortable if you wore the socks under your jeans.'

I sat in the tiny front room, testing my Dictaphone, while the kettle and Megan whistled in the kitchen. Her gran eyed me expectantly from an armchair.

'What's that thing?' she asked.

I showed her the Dictaphone and clicked a few of the buttons. 'It'll record everything you say and then I can write it up later.'

She seemed impressed. She nodded a couple of times and stared at the wall for a while, mouth pursed. 'Not going to give me cancer, is it?'

'No, Mrs Howells, it's safe.' I held it out to her. 'Do you want a closer look?'

She flapped a hand at me and tugged her blanket further up her chest. 'You keep hold of it. No reason why I should have to have it.'

The return of Megan had me fumbling pen and papers to the carpet. I think she knew the effect she had on me, but she was graceful about it and let me help her with the tea while she picked up my notes. Her gran sat and watched us through narrowed eyes as milky pale and faded as sea glass. 'Crumbs!' she barked as I took a piece of cake. Megan softened the command by winking at me as she leaned forward with a plate.

Once centre-stage, Mrs Howells set aside her suspicions of my character and modern technology and shuffled forward in her chair so that she could tap my wrist with her spoon whenever the fancy took her.

'It's way up in the valley,' she said. 'Up where the Arth is still more stream than river. She'll take you,' a nod towards Megan, 'though I don't like her going and I've told her so. There're a lot of ruined cottages up there, scattered through the woods. Most of them were crumbled down to nothing by the time I was born but that one was still lived in. My mother took me there every Sunday with a basket of bread and some potatoes. Christian charity, she said, but I knew it was because she was scared.' The quick, precise flick of her spoon against my wrist bone made me jump.

'You see, she was a witch. The woman who lived in the cottage. Nobody ever said as much but we all knew it. Once a month she'd come down to the village and stand in the lane, not looking at us, not speaking, just waiting. We'd all, each household, fill her sack with what food we had and then she'd go. She touched my mother once, laid a hand on her stomach when she was pregnant with me and blessed the bump. Four miscarriages before that but she carried me straight through and delivered me with barely a drop of blood spilt. But what you can give you can also take away, that's what my mother thought, and that's why she made the extra offerings. Just. In. Case.' Three more taps of her spoon. I had to stifle a grin and knew that Megan was smiling behind her mug.

'And then one day she had a child with her. A girl, not much more than a toddler and weak as a newborn. There was something wrong with her, you know, in the head. Constantly dribbling. She'd walk in circles if she were put down. Nobody could believe the witch had had her the usual way, no man would dare go near her, so the little one must have been dumped in the woods like people dump kittens they don't want. Either that or she stole her.

'Anyway, things carried on as they were and no questions asked. Blankets and firewood and vegetables in the winter, apples and fish in the summer. We all rubbed along and the child seemed healthy enough. Didn't like us though. I never saw her smile, not once. My mother made me give her a bag of my old toys one Christmas and she tipped them out onto the ground in front of me and stood on each one, grinding them under her shoes. I cried all the way home.'

She settled back in her chair and raised her eyebrows at Megan, who stood up and gathered the mugs. 'More tea?'

I nodded and murmured a thank you but was so engrossed in her grandmother's story I forgot to look up to watch Meg leave the room, and by the time I remembered she'd disappeared back into the kitchen. Mrs Howells thinned her lips and folded her arms, staring at me. We waited in silence until Megan returned and only then did she unfold her arms and carry on.

'Yes, she was an odd one, that girl. She used to spend her time sitting in the upstairs window of the cottage and gawking at the world around her. There can't have been much of a view, it was all trees, but she'd sit and stare and point the way you or I would if we were dropped onto the busiest street in

London. Who knows, maybe she saw things in the trees the likes of us couldn't see?

'When the witch died the girl couldn't have been more than half grown, eleven at most. We should have done something then, someone should have, it's not right to leave a little girl up in the woods all by herself. But, you see, we didn't want her. None of us wanted her. So, we never talked about it. Left the odd bag of potatoes by the door, that kind of thing, and pretended that she didn't exist. She made it easy for us, she never came to the village in the daytime, though there were some who said they saw her now and then after dark, digging through the allotments.'

She nodded at the memory and reached for her tea. 'Any more cake, Meg? I can't remember exactly when she died but it was a few years later. Some childhood illness she should have left behind with her pigtails, but I suppose she was a late bloomer for that kind of thing, what with being so backward. A few people said that they'd stopped seeing her at the window but none of us wanted to know so nobody knocked on the door. Nobody went in to check.

'A couple of tourists found her a few months later. Walkers, they were, and they raised a right fuss afterwards, trying to get the police interested. Made us feel like criminals. She'd been dead a while. Curled on the floor beneath the window in the upstairs room, fingers hooked round the edge of the sill. As if she'd tried to drag herself up for one last look out. Poor girl.'

I took another piece of cake. 'Did you ever find out where she came from? Did any relatives come forward?'

She glared at me. 'I haven't finished yet, young man. You

can ask your questions later. You wanted to hear a haunted house story and I'm just getting to that part.'

She acknowledged my mouthed apology with a slight movement of her head and cleared her throat.

'So there we were, all very sorry for the poor girl, but really, it wasn't as if we'd done anything wrong. She was taken away and buried in the churchyard on the top of the hill. You couldn't pay for a view like that these days. Meg can take you up to see the grave, I'm sure, if you can handle the walk.' The doubtful glance she gave me spoke volumes about her confidence in my ability to handle a walk even half that distance.

'After she was buried, we didn't give her any more thought, if I'm honest. It was over and done with. There were a few hardnosed types, mentioning no names, who went up to the cottage to see if there was anything worth taking, and a few ghouls who wanted to see where she'd died, but the rest of us left well alone. And then the troubles began.'

My Dictaphone suddenly let out a high-pitched squeak and I echoed it with my own chirrup of alarm. Megan chuckled quietly from her corner and her gran threw back her head and bellowed her delight.

'Got you scared, have I?' she asked, as I fiddled with the tiny machine. 'Like a ghost story, do you?'

I tried to laugh. 'Love them. I'm a big kid when it comes to a good ghosting and the scarier the better. Please, carry on.' I was desperate to press my hands to my hot cheeks but didn't want to draw any more attention to myself.

'So,' she continued, still smiling, 'during that autumn, a few months after she'd died, we had an outbreak of whooping cough in the village. It claimed nine young lives in a few weeks. They had to shut the village school; there was no one to fill it. In the winter we lost five souls at sea. Old Evans and his three lads first, in one fell swoop, all gone. There wasn't even a storm. Poor Aggie, his widow, she was never the same.

'By the next spring we were all of us wearing black in one form or another. I lost both parents to their hearts and the lady who lived next door broke her leg and got an infection that carried her off. There were whispers that the witch had put a curse on us for neglecting her child, and some folk even started leaving offerings up at the cottage. I got married and fell pregnant and barely left the house once I started showing, the looks I got. Everyone expected me to lose it, you see. But I didn't. Her mother.' She pointed at Megan.

'And then people started hearing things up in the woods. A courting couple came running down the lane one day, showing a lot more flesh than was decent and whiter in the face than my bed sheets. And you can trust me on this, young man, my bed sheets are the whitest things you'll ever see. They said they'd been sheltering from the rain in the cottage when they heard someone moving around upstairs. Before they could get their clothes back on footsteps came running down the stairs into the next room. The inner door burst wide open, ripped off its hinges. They didn't stop screaming until they were half a mile away and too out of breath to scream any more. Stopped their kissing and cuddling it did, though, which pleased the girl's mother no end because the boy was a bad sort and no good for her.

'Then young Tomos was found hanging from a tree next to the cottage. He'd failed his school exams and couldn't cope with the shame, so the story goes, but I'd seen him that morning and he told me that he was going to be allowed to take them again in a year. He wasn't cheerful but he didn't seem about to kill himself either. So, what do you think of that?'

I nodded and sucked on the end of my pen. 'Great, Mrs Howells. Not your usual haunted house story but it's definitely got me spooked.' My cheeks had died down enough by now for me to risk a joke at my own expense.

She bridled and raised her spoon. 'Not a proper haunted house? Tell me what you were expecting then. Go on. Not a proper haunted house! What would you say if I told you I've seen things with my own eyes?' She didn't let me answer. 'Now, I don't like to talk about this and I don't believe in ghosts like you see on the telly. Headless horsemen and the rest. But I do believe in bad spirits, and bad energy. I do now, anyway.' She shifted forward and lowered her voice.

'It was a couple of years later and there'd been a few more incidents. The hunt that went through the woods every Boxing Day came to a sticky end, horses bolting and bones snapped all round. A little boy went missing from Aberystwyth and was found wandering in the woods, covered in bite marks. Human bite marks. He wouldn't tell a soul how he got there. There was nothing that couldn't be explained away by ordinary men and their ordinary wickedness, but still. I'd taken to walking through the woods myself, to blow the cobwebs away. I was having some trouble with my husband and liked to get out of the house when I could. But I never went near the cottage. As soon as I could see it through the trees I skirted off the path and kept my distance.

'The day it happened I was alone and happy enough. I'd walked for a while and stopped below the cottage, on the river-bank, to cool my feet. I couldn't see it through the overgrown trees and barely remembered why I was avoiding it anymore. It was a warm afternoon and I was almost asleep when I heard something hit the ground behind me, so I turned to see. It was a wooden horse, about the size of your fist, and just like the one I used to have when I was little. I remember I was pleased and thought I could take it home for my girls. Then I saw something else, a few feet away. A tin pig, the kind you paint and add to a farmyard set. I stood with it in my hands and looked at it and I knew exactly where its ear would have a slight nick. You see, it wasn't just like the one I'd had when I was a girl, it was the one. The one I'd given to the witch's child all those years before.

'Well, my heart started beating fast then and I looked up at the cottage. I was still a way away but even so I could see there was someone standing in the doorway, just standing there, watching me. I forgot I was a wife and mother then, a grown woman, and I turned to run.' She swallowed loudly. 'And that's when I was grabbed from behind. Arms around my waist, and tight so I thought they'd split my ribs wide open. Someone pulled and dragged me towards the cottage. Words in my ear, wet words hard as pebbles. *Now you! Now you!* I screamed and kicked and heard shouting in the distance. It was a couple from the village. Incomers they were. I'd been as unwelcoming as the rest when they'd moved in but I was glad to see them then and never heard a bad word said about them after.

'By the time they reached me I was alone and scratched up, in a state. They had to half carry me back to the village. I was terrified I'd be pulled back to the cottage, so I clung to them all the way home.'

Her hands were shaking. When I cleared the fear from my throat she flinched and pushed them beneath her blanket, and I pretended I hadn't seen.

'So, that's my story. I've never been back to those woods since and I wouldn't again, not even if you paid me. I don't like Meg going but she's as stubborn as her mother.'

Meg shifted in her chair and glanced at me. 'Nearly time for lunch. I'll heat up the soup.'

I followed her into the kitchen. 'What a great story. She really believes it, doesn't she? Do you think she'll mind if I ask her a few questions?'

Meg moved close to reach a saucepan down from the shelf behind me. 'I think she's had enough for today. She's still there, in her head. I don't want to leave her scared.' She touched my shoulder, quickly. 'I've heard it before, anyway, so I can probably fill in any gaps for you. We should go in a minute. It's a long walk.'

I stood by the window and waited as she heated the soup and switched the television on, leaning over her grandmother with a murmured comment and kissing the top of her head. Mrs Howells accepted the tray placed on her lap with a nod. 'Thanks, cariad.' Her hands were steady now and her attention seemingly on the lunchtime news bulletin. Megan had been right about not wanting to be in the room when she started eating. Any appetite I'd had crashed into the wall along with the bits of half chewed carrot that exploded from her mouth.

As I squatted on the doorstep and wrestled my feet into my walking boots, she called to me from her armchair. 'You look after my granddaughter, do you hear me? Don't think of coming back without her.'

I craned my head around the frame and gave her my most reassuring smile. 'Don't worry, I'll keep her safe.'

Megan stepped past me and pulled the door closed, but not before I heard her grandmother's response. 'Patronising little city boy. He'll start running as soon as a cow moos at him, I know his type.'

True to my word, and stung by this slur on my manhood, I tried to help Megan over the first two stiles. We tussled, legs at extraordinary angles, until she laughed and pushed me gently away. 'I can manage, really. Save your energy for the uphill bits. And for the cows.' She winked at me and I imagined leaning forward, kissing her. I bent and fiddled with my boot.

The path narrowed through gorse and thorn, winding up the side of the hill. The village was soon no more than a grey slide of rooftops and chimneystacks. I was too out of breath to speak, too focused on not panting, but Megan seemed to float in front of me, twisting to point at the view as it fell away behind us, pushing her hair back with an impatient hand.

'You don't mind taking me?' I asked when the path had levelled out a little and I felt less sick. 'After what your gran said? It doesn't scare you?'

She stopped and pulled a bottle of water from her backpack. 'Don't be silly. I don't believe in ghosts and I've played in those woods since I was tiny. I know my gran thinks something happened to her there, but she was quite fragile back then.'

She offered the water and looked away from me, down over

the gnarl of treetops towards the flat grey of the sea. We'd climbed a fair way and cleared the woods, but they stretched ahead and beneath us, in the distance. I guessed that was where we were going, to rejoin the river and follow its rush to the cottage.

'My granddad used to beat her,' Meg said, still staring down at the sea. 'It got so she was too scared to be at home and too scared to stay away in case it made him angrier. She had break-downs and even went into hospital for a while. You wouldn't think it to see her now, so strong, but she used to jump at the buzzing of a bee in the garden. She thought it was him all of the time. She thought he was just behind her, even when he was in the next village, working. He became her entire world.'

We carried on walking, but slower now. 'Did she go to the police?' I asked.

Megan shook her head. 'I don't think she even tried. You just put up with it back then. No, he died. Heart attack. My mum was still a girl but just as relieved. She had her fair share of bruises too. She says they wore pink at the funeral and tap danced behind his coffin.'

She did a quick jig, clumsy in her thick layers, and laughed as she stumbled and I caught her arm to steady her. 'All downhill from here,' she said, gesturing towards the valley ahead of us. 'And that's where the fun begins. There's no real path anymore so we'll have to do a bit of clambering once we get into the woods. Take a good long look at the sky while you still can, Matt. The trees are so dense at the bottom, where the river is, you won't even know the sun's shining.'

'We need breadcrumbs,' I told her as she strode ahead. 'To lead us back out.'

'Oh, I can get us back out,' she assured me. 'If they let us go.' And she grinned.

That fear again, just a tickle between my shoulder blades but as addictive as anything I'd ever known. I loved it.

I followed Megan down through a sheep-scattered field to where the trees elbowed each other. She slipped under the fence and faded away, lost against the dim backdrop. As I scrambled after, skidding to my knees, I called out to her to wait. The pale angles of her face gleamed supernaturally white as she turned to me. 'Are you okay?'

I resisted the urge to take her hand. 'I couldn't see you properly. It's like the light's being squashed by all these trees.'

She nodded and peered at her watch. I wondered if she had plans for the evening. 'It's going to be steep for a while now,' she said. 'Be careful and if you start to slip just sit down.'

After the third skid had landed me on my back, I decided it would be easier to just stay seated and slide the rest of the way. I didn't know how Megan kept her footing. She glanced round a couple of times to check on me, but we didn't speak until we were at the very base of the valley, enclosed on all sides. I could hear the river toiling somewhere out of sight. It was several degrees colder and my jeans were heavy with mud. I tried not to shiver.

Megan pulled me to my feet. 'Not far now. If we can get to the riverbank, we can follow it to the cottage.' She started to force her way through the undergrowth, swearing quietly as brambles scratched at her legs. 'They caught a monkey in these woods a few years ago, you know. It had escaped from a private collection and didn't know how to survive by itself, out in the wild. A couple of kids saw it first and ran home to tell their parents, then two of the local farmers took their shotguns and went after it. Not much of a hunt, by all accounts. The poor little thing ran straight up to them. All it wanted was to be looked after. They took it into the pub afterwards, all puffed up like they'd done something clever. The little dead body dangled by its tail for everyone to see.' She grimaced. 'It trusted them to keep it safe and they killed it. Probably laughed as they pulled the trigger.'

We were at the riverbank now. I tipped my head back and could just make out tiny patches of sky between the thick layers of tree canopy above me. They looked a long way away. The movement made me dizzy and the leaf mould I was up to my knees in made me sneeze. Something had gone from the day. I was struggling to recapture that sense of anticipation and fun I'd felt before we entered the woods. If her sober monkey story was anything to go by, Megan's mood was dipping too. I didn't really have anything to lose.

'Maybe we can go for a drink afterwards,' I said. 'If you want to?'

She smiled at me and reached to brush something from my shoulder. 'That would be nice. You can tell me a ghost story over a pint.'

Before I could decide whether she was flirting she'd turned away and started walking upriver. I suppose I should have taken the lead and trampled the worst of the brambles, helped her over the fallen logs, but I was content to stay behind and enjoy the way her jeans tightened across her thighs as she kicked a path clear for us. I allowed myself a tiny daydream or two.

When she stopped I was so engrossed in my own thoughts

I barely registered the sudden stillness until I'd cannoned into her and almost knocked her off her feet. We were both warmed from the walk, cheeks pinked by exertion. She clutched at my arms to keep herself upright and pointed over my shoulder. 'There it is.'

And there it was. So tangled in ivy I would have missed it if I'd been by myself. Half of the roof was gone and the other half looked as if it was hanging by cobwebs alone. There was no door to keep the elements out, no glass in the window frames. They punctured the stone walls, blank and black, like eye sockets. I started to walk over, fumbling in my backpack for my camera, clicking off a couple of shots, and then something moved in the upstairs window. A quick, pale blur of something. I squeaked and took a step back, and behind me Megan laughed.

'It's a dove, look.' She clapped her hands and the bird launched itself from the sill, flapping wildly as it tore away. 'But I know what you thought. Just for a second it could have been a face. That's the window the girl used to sit at, before she died.'

She stepped past me and walked up to the doorway, pouting and draping herself against the frame like a model on a photo shoot. 'Do you want a picture of me?'

I thought I might as well fire off a few rounds, seeing as she was asking.

'And what about one from the window? I could sit up there and look out, the way she did.'

She ducked inside the cottage. I could hear her stumbling around.

'Be careful,' I shouted. 'The whole lot might come down on you. It doesn't look safe.'

She shouted something back, something unintelligible but reassuring, and I relaxed and scuffed around outside while I waited for her to reappear. Blocks of stone lay scattered, presumably loosened from the cottage walls by harsh winters. I prodded one with my toe. It was a chunky blue-grey, shot through with seams of milky quartz. Beautiful enough to take home and lay on my mantelpiece as a souvenir. I bent to pick it up.

Beneath it, something pink lay half buried in the earth. Pig pink. I held it in my hand and turned it over, wiping it clean on the front of my jacket. Its rusted face leered up at me. There was a slight nick to the ear. I shuddered with my whole body then, felt the shudder kink the hairs on my head and crease the skin across my feet. I dropped the toy and stepped back, looking to see if Megan was at the window. I thought I could hear her somewhere inside the cottage, I could definitely hear someone, but there was no answer when I called out.

This was usually the best bit for me, when the thrill teetered over into fear and that fear threatened to gallop away with my adult self and turn me back to a child. Monsters and werewolves flickering on the edges of my vision. But I suddenly wanted Megan outside, with me, where I could see her and know she was okay. Then I could let myself enjoy it, the getting spooked and the afterglow of safety when the grown man in me reasserted himself.

'Meg,' I shouted, 'just come down. I'm getting cold.'

My eyes were starting to water. 'Megan, answer me.'

When she appeared at the window, popping up in a flurry of hair and limbs to fill that dark space, I actually screamed, and then we both laughed and I couldn't stop.

'Did you think I was her?' she called. 'It smells really bad in here. No ghosts though.'

She hooked one hand around the frame and leaned out. 'Get one of me like this.'

I looked at her through the camera lens. 'Get back in first. If you fall and break your neck your gran will make mincemeat of me.' I adjusted the focus and watched as she hauled herself back inside the cottage, crossing her arms on the sill and smiling down at me.

'Better?'

I grinned at her. 'Much better.' I raised the camera again.

Then she turned her head quickly as if she'd heard something in the room behind her. When she looked back at me her face was almost mask-like with surprise. I started to say something, but she jerked with a sudden, vicious convulsion and her mouth opened wide. Loose masonry from the window scattered down to my feet.

I tried to laugh, still half convinced that she was joking around. 'Meg?'

Her lips clamped shut, teeth grinding, and then opened again, wide. But she didn't speak.

Over her shoulder a face appeared, chin resting on the curve of her neck. If we'd been anywhere else it would have looked like a gesture of affection, the two heads so close. But here, it was something else. 'Meg?' I said.

We stared at each other. Something twitched at her waist and I knew then that she couldn't move, couldn't speak, because of the arms encircling her ribcage. 'Meg?'

The face, the other face, turned to me. Young, pockmarked, and grinning as if she'd only just learnt how and now would never stop. That grin stretched her skin so that the corners of her mouth were torn and bloody and I could see the meaty length of her tongue. She looked at me and whispered something into Meg's ear, and Meg shut her eyes. They were glassy with tears when she opened them again. Her hands clung to the sill, fingers white and rigid, and then something snapped with a crisp rip and she sagged and let go. I thought of twigs crunching underfoot but knew it was one of her ribs.

I still believe I might have done something then, gone inside and got her out, but as we looked at each other, the three of us, I heard footsteps making their way down the stairs, somewhere in the dark cottage, and I knew the three of us would soon be the four of us. My body hijacked any conscious intention and threw me backwards, away from the footsteps and the grinning face, and from Meg.

She was still staring at me, tears on her cheeks, when I dropped my rucksack and ran back to the river. Up to my waist in it and plunging downstream, legs and arms thrashing, screaming Meg's name. But I didn't look back.

I don't know how long it took me to reach the beach and I don't know how long I lay there on the sand, monstrous in my seaweed wrappings. I was half drowned and hypothermic. The police brought Meg out of the woods, splintered through with broken bones. They worked hard to get me to admit to having killed her, to being high on drugs. They didn't believe me when I told them about the witch.

When they finally gave me my camera back, I sat for hours with the photographs, just looking at her. There were two that the police had missed. In both of them, the witch stood in the doorway of the cottage and watched me not watching her. Her child leaned from the upstairs window and grinned, not at me, but past me, at Meg. I burnt those ones.

But the photographs of Megan, twirling, posing, pouting, I'll keep them forever. She really was the most beautiful girl I've ever known.

DROPPED STITCHES

I was born with an extra two fingers on each hand, to a mother
with four fingers less than nature usually gives out. The
women in our family believed all things happened for a reason,
both good and bad. I was considered too young to have an
opinion on that but if I'd been asked I'd have said I was just
grateful I hadn't been born with an extra liver. There were a
few big drinkers in our village.

My mother, when I was still small enough to get a slap
around the side of the head for my cheek, took my spares and
sewed them onto her clumsy handshake with scarlet thread.
She said, flexing her new grip admiringly in front of the
mirror, that the intricate double feather chain stitches she'd
used were practical. I knew she thought they were pretty and
bold, turning flesh into art. And the thread matched the hem
of her best dress.

From that day the empty tips of my lost fingers itched and
tingled whenever I was tired or emotional. I'd stroke my
thumbs across their memory and look over at my mother
curved in her armchair, scribbling on sheets of paper or
making love to her embroidery frame. I'd watch the busy skill
of her patchwork hands and miss the fourteen messy whirls I
used to press into the grime of my bedroom window every
morning, miss being able to cradle a half dozen warm hen's
eggs in each palm without dropping any. I even missed being

called a circus freak by the other children in the school playground.

The way I felt my way through the world had been changed unalterably. My senses were stunted now, more two-dimensional than three-dimensional. Or maybe this was simply life as other people experienced it; I didn't have any way of measuring that. All I knew was absence, a dimming of my ability to connect with the world around me through touch and know it through its textures and its edges. I started to bump into things, get headaches, need thick-lensed spectacles. Ear infections plagued my winters.

The puckered scars of my lost fingers trailed ghosts that haunted us both. I'd see Mother wince and pinch a finger into her mouth, start gnawing distractedly, when my phantoms started their tingle. It was as though she were trying to chew the print right off them, erase those delicate skin swirls that shouted my name, my essence. Those unique marks that strained for me across the room.

She never looked up to meet my gaze, never acknowledged any discomfort, but would tell me sharply to fetch her a glass of water or run upstairs for her cushion. I'd mutter my way out of the room and lurk in the hallway a moment to watch her through the crack in the door. Only then, when she thought herself alone and unobserved, would she glare down at her no-longer-lacking hands, her symmetrical and normal hands, and threaten them with candle flame or pins if they didn't stop throbbing and let her get on with her work.

Mother was a dressmaker whose creations had been stunning even when the labour was arduous. My memories are all of her using her mouth to bridge the gap where her index fingers should have been, teasing needles through fabric with lips and tongue. Her smile was bloody more often than not. Her dresses had to be rinsed in salt water to loosen the stains before they could be shown to customers. *I've gained more than you've lost*, she told me once when I complained about my hollow knuckles. *You should be more generous-spirited, more grateful. Now you've got ordinary hands that look the same as everyone else's.*

But being ordinary, or not, had never bothered me. The doctor had called my extra fingers abnormal, and my aunts had knitted special winter gloves with smug pity. The priest had even gone so far as to suggest that my scalp be inspected for unusual marks. None of it had mattered when stacked against the fact that I could juggle five balls for longer than any of my friends, could keep them flowing up up, arcing from my hands to the clouds and back like a grubby Catherine Wheel.

When I grew older, and into the coveted bra my mother had made for me out of silk scraps, I realised that I had control over my severed identity. Well, within the limits imposed by the past use of sewing scissors and scarlet thread anyway. With a teenager's sly spite, I would flick the empty space above my hands where fingers had once been, and Ma would jerk and hiss pain through lips thin and pale as worms. I would make a fist around shadow tips, give a sharp twist, and she would bend and gasp, drum her feet. It was as though she were soft and boneless, my puppet mother, and I was tugging strings attached to fabric limbs, forcing her tortured dance across the kitchen's stage.

With each passing year, as I gained in strength and maturity, my mother weakened with the effort to hold onto who she was. Her memories floated like flotsam in the wreck of her mind, bumping up against mine, tangling in them. She held her hand out to me whenever I passed her chair and pressed her fingers, my once-fingers, against the pulse in my wrist to keep me close. She called me by her own name and spoke about herself in the third person, using my name. Those years of resistance, that refusal to acknowledge the mingled confusion of our identities with the theft of my body parts, had finally defeated her. Her hands became numb and chilled, only ever warm when they were tucked into my palms in a muddle of flesh, most of it mine. She was ravenous for affection and approval, just as I had once been.

I nursed her through her end days, staying by her bedside while my father tipped evenings down his throat at the local tavern. Shawl-wrapped against the frosted world, I sat and sang childhood songs to her, tapping out the tune across my knees with the handle of her sewing scissors. Her eyes followed the leap of metal as she shuddered against her heap of pillows. *You won't do it yet?* she asked me. I shook my head and cut the space between our faces a couple of times, enjoying the low, crisp growl the scissor blades made as they sliced ribbons from the cold air. *No, I'll wait*, I told her. *I've been patient this long.*

And I kept my word and waited until she was as cool as the room before I took my fingers back.

LIKE WATER THROUGH FINGERS

And you're here again and they still can't see you. But they won't even look, when I point they don't turn their heads and so how can they expect to. Stubborn is what they are. They refuse to fit their hands around mine and let me steer our cupped palms through you, to feel you spill like water through our fingers, they tell me not to touch. And when I plead and then I grab at them they press me back in my chair and tell me to *calm down, be quiet, stop getting so aggressive.*

And then you fade again and it's just me and them. It's easier for us all, when you're gone. They study my face and nod at each other and let me eat my dinner with the others. I've thought about pretending you're gone when you're not, wrapping you around me and wearing you like a shawl, knotted tight over my heart, but as soon as you're here I shine with it, with you, and I start to twitch and reach to pull you close. I can't help myself. And then they know you're here again and they stiffen and sigh, straighten up and put their cigarettes out. I'm starting to *become a nuisance.*

If I could stand I would, and dance with you like we used to. It wouldn't be as easy as back then, when you used to hold me pressed against your chest as if I might float away, and you'd slip your palms down past where my spine flares out to flesh, and flirt them there, and smile at me. Do you remember how you used to do that? Now it would be more tentative, even ludicrous. Me with my absent legs trailing nails and panic through the murk of what you are, terrified you'd drop me. Maybe I'd slide down you like a waterfall, cascade over your torso, the rush of your thighs, and collapse in the froth of your faint, almost-there feet. And I'd flail around on the floor until someone came and lifted me back into my chair and told me to stop crying.

But what if that didn't happen? What if we could hold ourselves, and each other, in that place before skin breaks the surface of liquid and disappears below it? When I fill the sink in the bathroom and rest my hand on the water there's a moment when it's solid against my flesh. Its weight pushes back at me, all those molecules tight and gathered and thrusting, I can feel them. But then the tremble begins in my arms and forces my hand down through that moment, and it's ruined and I have to empty the sink and start again.

They don't let me do that too often. They bang on the door and if I don't answer at once then they barge in. I've told them that one of these days they'll interrupt me in the middle of something they'd rather not witness, but we both know they've seen it all and there's nothing that could embarrass them anymore. It's the water they're concerned about. The *waste*. I sometimes think I must be personally responsible for the thirst of millions, the way they go on about it. They call it an *obsession* and ask me how many times I've filled and emptied the sink today. Last week I was resting my face on the water's surface, trying to see if I could hold myself still enough to dance cheek to cheek with you and one of them came in and pulled me up by the hair and shouted for help. They didn't understand when I tried to explain. They wouldn't leave me alone after that, not for days.

And you're here again and I think I'm close to getting it right, that balance between us, that skating on water, so that we can touch without merging. It's enough that you're here though, I don't mind if I never get it right, but I'm practising anyway, I'm practising every day. When you're here and you smile at me the way you do it's enough.

They think they can help me *get over you* as if you're some kind of obstacle, a fallen branch on the ground in front of me that, with their support, I can scramble over. I have to talk to a lady who comes in twice a week. I've never seen her legs, she's always sat behind her desk and when I knock on the door she doesn't get up to let me in, she just calls out. Maybe she thinks she's being kind, or respectful, but it just seems rude. I have to wheel myself in and twist to shut the door behind me without tipping myself out of the chair and she just sits and watches or writes things in her notebook. You're never with me when she is. Even when I close my eyes and wish so hard to have you here again, for her to see you, you stay away.

We go through the same things each time and I wonder if she's as bored as I am. She asks how often I've seen you. She asks whether you've changed. Whether you speak. In our last session she told me to explain why you don't look the way you looked when I last saw you. She said that, if you were really real, you'd be suspended in the moment of death, swollen and blue, and that's what I'd see. I asked her if she was an expert on the paranormal but she just smiled and gave me two books on grief to read and one on PTSD then wrote something in her notebook. I don't think she likes me at all.

The other people who stay here told me they've seen you too. Twice in the kitchen and once in the garden. I wanted to hit them. Why would you be doing that, giving yourself to them when you never even knew them? I think they're lying just to get attention but then I'm scared that they're telling the truth. It annoys the staff though. They call it *group hysteria* and glare at me as if it's my fault, like I'm doing this on purpose just to create problems. They say when I leave here things will settle down, because I'll take you with me and there won't be any more of these *fantasies*. But what if they're wrong and you don't come with me? What if you stay here and they won't let me come back to see you? All that's a long way off though, because I heard them saying that I couldn't be trusted by myself, away from here, until I'd *accepted what had happened and stopped trying to drown myself in the sink.* So I don't need to worry about it for a while.

And you're here again and I'm just going to sit by the window with you beside me and watch the afternoon filter through you, and we'll smile at each other and it's a perfect way to spend my time. I love the way the sun turns you dusty, like candlelight through a crystal-thick glass of brandy. I could sit here with you forever and never move, never want to move because you're here again, and it's only when I look away or someone speaks to me, that's when you go. So if they leave me alone I can concentrate just on us and you'll stay, for a while at least. I just need to concentrate.

I wish she hadn't said that, about the last time I saw you. She didn't need to say that when it's in my head all the time anyway. The swollen and blue. You're here right now though and that's all that matters. The other time, the last time, I don't want to think about that. I'd rather have no legs and the way it is now than have my legs and the way it was then, the last time I saw you.

Crushed. I knew they were crushed beneath the steering column. The car was reared over me and I wanted to move but I couldn't move and so I sat there, propped like a doll on a shelf, safe and strapped in, and I watched as your feet jerked and tapped on the car's bonnet, almost close enough to touch if I leaned through the shattered windscreen, but I couldn't raise a hand to touch you and you drowned without a struggle in six inches of water. Six inches of water. And I sat with you through the night as we sank deeper into the ditch and I watched you and said your name and my legs got colder and colder but your feet stopped jerking and then you didn't move at all. Six inches of water. They kept saying that afterwards, as if it were so slight an amount, so ridiculous a death, we would all find it funny. They'd chopped my legs off by then.

So I sat with you through that night and stared at the soles of your shoes and remembered the first time we danced together, and it was the first time we loved and meant it, and that's it really. That's what we are.

But you're here again and you're smiling and I'm so close now, I'm practising so often, soon we'll be able to dance together, properly. Until then I'll just keep reaching out to you, and that's enough to make me happy, it's enough for now, to stroke my hands over you and feel you spill like water through my fingers.

MARIA'S SILENCE

Maria was perched on the back of the stone horse. Cross-legged, chin in palm, scowling into the distance. The early risers, humming their way wearily work-wards, saw her first. They jumped and blinked and let out yelps of wonder. They turned and ran or approached on tiptoe and reached out a trembling hand to touch her foot. Stroked fingertips through nothing.

She sat and scowled and ignored them all.

Somebody thought to fetch her parents and somebody else thought to boil up a kettle and sell hot tea. Before the morning sun had even started to warm the chill stone flank of the horse, the town square was thick and writhing with bodies. The church bells grumbled above their deserted shell.

Her mother, when she arrived, broke apart and poured grief in salty shrieks onto the horse's hooves. Her father stood rooted to the flagstones and had to be carried home in the arms of four men: a cardboard cut-out.

Her best friend ran to join the throng, shiny with hope and love, panting with exertion.

'Maria?' she called. 'Is it really you? Have you come home?'

Maria turned her head a little, and sighed, and continued to scowl.

'Maria, please! It's me, Anna. Come down and talk to me, tell me what happened. We thought you were dead!'

Anna began to weep. People looked suspiciously around, anticipating a cruel and tasteless prank. The grocer and the butcher began to argue with each other, and the postman's dog started to whine. The sun groaned and heaved its swollenness higher into the sky.

Anna scrambled up onto the horse's plinth, clambered over its timeless trot, and swung herself with a cry of triumph into its saddle. She flung her arms out to embrace her friend.

'Don't ignore me, Maria!'

Her hug collapsed through the air as if through honey and she lost her balance. Men leapt forward to catch her as she tumbled from the horse and jostled with each other to clutch her famous curves. Maria narrowed her eyes and blew a wisp of hair from the corner of her mouth. She uncurled her long legs, stretched, and resettled herself.

Anna jerked her flesh away from the men's clammy pinches and straightened her dishevelment. She shivered and pointed.

'It can't be!' She turned to the people standing, staring. 'Did you see? I couldn't touch her. There was nothing to hold onto!'

And she knelt and covered her face.

Maria shrugged and gazed moodily over the terrified screams. She began to bite at her fingernail.

By lunchtime Maria's mother had returned, though her father remained in their kitchen, where he'd been carefully set down. Strings of onions now dangled from his frozen wrists and several sun hats crowned his bushy head. An energetic card game was taking place around him.

'Speak to her, Isabella. Ask her what she wants!'

Maria's mother was nudged through the crowd. When grief

burned the words from her lips, elbows jabbed impatiently at her ribs.

'Maria? Are you a ghost? Have you come home? Do you want me to make you some coffee? The stove is lit, Maria, and your bed is made up, ready ...'

Her words fluttered around like torn paper, swirled on the breeze across the crowds, and floated past her daughter's face. Maria pouted out her lips and blew the words away. She turned her head slightly and her mother's trembles were no longer in her sight line.

Elbows crooked and created hard angles, swung into readiness, and Isabella wrapped her arms around her tender spots and hastened on.

'I want you to come back with me, Maria, and tell me what happened. Shall I bake you some gingerbread? Would you like that?'

Everybody shuffled and whispered. Somebody giggled.

The cobbler's wife, a woman more ancient than the tooth fairy, shuffled forwards and glared upwards.

'Do as your mother tells you! And don't forget that I've still got your last pair of dancing shoes in my shop, re-heeled and waiting to be paid for.'

She brought her cane down, hard, on the flagstones, and the people nearest to her jumped and gasped. Maria flinched but kept her scowl in place. The cobbler tutted.

His wife shook her head and held up a twisted hand.

'Right! If you don't come in and collect them by next Wednesday then I'll have them myself or put them in the window. There're plenty of others who'd like the chance to own such a well-made pair of shoes.'

She began to move away.

'Come on! All of you. Leave her to think about *that*. Red leather they are. Lovely. She'll soon come round.'

The townspeople trailed reluctantly in the choppy wake of her limp. Maria's mother waited until they had all left and the square was empty of everything but the high-pitched backwash of chatter. She stood beside her daughter and cupped her hand around the emptiness of Maria's ankle, memory finding the delicate bone there and stroking it.

'I'm just glad you're back, my love. We'll be at home, waiting, whenever you're ready. I'll make a start on the gingerbread right now.'

She sniffed and squeezed the air before releasing it. There was a second's silence, and then she started to wail.

Maria swallowed. She stared over her mother's head and readjusted her scowl.

Day after day, Maria stayed on her stone perch, gazing at the muddle of cottages surrounding her, or at the distant sea, draped like a spangled shawl across the horizon. People started to lay gifts around the horse, approaching sheepishly and departing quickly, or lingering to take a look at the offers on display. Flowers, bowls of milk, and dried sausages appeared and disappeared. The florist's cheeks grew fat and the butcher always had a pink rose in his buttonhole. When the dairymaid appeared every afternoon with her two pails, she was greeted with impatient muttering and the tap of spoon on tin mug.

When squabbles broke out over the last fresh roll, Maria ignored all requests to mediate. The tooth fairy's grandmother returned on one occasion, swollen feet howling inside scarlet leather, and had to use her cane to prod apart two elderly men who had both dived on a plate of scones, each refusing to surrender their claim. She delivered energetic stripes to their backsides as they squealed on the ground and crammed their pockets full of cake.

After that incident, a ban was placed on all offerings and instruction given that no more than five people would be permitted to congregate at the town square at any given time. After some confusion and disagreement it was decided that this rule be amended to specify only living people, at least until the questions surrounding Maria's mortality had been satisfactorily answered.

Isabella ensured that she was always one of the 'no more than five'. Each morning, after she had prepared the breakfast and sent Katya off to school, she took her clothes off and tried for an hour or so to overcome her husband's catatonia, swirling and shimmying before his fixed stare, and then she packed a basket with warm bread and hot chocolate and set off to spend some time with her eldest daughter.

'Today will be a good day,' she would mutter to herself, as she walked. 'Today she will talk to me.' And her smile would firm and brighten, her back straighten with a mother's pride, as she turned into the main street and spied Maria's shadow-less silhouette.

Anna was often there and when the two women met they would embrace and raise eyebrows, shake heads and sigh. They shared the contents of their lunch baskets, carefully divided between three plates, and they sang songs, exchanged scurrilous gossip, or filled Maria in on what had changed in the town over the last year, since she had 'been away'.

Maria never turned her head to acknowledge even the juiciest piece of news, though her scowl deepened and lightened in rhythm to the chatter, sometimes almost lifting clear into the sky and darting up to the clouds before swooping back down to her face.

One afternoon Anna brought along Maria's death certificate and held it up in front of her friend.

'Look. Just take a look at it. It says here that you died on May eighteenth, two days before your nineteenth birthday. Do you remember? Please tell me, Maria. Why are you here?'

She drew breath and continued on with raised voice.

'Did you know that I found you? Did you know that? You were just lying there on the beach, no mark on you, and I thought you were asleep. But you wouldn't wake up. And then the doctor said that you'd taken tablets. Have you come back to tell us why? Are you angry with me? You are, aren't you? Please talk to me, Maria.'

Maria rubbed the side of her nose and began to pick at a loose thread in her dress.

'Maria, please! Think of your mother and what she must be going through. She's used up all the sugar in the village with her baking and the hens are exhausted from laying so many eggs. If you won't talk to me then I'll bring paper, and a pencil, and you can write it down. Will you do that?'

Two young boys wandered past and paused in their whistling to stare at the famous ghost. One nudged the other and hefted his half-eaten apple to shoulder height. Drew back his arm and sniggered.

Maria twisted on the horse and bared her teeth.

The boy's screams blew them right out of their school trousers and raced neck and neck with them all the way home.

'That has to be a good sign. Don't you think that's a good sign?'

Isabella stopped slapping her husband's face. She began to twist his nose.

'She reacted to the boys. She scared them off. Maybe she's ready to talk… Oh, come on, Gabriel, at least make an effort to snap out of it! My hands are sore from massaging you and I'm starting to suspect that you're enjoying being spoon fed more than you're letting on. I've got a good mind to leave you in the cellar and see how that suits you.'

She gave his ears a quick, sharp tug and then released him and turned away.

'I'm going to fetch my knitting now and go back to the square. Don't expect any dinner and don't wait up for me. Katya's with the neighbours. Oh, and there's plenty of cake if you get peckish.'

She bustled from sewing box to kitchen cupboard and then jerked open the front door and hurried out, slamming it behind her. Rays of early evening sunshine which had been pressed up against the door, jostling for a turn at the keyhole, lost balance and spilled across the kitchen floor, before picking themselves up and darting into the gloom under the table.

Maria refused to grip the pencil she was offered, and she refused to whisper in her mother's ear. She plaited and re-plaited her hair, counted the freckles on her arm, and began to wipe clean with the sleeve of her blouse an area on the horse's neck.

Isabella lost patience.

'I've had enough of this! I know you can hear me and I'll bet you can talk to me, so why won't you make the effort? How can I help you if you won't even tell me what the problem is?'

She waited.

'Would you like the last piece of date loaf?'

Maria continued to rub.

'Fine. If that's the way you want it… But I'm not going anywhere. I've got my knitting and a flask of tea, and I'll stay here day and night if need be, until you decide to speak.'

Isabella wrapped herself up against the chill and sat on the ground, huffing and muttering. Her hip quickly started to ache and she began to moan bad temperedly. Her knitting needles clattered as she worked out her frustrations on a jumper for Katya. Above her, Maria shifted in her saddle.

The evening shrunk and leapt into the arms of the night, which cradled it and then set it aside. The moon shivered and drifted across the sky. The tooth fairy's grandmother clattered from shop to home in her new red shoes. The butcher, the grocer and the blacksmith drifted into the lamplight around the square, to laugh and banter and snatch peaks at the girls walking by.

Doors slammed and windows trembled in their frames. The men finished their drinks and shouted their goodbyes. The girls pouted and stopped tossing their hair. Flowers folded in on themselves like fallen ballerinas. Cats shed their daytime personas and danced with the shadows, practised their spells. Isabella dozed for a while.

When she awoke, she was cupped in the palm of deepest night. For a moment she felt the panic of childhood but then she raised herself and looked around her, probing the thick layers of jet until she could see the stars. She glanced up at Maria but couldn't make out her features. The world was asleep. The silence was complete. Joy settled on her.

And then she heard it. The absence of noise, and beneath that, her daughter's voice.

'Mama, can you hear me now?'

Isabella threw herself against the stone flank of the horse and began to sob.

'Maria! I can't believe you're finally speaking! Talk to me! Tell me how you are! Tell me everything!'

Maria covered her mouth. She closed her eyes.

'Maria! Speak to me!'

Isabella fed her grief with howls until it peaked and burst. She collapsed onto her knees and nodded her head. Gave her daughter silence. Maria opened her eyes and rested her hands back in her lap.

'Thank you, Mama. I came back to tell you that I'm sorry for what I did, for hurting you all. And I came back to tell you that you must give Katya silence once in a while. Let her be quiet when she needs to be and listen to her pauses as well as her words. Please do that for her, so that she doesn't become me.

'I must go now, I've stayed longer than I should, and it's tiring me as much as it ever did to have to compete with the noise of this world. I've been speaking to you the whole time I've been here and I've been waiting for you to be silent so that you could hear me. I love you, Mama.'

She reached out and traced a finger across her mother's cheekbone, though neither of them felt it.

She smiled.

PIECE BY PIECE

When you walk into this room pause for a moment, please, and look around you. Don't simply scan for walls that can be knocked through, don't just take mental measurement of the march from skirting board to skirting board and wonder how your greedy four-seater sofa will ever fit. Look down first, past the scuff of your leather shoes, and see how rich, how varied, the brown of the floorboards is. The grain carries every shade between mocha and bistre depending on the time of day. When the afternoon sun warms the wood, believe me, you'll feel an urge to take off your clothes and lie stretched across it, legs splayed as wide as they can get. You'll sink into it, deep down to the memory of its living roots, and you'll dream of burrowing mice and earthworms. In the early morning chill you'll need slippers, or socks at the very least, before you'll dare to tread its sharp, forest length, and even then you'll think of wolves and thorns and fear for fragile toes.

It didn't get this gleam by chance, you know. It was me. It was love. And hours of polishing, sliding around on my knees, queasy from the fumes. I massaged and I stroked and I drew its colours back to the surface whenever they started to flatten and fade. I talked to it the whole time. My hands would be so cramped after I'd finished, I wouldn't be able to straighten my fingers for the rest of the day, but it was worth it. The floor-boards sighed their delight and rubbed themselves against the pat of my palms, nudging my flesh until there was nothing else to do but take my clothes back off and use my body to smooth in the topcoat of polish.

Look up now and see the painted walls lighten as they drop to knee height. I did that myself, by mixing firebrick into vermilion in increasing amounts. And admire the stencil work up there by the mouldings, so delicate it's almost shadow play. Please don't think about wallpapering over it the moment you move in, you'll never see this shade of red again. I cut my hand when I was getting the lids off the pots and I let my blood drip into the paint. It bled a lot and I stirred it in well. I think it added something special to the mix.

You're interested in the stairs, I can tell. Look at you, you can barely keep your hands to yourself. Go on, swing your leg over the banister and slide down to the newel post, there's no one else around. I used to do that every morning, at the beginning. The sturdiness of the rail between my thighs always made me gasp and shiver. Sometimes, when I should have been on my way to work, I'd run up and slide back down, again and again. I was so playful back then. By the time I was finally settled behind my desk, damp from all the laughing, my hair one long tangle, it would be time for lunch. They let me go in the end, but I would have left anyway. There just weren't enough hours in the day, enough days in the week, and I resented every moment spent outside my own front door. I think of them sometimes, my work colleagues, rutting mindlessly in their filthy homes, rolling across carpets stricken with mould, walls collapsing around their ears, and I pity them. Who cares that a house isn't a conventional lover?

You'll see from the flagstones in the kitchen, the cornices

101

in the bedrooms, that this house has been stroked and fondled as much as any human body could ever be. They're almost as perfect as the day they were first fitted, and they're original pieces. But the honeymoon period ended, as it does, and by the time I reached the top floor the easy loving was gone. It wasn't enough anymore to just polish and paint. Gone were the long and sleepless nights when we'd lie together and I'd whisper my dreams into its corners. Gone the naked jiving through from lounge to porch. When I arranged to meet a friend at the pub down the road, just a quick drink, the new pipes I'd installed buckled and flooded the cellar. Boxes of my old diaries ruined. If I hurried to the corner shop to get more milk I'd return to a cold so spiteful my breath gusted from my mouth in dense sharp spikes and the radiators shivered.

I knew I was becoming *less* when I had to stand on a chair to reach the top of the doorframes to dust them. I could slip my arms through the supporting pillars of the banister, right up to the elbow. And then my fingernails began to soften and fall like bruised poppy petals. My hair unscrewed itself from my scalp and flung itself across carpets, across floorboards, across windowsills. By the time I'd finished sweeping and sponging, I had to start over again.

I'd lie awake at night and hear the grunts, the sighs, as the house shifted around me. It groaned as it reached to pull me close and at the same time sharpened its edges to give any offered embrace the sting of rejection. Even the light switches shocked me when I touched them. We were lovers at war and it was too big a foe, too jealous a beloved, to take my softness and leave me uncrushed. My passion stripped the flesh from my skeleton and then started on the very core of me, sucking until I was nothing but gristle and nerves.

My brittling bones, so close to the surface now, elbows and heels piercing skin, more mortar than marrow, brought me down beside the fireplace, here. The house's gaping mouth. Its empty heart. And here I lay, and let it take me, piece by piece.

It was always going to end like this, for me. I loved too much. I didn't know where to draw the line. But for you it could be different. The house just needs a firmer touch, a woman with a bit more backbone. Don't take any of its shit, and don't let it see how much you need it.

And if you do move in, please don't plasterboard over the hearth, and don't touch the mantelpiece. That's where I am now, what's left of me. I huddle into the cracks, crumbled as thin, as dry, as cement dust. But I still remember the feel of the banister between my thighs, the wild joy of laughing for hours, and I don't regret any of it.

THE GLAMOUR

I didn't see them for a while, at the beginning. I just heard them. And for the first couple of times at least I assumed they were a passing noise from outside, so I ignored them. Then, when I realised the sound was more immediate, much closer, I made an appointment with the doctor to get my hearing checked. I never kept the appointment.

The first time I saw them was brief, and in my peripheral vision. I put them down to damselflies or dust motes dancing on the sunbeams. I didn't think beyond the obvious because at that time I couldn't. My mind had become bordered thanks to the modern magics contained in the many bottles on my dresser.

The second time was just as brief, but more revealing. A ragged flutter of wings, a suggestion of humanity. When I turned my head they were gone but their shadows remained, faint and sweet.

They left me for a while and I almost forgot them, except in those vulnerable moments when first waking or slipping out into sleep. In the quiet of my rooms, in the quiet of the night, I would lie still, body tense, ears straining to recapture their almost presence, but find only absence.

They'd needed time to watch me, to learn to trust me. I think also to judge me. And they must have found me worthy of the gift of them because they returned one night while I slept and crept through my dreams, leaving trails of glitter and sparkle. Little explosions of beauty that made my slack mouth twitch and my eyes jitter beneath their lids.

I woke without hunger, without need, and felt *held*, emptied of loneliness. They were scattered across my pillows, vulnerable and still. We watched each other silently for a few moments and then I blinked a slow hello and curved just the very corner of my mouth upwards, so as not to frighten them, and they rose all together in one flick of movement and settled on my face. They rested their fragility on my cheeks, my eyes, my lips, inside my mouth, and suddenly they were breathing for me, or I was breathing through them, and the world shimmered and divided into rainbow fragments. Then they were away from me again and I could suddenly feel the trudge of my heart, the gurgle and suck of my organs, the whisper of my lungs, and it was all too awful. The weight and processes of my human body too real.

While I wept I watched them and they waited for me to recover my composure, gathered above and around me like vapour trails, close enough to bathe in my tears yet keeping a sliver of air between us. They whispered a name that I knew to be mine, their name for me, my rightful name, and I echoed the word, let it emerge like incense from my mouth and slip back into my ears. I had been claimed.

As I got ready for the day they stayed with me, weaving and cascading to form a veil against my head, a bouquet in front of my hands, a train behind my feet. But they didn't touch me again and I knew they were denying us all the repeat kiss of our souls merging, until I had made up my mind whether to join them. That decision had to be mine alone.

When I left the flat they stayed behind. I heaved my human body out of the door and walked away from them, my spine grinding and creaking with every step I took. I didn't look back because I didn't need to. I knew they were still there.

Through the time that followed I learnt stillness. By slowing my breath and not moving my limbs I was able to slow my heart and escape the worst of the noise of its beat, the resultant rush and rumble of my circulating blood. By not eating, I was spared the horrors of my digestive system crashing through me. I lived for those infinitesimal seconds between the beating of my heart, between breaths, when I was less human and more like them. I lived and I died, and it took so much longer than I would have expected.

The end came with jolting suddenness. The unanswered phone. The missed appointments. There crackled into being a tentative disquiet, a narrow point of concern widening and spreading to encircle me and turn me away from the awful beauty of my gift. As I lay on my bed, surrounded by my future, I could sense the encroaching march of my saviours. I knew I could no longer submit to embrace, but must instead reach out myself and embrace my gift in turn. Their urgency was transmitted through the tattoo of wings colliding with wings as they arced and spun above my face and shivered against my skin.

The effort it took me to leave my bed and cross the room was as much spiritual as physical. Every movement provided a backlash of horror and disgust at the rampant orchestra of my human body and its toil. I pushed aside the bottles of untouched tablets at the front of my dressing table; several weeks' accumulation of untwisted screw caps and bridled thought, and reached for the bottle at the back. My Sleeping Beauty tablets. My poisoned apple. I swallowed and shuddered my way through the bitter task, until the bottle was empty and returned to its place.

We lay together and waited for the pills to purge the mortality from me and accelerate my progression towards forever, but even that took so long. At the instant of my last breath in, and my last conscious thought, they settled around my mouth and allowed the tiny channel of air to draw them inside.

They floated, and penetrated, and then it was over.

WICH

I only wanted to write my name. To create the letters with ink and feather or needle and thread, and look at them and know that meant me. I only wanted a spelling book to learn the shapes of A and B and onwards through the alphabet's march, understand the angles and the curves and how to put them all together.

My hipbones were bookends for a womb considered excellent for forming and birthing children. Two full hand spans from bony peak to peak; space enough to fit twin sons and room to spare. A man would travel a long way to wed hips like mine, never mind the face. A man would overlook the impudence of eyes that spent more time raised to the skies than lowered to the floor, for hips like mine.

Our hard grey valley was dug from slate, steep and cold. It was like living at the bottom of a tin pail. Crows scooped holes in the clouds above me and disappeared to softer, greener lands, to other valleys where the sun sunk slow and lazy after dinnertime and shadows crept in violet patches to meet the twilight. Above our village the sun set like a guillotine and the shadows sprang sudden, dark and thick as spilled blood. Without wings I would never reach these other valleys. Without wings I was my mother. My daughter would be me.

If I couldn't have wings then I wanted words. To pin down the names of the places the crows flew to, those foreign places that browned the skin of the travelling folk who came from miles and days away. I thickened stews with turnips and flavoured them with marrow so that I could set aside the tasty sheep innards and trade them for letters. I carved buttons from bones, stained them bright and bold with berries, and bought myself lessons in the scraps of time the travellers gave while they ate my nettle broth, resting on my step with their baskets of trinkets set between their feet.

I practised with a finger drawn through the flour on the table as I made our bread. I dragged a stick through the clay of the riverbank as our clothes slumped sodden and forgotten beside me. Creating words, destroying words, creating them again, wherever I went, until the shapes I made became less strange and started to spark connections inside my head; attach themselves to the world around me. Dog, and tree, and sky.

When I became more sure of my letters, more confident, I began to commit them to surfaces that would hold them through rain and wind and snow. I wanted to press them onto the spaces around me with sly discretion and know they would endure past my lifetime.

But a man could not tolerate a wife who stole out of the house in the mornings and cut rough shapes into the birch tree's silvered skin with the knife that gutted the fish, leaving scales sparking like jewels in the wounds. The nights spent wallowing between my thighs did not salve the sore of my presumption. The generous spread of my hips was no protection.

The local people took my scratched attempts at spelling to be spells. They called me wich. My husband joined them in inspection of my words and saw the devil lurking in every scrape and groove. He nodded at their fear. He called me wich.

That was their name for me and so that was my name. While they discussed my fate, before they unbarred the door and led me from the house, I went from room to room and scratched my name wherever I could. On tabletop, door frame, bedpost, lintel. Wich. Wich. Wich.

THREE FOR A GIRL

I phoned Georgie as soon as I left the clinic.

'It's okay, ladybug, it's over now,' she said, and made sooth-ing noises as I fumbled coins into the slot and cried into my palm.

'Was it awful?' she asked. And then, 'Where are you? You should be at home.'

I stared into the glassed windowpanes that framed me and watched my face float, stretched and featureless, in the grime. 'I wish you were here,' I said. My hand smelt of the antiseptic that had saturated the treatment room.

'I do too. I'm so sorry.'

She didn't remind me that I'd given her no choice but to be absent, only telling her my plan a couple of days ago, and only because she'd phoned when I was drunk and off-guard.

She was silent for a moment. I knew what she wanted to say. I could hear the words rattling in her quick intake of breath, the slow release. But I gnawed my fingernails and waited, with a strange, detached curiosity, to see how she would phrase it. There was an edge of cruelty to my waiting, I suppose, forcing us both to experience this reality.

'Will you be okay when you come to stay? With me, with my ... state?' she finally asked.

When I laughed, I could hear the shrill of hysteria and hoped she couldn't. 'Your state? Shit, pea, you're having a baby, not a fit. It's okay to use the word pregnant. I'll be fine. More than fine. I can't wait to be an aunt and I'm desperate to see you fat.'

I knew she wasn't convinced but she turned us both away from pursuing that particular thread any further. My big sister, always the diplomat. 'I'll meet you from the train, ladybug,' she said. 'I'll wait on the platform. It's a request stop, don't forget. Mark's away until after next weekend but he's looking forward to seeing you then.'

She sounded even less convincing than I had. But when she'd married the bastard I'd vowed, after locking her in a room and hiding her wedding dress for most of the morning, to feign neutrality. I couldn't stretch to actually smiling in his presence, but I didn't bare my teeth when I saw him anymore.

'I'll see you soon, pea. I love you.'

'I love you too.'

I hung up the phone before either of us could say anything else.

The kitchen window had been opened while I was out. The through-draught tugged the front door from my grasp and slammed it shut. I could smell scorched coffee beans and tobacco as I walked down the hallway.

My lover was sitting, smoking, at the table. The radio threw music into the room; something discordant that made me wince, though he seemed oblivious to the sound. A newspaper was spread in front of him, a crossword half-completed. I watched him for a moment, envying his serenity, the frown-creases on his face and the tapping pen as he puzzled over a clue. Then I moved towards him, and he stood and tossed the cigarette through the window. I imagined it arcing down through the bed of hellebores, scorching decay into the fragile cup of their petals.

'I hate you,' I said, reaching for him.

He nodded and put his arms around me. 'I know.'

'You told me you'd got rid of my key. You told me it was over.'

'I know. I couldn't do it.'

We didn't say anything else, just stood for a while and watched the day drift past the open window. I had no idea what he was thinking and I didn't ask. When he took my hand and raised it to his lips, tonguing my fingertips gently, I didn't try to stop him. This was always how our attempts at leaving each other ended.

By the time the train let me out at the tiny rural station I'd stopped worrying about what I was going to say, how I'd be, when I saw Georgie. I'd whiled the journey away watching the concrete and graffiti splashes of my urban life segue into a slide of auburn trees parading the boundaries of tiny fields, and lanes not much wider than the span of my outstretched arms. I'd napped and when I woke the savage grief that had walked beside me for the last couple of weeks had eased back. Not far behind but no longer linking arms. Relaxed into the comforting jitter and rumble of my seat as we crept away from my mistakes, I turned over memories.

Little Georgie with her arms raised, stick clasped in two hot fists, swiping wildly at a fabric donkey hanging from the ceiling. Her eyes slits of laughter and her hair a dandelion clock lifting around her head. Smiling parents, cheering children, the room a litter of paper plates. Little Marie, a year younger but already a couple of inches taller, twisting the stick from her sister's grip without asking, focused intensely on causing maximum damage to the poor donkey to get at the sweets swelling its belly. Every swipe connecting, the donkey careering back and forth, the birthday girl roaring her furious intent. The parents laughing, shocked, as they take her arm to calm her and blink down at her upturned snarl. Then one last thwack and the joy of sweets cascading over her head, her face plump with smiles, her hands filled with colour. She picks out the brightest ones and lays them across her sister's palms: a gift.

I hauled my bags onto the platform and looked around for Georgie. Somebody shoved into me, their suitcase heavy against the back of my calves, their hip a sudden solid warmth against mine, and I shuffled to the side, straining for a glimpse of the face I loved above all others. Only now, with the reunion just past the grasp of my fingertips, almost touchable, could I let myself feel the weight of the last months of missing her. It overwhelmed me for a second: the yearning and the panicked certainty that she wasn't here, that she'd got the wrong day or I'd got the wrong station, that she'd got ill or there was something wrong with the baby.

She appeared suddenly, from nowhere, and put her hands on my cheeks and said my name. It was as if she'd stepped through a rip she'd made in the air, entering my world by magic and sealing the jagged edges closed behind her. Her face was everything. I tried not to cry or cling to her but did both anyway. Her stomach was bulky against mine, hard and unyielding. My pregnant sister. I felt a moment's vicious resentment but didn't know whether it was at the prospect of a greater bond than ours or at the unapologetic display of her fertility. I kissed her and pulled back slightly to look at her again. Her belly jutted neatly into the hollowed space between my hipbones, and I thought of jigsaw puzzles and belonging.

'Ladybug,' she said, 'it's okay. Don't cry. Oh, Marie, I thought you'd never get here. I was so scared you'd change your mind and not come.'

I stroked her hair behind her ears and laughed as she grimaced. 'You still hate that. I always forget.' Her insecurity made me stronger, dried my eyes. 'Of course I'm here, darling. Now get me back to that shack of yours and feed me. I'm starved.'

I can't remember now what we talked about on the drive back to her home but I can remember laughing, holding hands, staring at her and thinking how well pregnancy suited her. She was glossed with happiness, beautiful, her hair shiny and the skin across her cheekbones plump and pink. It had been six months. The longest time apart in years. Too long.

'There it is,' Georgie said as we turned off the road and onto a long private drive. She tipped her head to indicate a house standing at the end of it; golden-stoned and ivy-wrapped. The setting sun blazed in window after window. A modern-day Manderley.

I leaned forward and gripped the dashboard. 'You have got to be kidding me.'

'Nope.' She giggled and glanced at me as we lurched into a pothole. 'I told you it was big.'

'You didn't say it was a mansion. It's gorgeous.' I couldn't take my eyes off it. 'How long does it take you to get from your bedroom to the kitchen? And how the hell do you keep it clean?'

She braked with a jerk that spat gravel from beneath the car wheels. 'Under two minutes if I do it at a fast trot. And I don't even try. Come on, ladybug, let's get you inside and introduce you.'

I followed her up the stone steps, through the huge, heavy front door and into the gritty half-dark of the entrance hall. All of the internal doors leading from it were closed, the staircase little more than a darker shadow that lurched upwards at the far end. The tiled floor was cold beneath the thin soles of my shoes and there was a damp tang of welly boots and anoraks: familiar and pleasant. The smell of childhood Sunday afternoons. Georgie was laughing as she turned around to grab my arm and pull me close. Her face was striped a muted yellow and green as she passed into the sunlight that filtered through a stained-glass arch set into the wall above the door. She floated like a nature spirit from the gloom around us.

'I don't usually use this main door,' she said. 'The side one leads straight onto the kitchen so it's easier, but I wanted us to make a grand entrance.'

'Christ, pea, you're in love,' I told her. 'Look at you, all lit up with it. Not that I blame you, I think my entire flat would fit into this hall. Tell me I get it when you die, please. You can cut Mark out of the will, I'm sure he won't mind.' I grinned at her.

She stroked her stomach. 'The little one gets it I'm afraid, if I'm carried off by a plague, but there's an annexe round the back you can have. Converted coach house. It's just a shell at the moment but you'll love it once we've done it up.' She squeezed my arm. 'Sorry.'

I opened the nearest door and peered blindly over the threshold. 'You can't apologise every time you mention the bloody baby. I'm not made of glass.'

She flinched. I smiled and kissed her forehead. 'I'm sorry, it's been a long journey and I'm tired. Let's pretend getting pregnant never happened to me, shall we? Just concentrate on you. Now show me where I'll be sleeping and then we can sort out dinner.'

I picked up my bag and shook my head as she tried to take it from me. 'Don't you dare. You're already heaving around enough extra weight.' I followed her through the entrance hall, past the carpeted thrust of the staircase, and into a long corridor studded with more closed doors. Following the bright crumbs of her chatter I rushed to stay close as she moved away, both of us stumbling over the uneven floor.

The old bell Georgie had left on my bedside table was a godsend. After I'd tried two different staircases leading onto narrow passageways that plumed dust beneath my heels, I retraced my steps back to the bedroom to get it and stood on the landing ringing it and shouting her name. I could hear her laughing somewhere below me for a good few minutes before she appeared from one of the intersecting corridors and waved to me to follow her. 'I'm sure I went down that one. This place is a maze,' I complained, rubbing flakes of rust from my fingers. Crescents of muddy red rimmed my nails.

We made our way back to the ground floor and she led the way through what would once have been a dining hall. Even with our mutual dedication to hoarding clutter it felt empty and bereft of purpose, throwing our voices back to us in thin echoes. Naked light bulbs faltered and buzzed above our heads and sealed cardboard boxes lined up beneath the windows. Twists of dead wasps littered the sills. I could have closed my eyes and spun in circles without worrying about falling over something.

'I don't remember this room,' I said. 'Did we come through here when you gave me the grand tour earlier?'

My sister nodded. 'I took you everywhere. You're probably confused because we came into it from the main staircase and cut through the far corner so I could show you the fireplace. Through that door there.' She pointed. 'The lay-out's strange in this house. So many add-ons and stairs and far too many twists and turns, as you discovered just now. The main staircase only goes up to the first floor; after that, on your floor and the one above, there's a choice of minor staircases to use. None of it seems to make logical sense. When I've got some time I'm going to get an architect in to look at redesigning the whole of the interior and then I'll run it as an artist's retreat, with courses and studios. I could put on exhibitions and maybe even start painting seriously again myself. It's pretty bare, I know; difficult to imagine at the moment.' She'd seen the look I'd cast around me.

'It must be so exciting,' I said, 'to think of all the changes you'll make.'

The remark was casual, off-hand, but she bristled a little. 'I'm lucky, I know,' she said, 'to have all this without having to work for it.'

'Mark's luckier,' I told her. 'Having you *and* this lovely house. I hope he realises how lucky. You'll turn it into a beautiful home and then fill it with dozens of babies, and adoring artists will make you their muse.'

I licked the palm of my hand, tasting the stain the bell had left on my skin. My tongue winced away from the ruddy smear, so much like blood.

Georgie was breathless by the time we'd moved through the rest of the ground floor and back to the kitchen. She climbed onto a high stool by the counter and propped her chin on her palms, puffing air. I watched her as I turned the gas down below the pan of soup and began to butter bread.

'Chest bad?' I asked. 'How often does Mark work away now?'

She shrugged and began to twist her wedding ring around her finger, grimacing as it clung to the puffy flesh, jamming and jerking from her efforts. 'Not as often as he used to since he moved up in the firm, and he's promised to be home a lot more when the baby comes. It's fine, Marie, it suits us both.' She smiled at me but I didn't smile back.

'I bet it suits him, to have his flat in the city and weekends at his country pile, but what are you going to do for the next six weeks, before the little monster shows up? You can't rattle around this bloody place all by yourself. What if you go into early labour or something?'

Georgie laughed and reached out a hand to me. 'I'm only about a mile from the village and I don't think it'll happen so suddenly that I won't be able to get to a phone. This isn't a Victorian novel. I love this house and I'm content, I really am. Don't worry so much, ladybug. You can always visit more, you know, if you want to check I'm okay.'

I stroked her hand and tapped my nails against the thick platinum of her wedding band. 'You should try and get this off now before your fingers swell even more. I'm sorry I haven't visited since you moved here. I wanted to, it's just been difficult.'

'Well, you've been busy.' She raised herself up and settled more comfortably on her stool, arms wrapped around her stomach. 'With the job and everything else that's been going on.'

She made the statement sound like a question. I spooned soup into bowls and joined her at the counter. 'Okay, you get five minutes. Ask what you want but after that we don't talk about me anymore. You're far more interesting.'

'When did you get so secretive? So shut down? You always used to tell me everything.'

I dropped a piece of bread into my bowl and pushed it below the surface of the soup with my spoon, watching it bloat and break apart. 'Four and a half minutes. And I'm not being secretive, there's just nothing to tell.'

Georgie licked the butter from her bread and wiped at her glistening chin. 'I've become such a pig these last months. Okay, tell me what his name is. Are you happy? Do you love him? When will I meet him? How are you feeling since the … ?'

'Abortion. You can say the word. And you won't meet him; it's not that kind of relationship. It's not a relationship at all. Yes, I love him. More than I should. Far more than he deserves. And I don't feel anything about the abortion. There's no point breaking my heart over it, is there? It was so early it was barely even a pregnancy and now it's not even that.'

I rested my spoon on the side of my bowl. 'I forgot the cheese! Do you remember how we'd refuse to eat our vegetables unless they came with a blanket of melted cheese on top? Mum used to sneak as many as possible onto our plate, knowing that if she dumped enough cheese on top we'd eat anything.'

Georgie laughed and nodded down at the shower of cheddar I grated over her bowl. 'More please. I'd forgotten that. I wonder what she'd think if she were alive now, whether she'd be proud. And Dad too.'

I kissed the top of her head. 'Of you they would. You managed to get a degree *and* marry well. Dad would be thrilled by the qualification and Mum would be thrilled by this place and the stone in that ring. She always was a snob.' I gulped wine and wound melted cheese around my spoon as if it were spaghetti. Georgie tutted gently but I didn't look at her.

'They'd be proud of you as well,' she said. 'I know they would. You were always Dad's favourite anyway. Way too clever for the rest of us and he loved that. You made all those extra shifts on the buses worth it.'

I looked past her, to the window. 'Yes, and I remember how thrilled they were when I dropped out of university to forge an obscure career making grotesque glove puppets for craft shops. It's getting dark. I've forgotten what true night looks like. Are you sure you're happy here, alone? You don't get scared?'

Georgie laughed. 'Of what? There's more to scare me in the city than the country, and we're both country girls, Marie, you can't have forgotten that. Anyway, I keep myself so busy there's barely time to sit down.'

I got up and switched the light on. 'Doing what?' I asked. 'What exactly is there to do?'

She shrugged. 'Getting the nursery ready. Sorting through the stuff in the upstairs rooms. Making lists. There was a lot left in cupboards when we moved here so I've been going through all that. It's mostly rubbish but I found that sweet old bell I put in your room. Oh, and I'm volunteering for the WI as well. I got nabbed the first time I went to the village.'

I rooted through one of the drawers in the dresser for matches. In the face of her enthusiasm I didn't want to point out how skeletal, how unoccupied, the house seemed. It was as if she'd moved here four months ago and then just forgotten to unpack. Apart from this kitchen which, judging by the cushion-bulky armchair and the pile of books on top of the television, she appeared to live in, none of the other rooms looked as though they ever witnessed a living heartbeat.

Once the lamp was switched off there was nothing to anchor me in the room. The darkness was absolute; my palm in front of my face a sensed rather than seen thing. I switched the lamp back on and opened the curtains to look out across the lawn, missing streetlights and traffic, missing car horns and alarms. Even missing the noisy spill of drunks from the pub on the corner of my road. But missing him most of all.

The night was thick with drizzle, the moon nowhere. I'd been cherishing romantic notions of a rural sky, vast and star-spangled as childhood memory, but the dense, claustrophobic reality made me sneeze and shiver. With the room lit up behind me I couldn't see anything beyond the dark, flattened outline of myself against the glass, all broad, anonymous strokes. The house made wheezing, ticking sounds beneath and behind me. I didn't know how I was ever going to be able to sleep.

I turned the lamp back off and pulled one of the pillows into a hug, curling tightly around it. Then I tugged the duvet over my head, shut my eyes and began to cry. The grief was back, tight around my ribcage, pummelling the dead air at the centre of me. I tried to breathe through it, filling my lungs to loosen its grip, but then after a while gave in and let it pull me down.

I'd been dreaming strange flickering dreams, of Georgie and her baby, of my parents, when the child woke me. I lay for a few stupefied seconds while my consciousness guided me back inside my own body and re-grounded me in the now. There was a whimpering sound by my side: steady, low, miserable. And now pressure from a tiny hand on my cheek, patting with soft taps as if secretly scared of waking me, scared of what I might do, of my anger.

I lifted the duvet and reached out, folded the small, shuddering body against mine. Warmer than a pillow, softer than my lover and less likely to break my heart. This is what my child would have one day felt like in my arms, if I'd let her live.

We fell back to sleep immediately, wrapped into each other, and my dreams were right where I'd left them, waiting for me.

There was a thin, damp dawn when I woke again, and my pillow was on the floor; the space beside me empty. I rolled across to cover it with my heat, half remembering the warmth of another, and I slept again for a while then woke with a start, full sunlight in my face. I checked my watch: gone 8am.

I stared at the ceiling for a few moments and tried to disentangle last night's dreams. There had been Georgie, with a child, and then my parents with their disapproval and their need. Or had they had a child? It was all slipping away, in that way dreams do. It had served its purpose and purged me clean.

But something still remained, jangling behind my eyes. Something sweeter and safer than that. I tried to regain the feeling and then gave it up as pointless and swung my legs into the chill air of the room, fumbling for my dressing gown. It was enough just to have the echo of it, to almost remember contentment.

It was the burning smell that led me to the kitchen, and my sister. She was standing in front of the huge stove, breaking eggs into a pan and swearing. I stroked the jade flannel of her shoulder and she shrieked and swung round, thrusting egg shells at me. 'You do it,' she said. 'I can't get anything to fucking work this morning.'

I pushed her gently into a chair and began to prise burnt toast from the grill. 'Bad night?'

She nodded and rubbed her eyes with the sleeve of her dressing gown. 'Yes. Nightmares. I think they were nightmares anyway, I can't really remember them. I kept waking up thinking there was someone in the room, someone wanting to hurt my baby. It's probably just hormones. I've had an easy ride so far with the pregnancy so it was bound to catch me out.'

The phone shrilled beside her and she shrieked again, then

laughed and scooped it up. I watched her as she spoke into the mouthpiece, watched her face soften and smooth with delight. She half-turned away and lowered her voice to a murmur, playing with her hair. I should have stepped back and given her some privacy but her happiness transfixed me, kept me close to her warm body. I suddenly wanted what she had, and so fiercely. I wanted to shed my life and step into hers, step right into her skin and be her.

She glanced up and saw me staring. Her expression changed, briefly, to something close to shock, but then she smiled and stuck her tongue out, shooing me away with a hand. The bones of my face felt rigid with the force of my want, my jaw welded tight, but I managed to grin at her before turning back to the stove, still straining to listen to her words as I fried the eggs.

Georgie hung up the phone and joined me when I slapped the plates down onto the table. 'Thanks, ladybug. That was Mark.'

I reached for the pepper. 'I'd assumed that. Do you want any sauce?'

She shook her head. We ate in silence for a while, her sliding looks at me as I chewed and smiled and stared at the world yellowing into sunlight over her shoulder.

She sighed and rubbed her stomach. 'That was lovely, thank you. I'd go for seconds but the little one's twisting around too much right now. Do you want the rest?'

I shook my head and reached for her plate, but she moved it away. 'No,' she said, 'you cooked so I'll clear.'

I shrugged and watched her walk to the sink, feeling miserable about resenting her happiness so much. But not able, not willing right now, to retrace those mental steps back to simple joy at being with her. It was so much easier to love her when we were apart. Together, I couldn't step outside of the shadows I filled my life with, the ghosts of my disappointed parents, the vicious unhappiness I chose as my lot. Contentment had always been something Georgie found effortless to achieve, wandering with an almost thoughtless serenity through a life that in turn made way, welcomed and provided for her. She chose the lit spaces and set up her easel while I chose the dark corners, hunched over my sewing machine to create deformed puppets for stranger's hands.

While Georgie filled the sink and fussed with the taps, I thought about inventing an emergency and heading home. The lure of my own domestic space, the joint thrills of indulging my misery and hoping my lover might visit, dangled like baubles in front of me. I watched her and slipped my foot out of its slipper, resting my naked sole on the tiled floor, pushing against it, curling my toes into the earthy cracks. A shock like static tingled across my ankles and my arms were suddenly warm and full, closed around last night's dreaming comfort. I felt a jolt of love, primitive and fierce, a love for the very foundations of this house. If it were mine I'd dance through every room, every day, and throw open every door. I wouldn't keep it shuttered and shrouded in darkness, or store my life in boxes. If it were mine I wouldn't need anything else.

Above Georgie's head the mug-cluttered shelf groaned free of its bracket and tipped slowly from horizontal. The mugs at the very end of it plunged, pottery lemmings, onto her head and shoulders. She screamed and stumbled backwards as I jumped up and steered her away from the sink. The shelf gave way completely, mugs tumbling down. The sound of breaking china was tremendous. The sight of it all shattering, spitting coloured shards across our feet, quickened my heart. I held my sister against me until the room was quiet.

Georgie's right cheek puffed up and darkened against my fingers as I examined her face, her eye narrowing as the skin around it swelled. She was shaking as she stared at me. 'What the hell just happened?' she asked.

'You're going to have a nasty bruise but I don't think you've fractured anything.' I led her to a chair and got ice from the freezer, wrapped blocks of it in a tea towel. 'Sit there and hold this against your cheek until I've swept up.'

I crunched my way over to the sink and looked at the shelf. 'Years of cooking and condensation finally did for it, the brackets are totally rotted through. It was quite spectacular though; I don't think there's a single unbroken mug. Shit, wasn't this one of Mum's favourites?' I held up a piece of poppy-red china.

Georgie nodded behind her tea towel. She looked close to tears. I smiled at her as I began to open cupboard doors, looking for a broom. 'It could have been worse, pea. At least now you can go on a shopping spree and buy some more.'

She started to cry. 'It was the last of the tea set. Dad bought it for her when she had me and everything else got broken or lost over the years. I knew I should have left it in a cupboard. At least it would have been safe then.'

'Better to use it and take the risk, darling,' I told her, dropping the broken teacup onto the floor. 'Even if it does mean things get destroyed.'

We spent the rest of the morning drinking tea from plastic beakers dug from Georgie's picnic hamper and talking about going for a walk. Still jittery, Georgie jumped at every sound and examined her face in the mirror every few minutes. I was itching to be alone for an hour.

'Why don't I pop out to get us something nice for tea?' I suggested. 'You can have a bath and a lie down. Just point me in the right direction.'

The instructions for finding my way to the village covered both sides of a piece of paper and involved warnings not to run if I came across the bull in the field at the bottom of the lane. By the time we'd found a pair of ancient walking boots that almost fit and I'd waved goodbye to Georgie, the afternoon was all around me. I walked beneath the trees that lined the long driveway, enjoying the solitude and the leaves that swallowed my ankles.

I wondered whether there would be a public phone box in the village; whether, if there were, I would have the strength to resist calling him despite our agreement not to have contact while I was here. I shook my purse lightly to see how heavy with coins it was and felt pained relief when it didn't rattle.

The end of the drive was guarded by stone posts. Loose bricks scattered in the ditch and a rusted metal gate faded away, belly up beneath nettles. The house name, Magpie Hall, was painted on wood and screwed into one of the posts. This was one of Georgie's additions, I just knew; her attempt to soften the Gothic creepiness of this decayed first impression of her home. The lettering was bold and green, the plaque scuffed at each corner where the screw had skidded across the varnish before it bit, tunnelling wounds into the wood. Dirt and damp had started to peel back layers around the punctures. I doubted it would last the winter.

I turned to look back at the house, feeling the same tug of possessive love I'd felt this morning in the kitchen, almost wanting to walk back into it and lock myself inside. I counted the windows on the second floor, left to right, trying to work out which bedroom was mine. It had to be one of the middle ones as the morning had given a direct view down the sweep of drive to where I now stood.

As though on cue a figure appeared in the window of the room I'd just decided must be the one. Smaller, much smaller, than I'd expected my sister to be, even from this distance, she stood frozen in her frame of wood. I waved and spun around, arms outstretched, but there was no answering wave. She had to be able to see me, I was standing directly between the gate posts in full view of the house. I waved again and saw movement as she pressed herself against the window, white cloth a shock against the glass, face a pale disc above it. Surely she was looking straight at me.

As I lowered my arm and turned to go, I saw Georgie pass the window in the kitchen, her jade dressing gown a vivid flash, there then gone. I stumbled and stared upwards. All of the upstairs windows were empty. The curtain in my room smeared across the glass then billowed away, breeze-stirred.

The village was a café, a shop, and a pub, bordering a triangle of green. Ducks splashed in a tiny pond and wooden signs pointed the way to a church and bridle paths. It was charming, and as far removed from my own life as it could possibly be. A bell chimed above me as I went into the shop and heads turned my way. I walked the narrow aisles self-consciously, filling a basket with treats for Georgie.

Next to the counter stood a table covered with books about the local area. There was a black-and-white photograph of Magpie Hall on the front of one of them. Just a small photo in the top corner, fanned between images of other grand-looking houses, but the thrill of recognition made me exclaim with pleasure as I picked it up and joined the queue to pay. The woman in front of me eyed me over her vegetables. 'Visiting?' she asked.

I nodded. 'My sister lives here. I'm staying with her for a few days.' I tapped the book. 'She lives at Magpie Hall, a mile or so out. I'm hoping to get a bit of history about the place.'

The woman's eyebrows rose. 'So, you're Georgina's sister, then. She's a sweet girl, very involved with the village. We haven't seen her for a few days now; I was going to go up and check on her tomorrow. Don't like the thought of her all alone with the baby so close to coming. We've never met her husband, you know.'

I ignored the criticism implicit in her last words, the veiled invitation to add my own and make it a dialogue. The effort was tremendous.

'She loves it there,' I said. 'I can see why; it's a gorgeous house.'

The queue shuffled forward a few steps and then stalled as the assistant began to weigh dried herbs shaken from a huge glass pot, dusting the air with ancient oregano. I smiled at my companion, who was watching me closely.

'You don't think she finds it a bit overwhelming?' she said. 'It's a big house when there's just a small family to fill it. We all assumed it would sell as a hotel, it was empty for years, but then Georgina turned up in the shop one day and asked to join the WI. She volunteers for everything, very generous with her time. I don't know how she does it, to give so much to us and also manage a home of that size. Did she tell you it used to be an orphanage, the Hall? Most of the children had parents that couldn't afford to keep them, so it was more like a poor house, a foundling hospital for the unwanted, but locally it was called the orphanage because they never went home once they were left there. They were treated kindly enough, by all accounts, there wasn't more than the usual cruelty you'd find at an institution like that, but it was a sad place.'

She nodded at the book I was holding. 'There are pictures in there of them all lined up in the garden on public holidays, holding bags of sweeties, and dolls. They were paraded in front of the great and the good twice a year to show how grateful they were to have a roof over their head.'

She nodded her head towards an elderly woman standing ahead of us in the queue. 'Her mother was in there. Left at sixteen to go to London and seek her fortune. She came back a year later with a little bundle of her own to add to the household. As if they weren't full enough.' An eyebrow was raised meaningfully, another jerk of the head towards the older woman. I hoped we weren't being overheard.

'Georgie didn't tell me anything about the history of the Hall,' I said. 'Apart from when it was built, that kind of thing.

She's really contented there though, she loves it. And she's made it into a real home.' I sounded defensive, I knew, and smiled again to soften my tone. I thought about the empty, echoing dining room we'd walked through last night, the unopened boxes and closed doors. As if Georgie were scared to get too comfortable in the house. As if she didn't quite feel as though it were really hers.

The people in front of us peeled away. The woman stepped forward to take her turn at the counter. 'It's nice to have her living there,' she said as she thumped carrots and onions down. 'It'll be nice to have the baby there too, and maybe more in time. Happy children running across the lawns, that's what that place needs. Give her my best, won't you? Tell her Sylvia will be expecting a visit very soon.'

The day was drawing itself in as I started back to Magpie Hall, an early dusk scratching at the edge of things. The sky was lowering with rain clouds and the air felt damp against my face. I shouldered my bags and walked as quickly as I could.

The book banged against my hip with every stride. I'd slipped it into my coat pocket so that I could take it straight up to my room when I got in and sidestep showing it to Georgie. I wondered why she hadn't told me about the house's past. Surely not disinterest, though I could see how it would unsettle her: the knowledge that her home had once sheltered unwanted, probably unloved and unhappy, children.

The first rain drops started falling as I turned into the long driveway. Despite the gloom and chill, I stopped to look at the house. Its lower level squatted above the lawn and glowed a welcome, lamplight in each room. Its upper levels reared into the sky, as insubstantial as shadows, each dark window throwing twisted clouds back into the twilight. I could have stood and stared until I lost the day completely.

The rain, heavy now, forced me into movement, and I half-ran the length of the driveway, stumbling a little in the potholes but never falling. Running for home, I thought. Nearly there.

Georgie was curled in an armchair by the Rayburn in the kitchen, reading, as I let myself in through the side door. She made to get up but I waved her back. 'Don't be silly, pea. Stay where you are. Thanks for turning all the lights on, it made the house look so lovely and welcoming.'

She frowned and slipped a finger into her book to keep her page. 'I didn't realise I had. I can never work out which switch does what and half of them shock me when I touch them.'

I shrugged my coat onto a peg and unpacked my bags, spilling chocolates and cheeses onto the table, loving Georgie's greed as she pounced on things and heaped them onto her lap, ripping through wrappers. I dragged a chair to sit beside her, taking her chin in my palm for a moment to look at her bruises. 'You've got quite a shiner going on there,' I told her, patting the chocolate-bulge in her cheek.

Her fingers covered mine, squeezing briefly. 'I'm a walking disaster zone at the moment. I almost fell down the stairs when you were out. These bloody slippers are lethal, it felt like someone suddenly stood on the heel when I was at the top of the staircase. I nearly tore my arm out of its socket grabbing at the banister.'

I took the last chocolate truffle before she could. 'You were always the graceful one when we were kids, you floated through the days. When did you get so clumsy?'

She started popping olives into her mouth. 'Just recently. I blame the baby; it's thrown my co-ordination out completely.'

I laid a hand across her stomach, quickly and lightly. 'I'm not surprised. It looks like there's an elephant in there.'

Georgie groaned. 'It's mainly fat. All those years of self denial, now I'm eating everything I can get my hands on. I don't know how I'm ever going to be able to lose weight after the birth.'

'Stop it. You're beautiful. Your baby will be healthy and gorgeous, and I bet Mark loves the way you look.'

She handed me the empty olive pot and reached for the crackers. 'I don't know. I think he's found it all a bit scary, the thought of being a father. He doesn't seem to want to look at me since I got pregnant. And he doesn't touch me anymore.' She looked at me quickly, testing my mood for confidences.

I got up and went over to the fridge. 'Probably because he knows you're too good for him. Which you are. Right, I'm going to cook you a proper meal before you eat everything I bought today. It was meant to last at least until tomorrow.'

Georgie heaved herself up and came to stand beside me. 'Don't, ladybug. Be nice. You're going to see him in a week and I want you to try and get along. Please be nice, for me.'

The mushrooms in the salad box had started to slime over. I slid my thumbs across their swollen heads and stared at the muddy trails under my nails. 'Of course I will. I promise. Now sit down and let me cook for you. I want to make the most of having you all to myself.'

I kept the curtains open when I went to bed and lay awake for a long time, watching the shadows shift across the room as the sharp half-moon plunged from cloud to cloud. I was tired but I didn't want to sleep. I was waiting, while pretending I wasn't.

Once I closed my eyes and stopped hoping the child came to stand beside my pillow. She was still whimpering but the sound was less depthless in its misery, as if there might be an end to the sorrow. I lifted her to lie against me and held her close under the blankets until the shudders left her body and she slackened into dream-twitches. Her hair was coarse as teddy bear stuffing against my cheek and smelt of long-rotted leaves. I pressed a smile to her temple and finally slept.

I don't know whether it was Georgie screaming or the little girl crying that threw me into wakefulness and across the room. I was by the door and calling my sister's name before my eyes were fully opened, snatching at the door handle and twisting it, my hands slipping off and cracking against the wood panels. I slapped at the light switch to orientate myself but there was nothing beneath my groping fingers except the silken chill of wallpaper. The screaming went on and on.

The little girl wrapped her arms around my waist and hung on, bracing her feet against my ankles and pulling me as hard as she could back to the bed. We slithered across the floor a few steps before I managed to prise her fingers from me and push her gently away. She fell to the floor and lay there with her arms stretched out, her hands flailing at the air in panic, her face torn by sobs. I almost turned back to kneel beside her, aching to hold her, but the screaming went on. I left her lying on the rug, collapsed and heartbroken, and ran to the door.

The night was deep, almost airless, as I stumbled through it. The screaming had stopped; the silence terrified me more. I shouted Georgie's name, floundering to the staircase tucked at the end of the landing and plunging down, two steps at a time. Her bedroom was one floor below mine and on the main landing facing the woods at the back of the house. I turned left at the bottom of the stairs and shouted again. And the screaming started once more.

I ran without any sense of direction, steered by terror and panic, ricocheting off door frames. The noise was everywhere, I couldn't locate where it was coming from. The doors I opened gave access to rooms empty and still. I slipped on the edge of the worn runner and fell onto my hands and knees, the breath jerked from me in a high-pitched squeal, and then I gave up, just for a moment, and lowered myself flat to the floor and put my hands over my ears, screwing my eyes tight shut.

Silence again, sudden as if sound had been choked in an instant from my sister's throat. From somewhere above me a bell sounded, faint and sweet. I turned my head to the side and opened my eyes. The gap beneath the door nearest me, a chunky dark strip level with my face and slatted by floorboards, was filled in its centre with the tips of ten small, bare toes. I watched as they shifted and settled, close enough for me to touch if I stretched my hand out. I craned my neck and looked at the next door along. More toes.

The bell sounded again. More discordant this time, harsher, as if impatience was getting the better of the ringer. The toes jerked in response and began to tread the floor, marching on the spot, waiting to be let out. Shadows flickered along the length of the corridor with the rise and fall of feet behind every door. I hauled myself to my knees and reached for the handle nearest me, responding to the urgency of the movement and the jangle of the bell without thinking.

Georgie called out my name, her voice raw with panic. She was close. I dropped my hand, scrambled to my feet and ran towards the vast window at the end of the hall, banging on doors as I passed them, shouting for her. Behind the fourth door she called again and I opened it onto lamplight and the smell of rose perfume.

She was curled high against the pillows, knees up to her chin. Across the bed her hair was scattered in clumps and straggles, bloody at the roots. We stared at each other for a moment, and then she held her arms out to me and began to sob.

I climbed onto the bed and hugged her. I was kneeling on her torn hair, I could feel it sliding over my bare shins. 'What happened, pea?' I asked, trying to keep my voice low and calm, trying not to cry. 'Who did this?'

She lunged in my arms to stare past me at the open door and lunged again to stare at the window. When I shifted, she flinched and brought her hands up to her face, covering it. Blood dribbled from her scalp. 'There was someone in the room,' she said. 'I woke up and there was someone on the bed with me. They grabbed me by the hair. They were so strong, Marie, and they wanted to hurt me.'

I held her wrists and pulled them away from her face, laid her hands across my lap and stroked her fingers until they straightened. 'Look, Georgie,' I said. 'Look at your hands.'

Spiralled around her knuckles and knotted across her palms,

her hair gleamed like gold thread in the lamplight. There was blood crusted under her nails. She jerked and bent forward, ripping at her skin. 'No, there was someone in the room with me. It wasn't me, there was someone else here, Marie. You've got to believe me.'

I tried to pull her hands apart but she slapped at me. Her face was a gargoyle-twist of terror and hysteria. We wrestled across the bed until she finally sagged and lay quietly.

'I think you had a nightmare, pea,' I said, wrapping my arms around her so that she couldn't move away. 'There's no-one else here. Come on, let's get you cleaned up.'

She was stiff with resistance for a moment, then she nodded wearily and let me raise her so that she was leaning against my shoulder. 'You won't leave me, will you? Promise you'll stay. I don't want to be on my own.'

I hesitated for a second, already missing what was waiting for me in my own room, sore with the memory of so much distress. 'Of course I will,' I told my sister.

Georgie was still crying when I woke up the next morning. I turned onto my side to look at her. 'Have you slept at all?'

She shrugged and wiped her eyes on the sleeve of her dressing gown. 'Not really. I was too scared to.'

We were both silent for a while. I stroked her arm while she sniffed and stared at the wall. She reminded me of a discarded, unloved doll, propped limply against the headboard with her scalp raw and bald in patches and her bruised face puffed into a mask of sorrow.

'I know you don't believe me,' she said, 'but there *was* someone in the room last night. I didn't have a nightmare and I didn't hurt myself. I didn't.' Tears rolled down her cheeks. 'I don't understand what's going on, why someone would want to hurt me.'

I propped myself onto an elbow so that I could look at her properly. 'No-one's going to hurt you, pea. I promise you. If anyone even tried to, I'd kill them. It was just a nightmare; you saw your hands. You did that to yourself.'

Her fingers rose to pat gently at the livid pink of her scalp. She turned away from me, swung her legs from the bed and stood up. 'I'll go down and put the kettle on. Thanks for staying with me last night.'

I reached out to touch her shoulder but she stepped away and walked out of the room without looking back.

I went up to my own bedroom and opened the door quietly, hoping to surprise the child, hoping to see her curled on the bed. But she was gone. I'd known she would be, but it still hurt.

My pillows were tumbled on the floor, the duvet half dragged from the mattress. My glass lay on its side on the rug, emptied of water, and the bell was dented where it had been thrown against the wall. It could have been me, I remembered the panic of last night's waking and the struggle leaving the room, but I was sure it was her, working out her anguish when she realised I'd left her and wasn't going to return.

I picked up the pillows and opened the curtains, flooding the room with the morning. Then I wrapped myself in my dressing gown and went downstairs to find Georgie.

After breakfast I insisted on both of us walking the grounds of Magpie Hall. 'I want to see the gardens and you need some fresh air,' I told Georgie as I pulled on my coat. She'd barely spoken to me, would hardly look at me, but my impatience shrivelled before her trembling hands and furtive glances around every room. She clearly hadn't wanted to go upstairs alone for her bath and, knowing how proud her hurt feelings could be, I'd made a fuss about wanting to look around the bedrooms on her floor; hanging about loudly as she splashed in her bathroom. I'd been curious too about the children who had stood behind each door last night, but every room I'd checked was empty, curtain-less and heavy with dust, the floorboards unmarked by footfall. Her bedroom was the only one on the floor that even had a bed.

We left through the side door and walked the walled kitchen garden with its remains of herb borders. A glassless greenhouse was matted with vines, half propped against the side of the house. We followed the path around the vegetable patch to the arched doorway at the far end, skidding a little on the moss that crept over the cracks in the slate. 'Shit, this will be lethal in the winter when it's icy,' I said to Georgie, tucking my hand into the crook of her elbow to steady her. 'Promise me you'll take care when you come out here, pea.'

She pulled away and walked ahead. 'I wish you'd stop calling me that, it's so childish.'

I hurried to catch her up as we trod across a vast lawn gnarled with magnolia and rhododendron, towards the wood at the back of the house. 'But you've always been pea, you loved being called that when we were kids. Mum was the pod and you looked so like her you were her little pea. I was the one who hated it, remember, feeling so left out.'

She smiled and let me take her arm again. 'Yes, and so I started calling you ladybug. Then Dad felt left out as he was the only one without a nickname. What was it we tried calling him for a while?'

I thought for a moment. 'Daddy Long Legs, wasn't it? But it never really suited him. He was stuck with just being Dad. I don't think he minded though, not really.'

Georgie stopped as we reached the gate that led into the wood. We both turned to look back at the house. Its front was skewed away from us, the side view far less imposing. There were only a few windows pressed into the walls and the chimney stacks had been rendered an ugly grey, starkly seamed into the yellow of the original stone. I wondered whether we were being watched, wondered whether I'd find my bed clothes dragged across the floor again when we got indoors.

'I still miss them,' Georgie said. I didn't follow her train of thought immediately, assumed she was talking about the foundling children, but then realised she was talking about our parents.

'I don't think about them much,' I told her, leading the way into the fold of trees. 'We barely spoke for the last few years before they died. I just didn't have the same closeness with them that you had.'

The wood was smaller than it looked from a distance, and fenced round; knee deep in ferns beneath the oak and elder, the rowan dripping berries. The trees were at the peak of their death throes, flaring colour and loosening leaves that eddied softly around us. We followed the main path to a clearing in the centre, and then onto the furthest point, where the fence bordered the lane that led to the village. Georgie hadn't replied to my last comment and we walked in silence, her a little way behind me. She'd pulled the hood of her coat up and wrapped a scarf around the lower half of her face so when I paused to let her catch me up I couldn't see her expression.

'Your own private wood!' I said. 'You're so lucky. All you need is a spaniel at your heels now. Do you walk through it often?'

She shook her head and looked around her as though suddenly realising where she was. 'I've been too busy lately. I came in here a couple of months ago to try and paint and some children were climbing trees. I couldn't see them, but they thought it was funny to throw twigs down onto me and laugh. It wasn't very nice.'

We turned to walk back, following the path around the boundary. The fence was rotted in places, missing in others. Animal tracks tunnelled through the undergrowth and in a tiny clearing the skeleton of a bird was draped over a tree stump, delicate as old paper when I touched a finger to it. Leaves floated and turned on the air currents like ghosts. The house appeared and disappeared in glimpses as we followed the turns of the path, its presence a comfort even when the sight of it was obscured. I realised that I felt at peace for the first time in months and turned to tell Georgie, to thank her, but her head was bent low over her chest, her shoulders hunched inward as if protecting herself from the world, and I didn't break the silence.

As the path tipped into a little dell just in sight of the gate I stopped her. 'Look, someone's made a den out of fallen branches.' I knelt down and lifted a corner of the dirty cloth to peer inside the little shelter. It was an old sheet stamped MH over and over along the hem, ragged and dull with mud, offering no real protection against the elements but lending a shady privacy to the triangle of dark space beneath. Twigs were piled into the corners of the den and cracked glass bottles, thick with a greenish stagnant water, lined up on one side: a careful parade of the smallest through to the largest. Feathers poked from their tops as though someone had tried to create something pretty and lasting to decorate their hiding place.

I shifted back onto my heels to peer up at Georgie. 'It looks like it's not been visited for a long time. Maybe the parents of the little hooligans who upset you when you were painting?'

I was giving her an opening to tell me about Magpie Hall's past but she didn't take it, just shrugged vaguely and without interest. 'Probably. It doesn't smell good; I don't know how you could bear to touch it. I'll get Mark to make a bonfire when he's back. There's a lot of old rubbish lying around the place that needs burning.'

The wood itself seemed to wince with me, wind rushing with sudden force through the trees so that they whispered above us and loosened more leaves. My sister's tangled hair lifted back from her cheeks and she coughed and hugged herself, kneading at her chest. 'Let's go indoors, it's getting cold.'

Georgie spent the afternoon reading in the kitchen. She'd swapped the coat for her hooded dressing gown so her head was still covered but she slipped a hand under the fleece every few minutes, absent-mindedly, to pat at her scalp. Her mood was still fragile, faintly reproachful. I tried not to notice the glances she cast around the room as if reassuring herself that nothing would leap out of a corner to attack. When our eyes met she sighed gently and returned to her book. That had always been Georgie's way: to have you feel her sorrow at being let down, her gentle disappointment. So much like our mother and so at odds with my own snapping, raging furies. Her passivity humbled me even as it infuriated me.

After making her a mug of sweet, weak tea I left her to read alone and wandered around the house, taking my time moving through each room, looking out of windows to get my bearings and imagining how I would decorate if it were mine. I deliberately left every door wide open behind me, letting light and air trace a course through domestic spaces that had been stale and shuttered for too long. I meandered up the main staircase to the first floor, then up again via what I supposed would have been the servants' route: steep and uncarpeted steps that taxed the muscles in my thighs as I fumbled for each narrow tread, hidden behind a heavy door at the far end of one of the stems of minor corridors.

The second floor, my floor, had two bathrooms and five bedrooms along the main passageway, though mine was the only one that had been furnished much beyond stacked bed frames and the odd chair not quite tatty enough to be thrown out. The effort made to ready my bedroom for guests appeared to mark the beginning and the end of Georgie's attempts so far at home improvement. Two more corridors pierced the main one, running the length of the floor in opposite directions, each ending in a staircase that dropped straight down to the lower floors without trespassing into the luxury of the comfortable centre, the carpeted areas.

I walked these minor corridors, stumbling a little over the warped floorboards, opening doors as I went. Room after room a copy of the one before. Identical squares of faded-paper walls peeling at the edges, dusty floors, windows grimed and dull. Decades of being nothing, harbouring nothing. The trapped air damp with the sadness of this house abandoned to become less than a shell of a home, for a shell at least serves a vital purpose: to shelter life within it. The house must have felt the vibrations when Georgie moved in; the feel and sound of feet and voices on the stairs, in each room, after so long without either. But after that initial flurry of movement, a return to nothing. My sister didn't really live here, she just haunted a handful of rooms on the lower floors, leaving the rest of the house still waiting to be reclaimed, to become what it was built to be.

I doubted, meanly, whether she would ever turn the Hall into a boutique artist's retreat and fill it with the smells of oil paint and turps. Before she'd even unpacked she'd let its size defeat her, pushing away its history and contenting herself with the vague conceit of future schemes.

Angry now, unfairly angry, I tore a strip of ancient flowery paper from the wall and folded it into several brittle wads, pushing each one into the crack at the foot of every door so that they were wedged wide open. Sunlight striped the corridor floor as I worked my way along roughly, muttering as I lowered myself down onto my knees over and over, scraping splinters into my fingers.

Then I did the same for the other corridor, stopping only when every door was open and the air from each room released itself into the wider space. I could almost feel the breeze of it circling me as I finally stood back in the crossroads of the main landing and looked around, left then right, noting with cross pleasure how the light leapt from room to room, rushing the length of the house to join me.

I pushed a fist into my aching back and went downstairs to do the same on the first floor.

I told Georgie I'd napped through the afternoon. As we ate dinner and talked in subdued bursts I made plans in my head to start cleaning the rooms on my floor. To at least make a start on the windows, so the world and the house could see each other more clearly. Maybe sweep the floors of their bluebottle carcasses and then place something solid and definite in each room: a picture or an ornament, even a book. An object to give the walls something more substantial, more *real*, to close around than air.

After I'd washed up and lit candles to fend off the darkness settled at the windows Georgie leaned forward and reached for my hand across the table. 'I'm sorry, ladybug,' she said, 'for today, being so cold with you. I don't know what's wrong with me at the moment.'

Instantly ashamed, contrite, I squeezed her fingers. 'You had a nasty shock and I've been a dismissive bitch about it. I don't know how you put up with me.'

We smiled at each other in the flickering light of the candles, brimful of love again, re-cocooned safely inside our relationship. I felt a surge of gratitude for Georgie, the easy way she shrugged off disagreements and turned us both away from any festering resentment.

'I'm going to bed,' she said, standing up with a look of resolve on her face. 'I'm exhausted after last night. No, I'll be fine.' She waved me away as I got to my feet to accompany her upstairs.

'Are you sure? I can bunk in with you again if you like.'

I hoped she'd say no, and she did, blowing me a kiss as she opened the kitchen door. 'You were probably right, it was just a nightmare. I need to stop being such a baby. Could you switch the lights off down here when you go to bed?'

I wasn't long behind her; suddenly bone-weary and longing for sleep. I moved through the house slowly, flicking off lights and lingering at windows to look out at the skinny moon. Pausing on the first floor to listen outside Georgie's room, and then up again. In my room I closed the curtains against the frosted night and climbed shivering into bed. The little girl slipped under the covers to lie against me as soon as I turned my lamp off, nuzzling into the crook of my arm.

'You let them out,' she mumbled into my shoulder sleepily.

I stroked her hair back from her face. 'Let who out?'

'The other children. You opened all the doors and let them out.'

The bedroom was freezing when I woke up the next morning. Sunlight slipped in shreds through the worn patches in the curtains, spilling a hazy kaleidoscope across the floor. I didn't have to move to know that the child was still beside me, curled tight and foetal against my ribs. We lay for a while, warm beneath the heavy bed covers, dozing our way to full waking. When I jolted from another half-dream she was gone and it was time to get up.

The house groaned in its pipes, thrusting heat valiantly through the rooms, as I made my way downstairs. Georgie wasn't in her bedroom or the kitchen, but the kettle was warm and the radio was jangling quietly on the top of the dresser. I stood at the open door, drinking coffee and looking for her, enjoying the bracing rush of cold air against my still-sleepy skin.

The walled garden was crisp with the autumn's first frost, the flagstones treacherous when I placed a foot on them. In the distance I could see the wood's dark huddle of trees and above it a faded stretch of sky, as if early mist had yet to fully clear the corners of Magpie Hall's boundary. A few rooks clattered overhead, surging towards a sun as dim and formless as if it had been wrapped in muslin.

Another coffee shored me up enough to brave the icy bathroom, and then I began to look for Georgie in earnest. I couldn't remember her telling me she'd be going out this morning and her car was still parked by the front steps. Her coat was still on its peg beside mine, though her woolly hat was gone.

Calling her name, I wandered through the kitchen garden and around the side of the Hall to the coach house tucked into a yard that faced away from the driveway and the elegance of the front view. It sagged around stores of neatly chopped wood, its frame now little more than a rotting skeleton shedding loose chunks of stone from the tumbled walls. A warped slate roof slid in dips and humps from apex to guttering, shattered in places. Torn tarpaulin flapped and tightened across the windows. I peered through the arch of doorway to the shadowed spaces at the back, worrying in case Georgie had come out to fetch something and slipped over. Rusted garden tools clung to nails on the back wall and an upturned wheelbarrow squatted in the corner, but apart from that the place was empty. It didn't look as though anyone had been in here for decades.

Anxiety had settled on me, vague but pressing, by the time I'd circled the house and gone back inside via the kitchen to see if Georgie had reappeared. I couldn't believe she'd taken a walk to the woods or the shops; her boots were still in the entrance hall and, besides, she would have waited for me to join her.

The house was cooling now, warmth ebbing from the radiators as the boiler in the storeroom settled into silence after its morning work. The Rayburn had gone out at some point in the early hours. By lunchtime we'd be freezing in the kitchen if I didn't get it relit. I shovelled coal from the scuttle and laid a clumsy pyre behind the door, flicking a match onto the twists of paper. I didn't stay to watch it catch, just hoped it would fire up. If it was as temperamental as the one I remembered from our childhood it would need hours of coaxing before it co-operated, but I didn't have the time or the patience to woo it.

Every door on the ground floor had been closed, every room returned to lonely isolation. I guessed Georgie had not liked my expansive march through her home yesterday, flinging doors wide as I went. In that case, I thought with a wince, she was going to hate what I'd done upstairs.

I hurried up the main staircase and back to her bedroom, whistling and calling. Her bed was neatly made and her dressing gown hung from the hook behind the door. No sign of life in her bathroom and the huge bath was dry and cold to the touch. The other bedrooms on the central corridor were empty, each door closed.

The nearest staircase to the second floor was the one at the end of the landing so I headed for that, then veered back and plunged along each of the side corridors, checking each room. She must have been through the entire house closing the doors I'd opened. The thought of her getting down onto her hands and knees again and again, contorting herself around her bulky stomach to prise my homemade wedges out, made me feel guilty and resentful.

On my floor I repeated the search and then, temporarily defeated, went back to my bedroom. It was strange to think I could be the only adult in the house. As if it were mine alone, for a while at least. I didn't want to linger too long before finding Georgie but knew there was a part of me that was enjoying the solitude that didn't feel like solitude, within these walls.

The book I'd bought was lying open on the bed. The child was perched on the edge of the mattress, staring out of the window and chewing on a braid of hair, but she turned and spat it out when I sat beside her and pulled her onto my lap. Her arms snaked around me and she burrowed her nose into my armpit.

'Have you been reading this?' I asked her. I picked up the book.

She nodded against my chest, eyes closed. Her thumb crept into her mouth. I rocked her and leafed through the pages, stopping at the photographs of Magpie Hall in its former incarnation.

She was there in the front row, this little girl I was holding; kneeling on the gravel driveway with her fellow orphans. She looked fearful and sad; sadder than any child should ever look. A rag doll lay across her long-ago thighs, her fingers entwined in its wool hair as though she were scared it would be taken from her. I closed the book and pushed it away, and we just sat for a while, me murmuring while she clung and relaxed into me.

When she spoke her voice was sleepy, low and soft. 'Stay with me.'

I looked down at her. 'I can't, I have things to do. Tonight.'

She pulled air noisily into her lungs and shuddered, biting down on her thumb, but she didn't cry. 'What things?'

'I have to look for my sister.'

Her eyes opened wide and we stared at each other for a long moment. She dipped her head back to its resting place but I raised her so that she was propped away from my body and I could see her face clearly. 'Do you know where she is?'

The child shook her head slightly, barely a movement, then, when I raised an eyebrow and asked her again, she pointed to the ceiling. 'She went up to the attic.'

I thought of asking her why, thought of making her promise me Georgie was okay, but instead I kissed her and laid her down on the duvet, and then walked to the door. When I turned back to say goodbye she'd gone.

It took me ages to find the stairs that led to the attic. I hadn't even considered that the house had yet another floor, so used to living as I did in a handful of cramped rooms with strangers layered above and below each other. I was swearing loudly, sweating panic, when I finally pushed through a narrow door set into the top of one of the servants' staircases and saw the steps leading upwards.

The cold became denser the higher I climbed. There was no light to see my way and I didn't know I'd reached the attic floor until my palms met a solid barrier. Fumbling for a handle, thumping on the door and shouting for Georgie, I felt the solidity and might of the house behind and beneath me, almost as if I were balanced on a cliff edge or the topmost turret of a castle, wavering between security and free-fall. Fear thrilled its way from my scalp to the bottom of my spine.

When the door jerked open, its brittle catch no longer able to resist my urgent shoving, I spilled through and landed on my knees with a grunt. Dim sunlight sourced from windows set into the end wall showed me a space vast and cluttered, the air thick with cobwebs. Furniture reared from the shadowed corners, dripping dust and rotted sheets. I got to my feet and called out for my sister, picking a route across the floor. Something crunched unpleasantly with every step I took: an almost elastic stretching beneath my soles and then a small crack and pop, a giving way. I bent to look, sweeping my hands over the floorboards to collect what was there.

The folded skeleton of a dead bird dangled from my finger-tips, shell and fluid clinging greasily to patches of fine down across the curve of its back. The stench of decay stayed on my skin after I'd dropped it with a squeak of horror and wiped my hands on my jeans. I resumed my crunching shuffle, wincing as I trod through what sounded like nest after nest of eggs abandoned just before the point of life.

The noise of Georgie coughing tugged me across the attic. I followed the sound, calling for her, ducking beneath blankets draped over beams. She didn't answer me but continued to cough somewhere out of sight; a hacking wheeze that ended in a dry, barking retch. I had to clamber over an avalanche of bed frames that had at one point been stacked against the wall but must have eventually succumbed to their own tilted weight and cascaded across the floor. I still couldn't see my sister and the coughing had stopped. There was nothing to guide me and I was losing what little light the windows at my back had offered.

A crude plywood partition had been hammered into the attic space, dividing it in two. Through the ragged gap that served as a doorway the other half of the attic stretched ahead of me, similarly vast and just as cluttered as the half I had just crossed. I was in the darkest part now, the deep middle, but heading towards the lit edges and towards her; steering around boxes as much through sense as sight, tripping over rolled carpets. Ahead of me, silhouetted grittily against the windows set into the far end wall, I could make out a hunched, still shape. Standing but somehow sagging; limply upright like a bundle of clothes strung from string.

'Georgie? Is that you, darling? What are you doing up here?'

When I got nearer I could see it was definitely her. Motionless, she stood half-turned away from me and looking down.

Even when I kicked against a wooden crate of pots as I struggled forward, the noise crashing in my ears for moments after the impact, she didn't move or speak.

I could hear the rasp of her breathing when I reached her, her lungs toiling to filter the dust and chill of the attic. She'd always had a weak chest, had spent childhood winters bundled into woolly layers, watching from the window as I charged through the snow with my coat unbuttoned and my hands bare. I thought I'd softened through the years and she'd toughened, each of us finding a more natural balance with maturity, but I remembered now seeing her asthma inhaler in the bathroom earlier, something I'd not known her to use for years, and I wondered how long she'd been needing it. Since she moved here? Since I arrived?

'Pea?' I reached out to touch the hand hanging loose at her side. 'Are you okay?'

Her skin was cold and pliable beneath my fingers, putty-like, as though the blood had congealed to paste and the bones had gone. She didn't respond to my tentative patting so I squeezed hard and put my other hand on her cheek to turn her to face me. I bent at the knees and crouched a little so that we were eye to eye, close enough to brush noses. For a few seconds she stared through me as blankly as if I didn't exist, her lips moving to some monologue I couldn't hear, and then she blinked and saw me. She frowned and pulled her hand from my grip.

'What are you doing?' she asked, rubbing at the tender spot below her thumb where I'd applied pressure. 'That hurt.'

'What are *you* doing?' I replied. 'I've been looking all over for you, pea. What are you doing up here?'

She shifted back a step, glancing around her, raising her hands with a wince to rub her neck. We both heard the creak of her limbs moving in their sockets after God knows how long frozen in place. She stumbled slightly and hissed, bending to rub her calf, and then her thigh. 'I'm fine,' she said, pushing away my concern. 'It's just cramp. You didn't need to come up here, I was about to head down after I'd got …' A look of panic tightened the muscles of her face. 'After I'd done what I needed to do.'

I started to turn away, a hand around her wrist to steer her towards the stairs. She pulled back for a second but then I tugged harder and she let me lead her through the attic without protest.

'What did you need to do?' I asked. 'It didn't look like you were doing anything at all. I've been worried, pea, you just disappeared.'

She didn't answer me and I couldn't see her expression when I glanced back. Her free arm was wrapped around her stomach as if protecting the baby tucked beneath the skin. Even when negotiating our way around the hazards strewn across the floor she didn't move it out to her side to help balance her. If she'd tripped she would have fallen straight onto her face.

By the time we reached the top of the stairs the cold had settled into my bones, forcing periodic shivers from me. I dreaded to think how chilled Georgie had got, how long she'd been up here. The way she'd just been standing when I found her, scarecrow-vacant, frightened me more than my cheerful coaxing would have led her to believe.

In her bathroom, I filled the tub with hot water and un-dressed her. Naked, she stood pliant and silent while I draped her in her dressing gown and began to rub her hands. It had been years since I'd seen my sister's body. The shock of her stretched belly, the dimpled corrugations across the plump flesh of her thighs, made me stare with a child's open-mouthed lack of discretion.

Pre-adolescent, we'd been almost identical in our bony-smooth skins, and post-adolescence we'd both been secretive and shy, uncomfortably aware of our curves and the curls of hair between our legs. Mum's pursed-lip disapproval of my breasts swinging like fists inside my school blouse had been double-pronged: I wasn't supposed to be overtaking my older sister in maturity, and not with such an unabashedly swollen display of womanhood. I remembered how she'd make comments about attracting the wrong sort of attention while we shopped for bras in the next size up; remembered too finding Georgie in my bedroom one evening, standing side-on at the mirror, hands on hips, my sock-stuffed bra fastened over her narrow chest. I'd been cruel and mocking at the time, accusing her of wanting what I had, scribbling crude drawings on the covers of her schoolbooks, making her cry.

Now, as I helped her into the bath and began to stroke water over her back while she sat and stared at the taps, her hands splayed loose across her thighs as though they'd been abandoned there, I yearned to cradle the dome of her belly with my hands and feel the leap and tumble beneath my palms. I stayed with her and murmured nonsense words, topping the bath up with hot water, until the muscles in her shoulders began to loosen and her lungs quietened their noisy, rhythmic, growl.

The Rayburn had gone out again when I went to check it. I'd left Georgie in bed with promises to return with tea and hot water bottles. My sing-song prattling was starting to get on my nerves but in the face of her passive inattention I couldn't seem to stop. The most she'd been able to offer me was a nod or a shake of the head and only after I'd repeated a question more than once. When I'd asked her, again and again, what she'd been doing up in the attic she didn't even do that.

As I threw more twists of paper into the bowel of the Rayburn I thought of phoning Mark and telling him about Georgie. But tell him what? She's acting a bit weird? She's having nightmares? I decided to leave the phone call until it was absolutely necessary. I knew there was a chance I wouldn't even do it then.

There was a crowd of children along the landing when I went back upstairs. My little girl was in the centre of the huddle, whispering and urgent. Her face lit up when she saw me and she ran to my side to hold my hand, swinging our arms and pressing herself against my hip. She tipped her head back and laughed up at me, thrilled. The other children watched with pinched, hungry jealousy, edging against the walls as I walked among them.

'What's going on?' I asked, clamping my free arm tight against my ribs to prevent the hot water bottle from sliding down onto the floor. I looked down at my girl, then around at the rest of them. 'What are you all doing?'

Nobody answered me. 'Okay, just stay out of Georgie's

room,' I told them, tugging my hand gently from the little girl's grip and patting her cheek to soften the rejection. 'Go and play in the garden or something.'

I shooed them away and waited until they'd gone downstairs before I opened Georgie's bedroom door and went in. She was lying on her side, facing away from me, but she shifted onto her back when I lifted the covers and tucked the hot water bottle into her folded arms.

'There you go, pea. I'll bring you some tea and toast up in a minute.' I bent and kissed her forehead then stood back to look at her. Her empty gaze fixed on the ceiling, her face slack and expressionless. With her patchwork scalp and bruised eye, that vacant stare, she looked like the victim of some terrible accident or trauma. Helplessness rose in my throat and released itself from my mouth as irritation.

'For God's sake, Georgie, either tell me what's wrong or make an effort to snap out of it,' I said, pulling the duvet sharply up over her shoulders. I walked out of the room, leaving the door wide open behind me, knowing she hated it left like that, hoping she might be prompted to get up and shut it. Anything to provoke a response.

The children were clattering around in the dining hall, whooping and giggling, as I slapped slices of cheese between bread and sat at the kitchen table to eat, sullenly determined to make Georgie wait for her tea. Maybe if she had to wait long enough she'd get up and come down to fetch it herself.

The noise of their play rescued my mood a little. It sounded as though an involved game of chase was unfolding across the hall. The door was ajar but apart from a steady flicker of shadows in the narrow gap I couldn't see the action, though I could identify the low chuckle of my girl through the shrill squeals of her friends.

I made toast and hunted through cupboards for a flask. The children's game spilled from the dining room and onto the staircase. I called to them to keep the noise down but judging by the stampede of feet above me as they charged across the landing I doubted they'd heard. It was as if some silent permission had been granted to them to claim, or reclaim, every part of the house and they were making the most of being merely children; pursuing childhood pleasures now without fear of repercussion.

Trailing after them once I'd finally found a thermos jug that would keep Georgie's tea hot through the afternoon, stacking the radio and her half-finished novel on the stairs to fetch later, I walked into a silence thick as fog on the first floor. I hadn't consciously noticed the children had stopped their games but now the absence of jostling laughter pierced me like a loss. I stood for a moment in the crossroads of corridors and listened for any sound: stifled giggles, scuffling feet, that meant they were still somewhere around. The quality of the silence, as if the house itself were bursting with held breath, made me uneasy but it also made me feel less alone.

Georgie's door was still wide open, just as I'd left it. Her bed was empty; the covers neatly folded back, hot water bottle on the floor. I checked the room in case she'd got out of bed and fallen, and then crossed the landing to the bathroom. I knew it would be empty even before I stepped inside.

This time I didn't bother searching through the house. I headed straight for the stairs to the attic.

I had to push hard against the warped door that opened onto the staircase leading to the attic, shoving again and again before it parted company with the frame with a groan that was almost human, and let me through. The children were a solid barrier lining the stairs, each step crowded with little bodies, angelic in their long night gowns as though they were part of some old-fashioned play. I realised that they'd been leaning against the door as I pushed against it. They'd been trying to keep me from getting through. I began to move them aside and force a path, one step at a time, but as soon as I'd moved one child another slipped into the space left behind. Smiling, giggling, they grabbed my hands and hung from my arms, pulling me back as soon as I'd gained a little ground. I forgot that they were just children, just playing, and began to shout and slap at them, demanding they let me through.

By the time I'd got halfway up the stairs I was trapped, unable to move forward or back. Some of the children had scrambled onto the shoulders of others so they loomed above me and I had to tip my head right back in order to see them. Behind me fingers poked into my ears and twisted around my hair, pulling it with sharp tugs that jerked my neck back in a steady rhythm, as though I were one of my own puppets. I was too angry to be frightened as I dug my elbows into soft bodies and scrambled up another step and then another, not caring if I hurt them. I knew I had to reach the top of the stairs, for that was where my girl would be, and she loved me and would stop her friends from behaving like this. She would let me through to fetch Georgie, and then all of us would go back down into the heart of the house and everything would be as it was.

My legs were weak and shaking but if I stopped pushing forward for even a second I wouldn't be able to keep my balance in the trample. I didn't know what they'd do to me if I fell down, I didn't seriously believe they'd intentionally harm me, but the sheer numbers crammed into the narrow space would crush me if I ended up underfoot. I heaved myself onwards, using my greater weight to ram a way through, kicking and thumping when I had to. My awareness was reduced to nothing else but the stench of my sweat rising from my skin and the sweet, joyful trill of laughter all around me. When I could see the dark panels of the attic door the children were suddenly kinder in their play. Fingers unlaced themselves from around my throat and my ankles were released. There was space around me and I could take deep breaths in without constriction.

Standing with her back to the door, hands stretched to me, my girl stood and waited for me to reach her. Her friends fell back, silent, watching us. I didn't know I was going to slap her until I'd done it, raised my arm to shoulder height and then brought my palm down hard and furious across her cheek. The force of it spun her sideways and thrust her back into the door frame. She yelped and covered her head as if scared I'd attack her again, then lowered her hands and flung herself on me, wrapping her arms around my waist. 'I'm sorry, I'm sorry, please still love me,' she sobbed. 'Tell me you're not cross.'

Something swelled in my heart then, filled it to overflowing and spilled into my sore, hollowed-out womb. I knelt and cradled her in my arms, hushing and rocking, telling her I loved her, of course I loved her, and I was sorry too. We stayed wrapped together until her body stopped shaking and she was breathing quietly, and then I raised us both to our feet but didn't let go of her hand.

When I turned to the door she stepped in front of me and shook her head, gently tugging me away. 'I did this for you,' she said. 'You know deep down what you really want.'

I thought of my sister, standing in the dark and the cold on the other side of the door, confused and lost, sealing herself in the attic but not knowing why. I thought of the house without her, just me and the children. Our home. Our family.

I nodded at my girl and let her lead me back down the stairs. The other children parted to let us through and fell into step behind us, so that when we reached the main landing and the steady comfort of lamplight in the early dusk, I didn't need to look round to know we were all together.

We sang and danced and laughed through the next week. Meals, picnic-style, kneeling on blankets in the huge dining hall, passing jugs of water and juice from glass to glass, a happy circle of please and thank you. Games of chase and hide and seek across the lawns and in the woods. We began to clean the small bedrooms on the minor corridors, decorating them with anything we could find: leaves piled into corners and berries on the window sills. At 10pm it was lights out and I slept in my room with my girl, shutting the door against the rest of them. She was happy enough to share me during the day, she enjoyed the greater status this gave her among her friends, but the nights were ours alone.

Lying awake while she dreamed beside me, her hand clutching at my night shirt to stop me from moving away, I sometimes thought I could hear faint creeping noises above me, as though someone were walking the floorboards over my head or pushing against a door. I thought of Georgie then, even though I could let hours slip by during daylight without thinking of her at all, and I wondered when she was going to come back downstairs. Once, when we were walking back to the Hall after a breathless afternoon romping around the garden, I thought I saw her at the end attic window. Just a brief flicker, gone when I blinked. The children caught my arms as I stumbled, righting me and then cavorting by my side, cartwheeling and leap-frogging, pretending to fall over as I had nearly done.

The phone in the kitchen started ringing on the fourth day and didn't stop; just once or twice at first, shrilling through mealtimes, and then every hour from morning onwards. We never answered it; the children didn't seem to hear it and I felt no need to speak to anyone outside the house. Somebody came to the front door and knocked for ages, calling my sister's name, peering through the letterbox, and we all huddled on our knees against the walls in the darkened hallway, stifling giggles against each other's shoulders. I'd made sure all of the doors were locked, should anyone be curious enough to try to gain access.

'Will this be forever?' my girl asked me one night, tucking herself into the fold of my arm as we lay together in bed. 'I don't know,' I told her. 'I don't see how it can be. But we're here now, that's all that matters.'

She squeezed her cold toes into the sliver of gap between my calves. 'It can last forever if we want it to. Just don't ever go up to the attic. If you loved me you'd want it to last forever.'

We'd become so self-contained, so independent of the outside world, I didn't even recognise the sound as a car's engine when it pulled up in front of the house on the eighth day. I looked first up to the sky for an aeroplane, opening the kitchen window to lean out. I saw Mark at the same time as he saw me and he called my name and began to walk across the drive towards me, even as I slammed the window shut and ducked down below the level of the sink. The children, who had been somewhere else all morning, appeared at my side. The smaller ones were crying, shaking their heads, waving goodbye to each other.

'Stay in here,' my girl begged me. 'Just stay in here and keep the door closed.'

'Maybe it'll all be okay,' I told them. 'I think it will be.' I couldn't meet their eyes as I stood up and walked into the hall. They already knew, of course they already knew, and the crying got louder but no-one tried to hold me back.

I didn't need to unlock the front door; Mark used his key and rushed in. We met under the green and yellow glow of the stained-glass fanlight. 'Where's Georgie?' he asked. 'Is she okay? The baby? I've been phoning for days, why didn't you answer?'

He pushed away the hand I held out to him, stepping back from me as if I were contaminated. 'You've told her, haven't you? You've told her.'

I shook my head and reached out again. 'I haven't told her. But she's not here. She's gone away and I don't think she's coming back. Mark …'

'No. She wouldn't have just gone, she wouldn't have done that. Where is she?'

He shoved past me and through to the kitchen, shouting for his wife. Standing in the doorway behind him, I saw the room as he must have seen it: tin cans and vegetable peelings spilt across the work surfaces, stinking and stained, dirty plates stacked on the table and floor. The chairs were upended, the table on its side; left like that after one of the children's games. I'd never been one for housekeeping.

Mark turned to look at me, his expression a mix of shock and confusion. 'Tell me what the fuck has been going on here,' he said. 'Tell me what happened.'

'We were just playing. I should have cleaned up.'

I tried to move past him, to start the process of tidying the room, but he put his hands on my shoulders and held me in place. 'You were *playing*? Jesus, look at the state of you, Marie, you look feral.'

My hands went instinctively up to cover my face, to hide from the horror on his. I knew how important it was to find just the right words to keep us all safe, keep us here exactly as we were and our life unchanged, but I couldn't focus on anything beyond the awful way he was looking at me. I started to cry, hating every tear as it welled up but not able to stop.

'She went by herself. I didn't make her, I even fetched her

down once but she went back up. It was her choice. I didn't tell her, Mark, I promise; she doesn't know anything. But can't you see what this means for us? For me and you, and for the child? For all of us?'

I clung to him even as he released me and tried to get past. I braced my body against the door frame and hung onto his waist, burying my face against his back, dragging him into my arms. This was how the girl had experienced my love, before we'd been freed by Georgie: always scrabbling to hold onto me while I set her aside. There was a dark blank void in my head between what was happening and what should be. The path had been cleared, for him and me. There was no need for this.

Mark forced my wrists open with a sound of disgust and thrust me backwards so that I stumbled into the kitchen and collided with the upended table. 'Where is she, Marie?'

The table leg was digging into my hip, hurting me. I concentrated on the pain as I faced him and pointed up at the ceiling. 'She's in the attic.'

He laughed then, without humour, waiting for me to add something further or say I was joking. Waiting for me to whip open a cupboard door and reveal my sister, safe and right here and happy to see him, as she always was. When I didn't speak he began to shout her name again as he ran to the staircase, pausing at the foot to point a finger at me. 'You locked her in the attic?'

'No! Of course I didn't. The children ...' I looked around me for my girl and the others. They'd been here, with me when Mark arrived. They couldn't have gone far. 'The children will tell you. You'll understand when you see them ...'

The pity that flickered across his face then was worse than any contempt. 'Just go,' he said, turning away from me. 'Get your things and go before I bring Georgie back down. This has to end now, for us. And this time for good, Marie. I don't want to see you again.'

After he'd disappeared, after I'd heard the last of him leaving me as he stormed through the house in his efforts to find the stairs that led to the attic, his frantic yells that were my sister's name and not mine, I waited for the children to show themselves from wherever they'd hidden. I waited for my girl to appear at my side and slip her hand in mine. I waited until I could hear the distant sound of Mark screaming, somewhere far above me, and then I went to the heavy, huge front door and opened it. I stepped outside and pulled the door closed behind me. I began to walk down the long driveway, towards the rusted gates and that bright painted sign that Georgie had painted for our home, for Magpie Hall.

PERSPECTIVES

She comes to the house three days after your son is killed in a climbing accident, floating out from the backdrop of your world, easing herself away from the grey wallpaper of those people you're vaguely aware of but don't ever think about, to stand on your front doorstep and stake a claim in your life. When you see her waiting beyond the thick glass door, her body wavering and separating as she shifts from pane to pane, you assume that she'd been a friend of your son's, yet another stranger compelled to pay ghoulish respects to the bereaved mother. When you open the door and she spills towards you with her hands outstretched and her mouth a crimson crumple you recognise her as the quiet girl from book group, the one who'd watched faces closely whenever anyone spoke, and nodded with eager, hungry agreement as though she'd been about to say just that, that very thing, herself. She'd never once offered an opinion on a book, and you used to wonder idly whether she even read them, why she bothered to be there. She'd stopped coming a few months back, or had you forgotten to include her when you sent round the latest list of dates and titles for the new season? Had you forgotten to tell her about the change of venue?

You can't remember her name and are mildly startled to see that her hair is a rich acorn brown, not the muted mouse of memory. Her eyes are pink-rimmed, and she pursues the drift of your body as you step aside to let her into the hallway, pressing her arms around you and her face against yours, hard enough for her cheek's bony peak to leave behind a dull smear of pain that you rub away. The hug feels jerky and unpractised, a lunge that you're required to catch and make safe. You pat her with the tips of your fingers before releasing yourself and leading the way to the kitchen.

The huddle of people crowded around the table, the neighbours and friends and morbidly curious, stop chattering and shuffle aside to create space. They eye the new arrival with interest and she stares back at them with a grimace of horror before scampering to your side. You fill the kettle for the fiftieth time today and wave a hand to indicate the plates and baskets of cake and sandwiches stacked along the counters. 'Please help yourself to something. It'll just go to waste otherwise. People won't stop bringing me food.'

Her skin flushes the same raw pink as her eyes and she slaps her palm to her mouth with a loud fleshy pop. 'I didn't bring you anything. Oh god. I'm so sorry.' She won't sit down, even when you try to point her towards an empty seat, fidgeting instead at your side and fluttering her fingers back and forth over the mugs and kettle so that the task of making a pot of tea is fraught with danger. 'Let me help. Please let me help,' she keeps saying, stumbling over your feet as you move around her to empty and swill the teapot at the sink.

Your cousin stands up and taps the back of her chair. 'Sit down, will you. You're making me nervous. Here, Kath, I'll have another.' She hands you her mug and takes the girl's arm. 'Sit down and tell me how you know Pete.'

'Pete?' The girl looks around the group with little pecking

glances, searching out a familiar face. 'I'm sorry, I don't think I do. I'm here to see Kathy.'

'Pete, as in my dead son,' you interrupt loudly. 'That's his name. Was his name, before he fell off a mountain.' You fill the teapot and lean with your back against the counter so that you can look at her properly. You want to watch the mortification drench her, you want her to drown in it. Spite rises in you and it's a blessing to feel something other than the bewildered, hollowed panic of the last few days. Maybe this will be my future, you think. I'll turn into one of those cruel, vicious women who make shop assistants cry or report them to their manager for not serving me quickly enough. I'll live to be as joyless as possible. My son, my only child, is dead and so what was the point of the day-and-a-half's labour, the worrying over every sniffle, the slump of relief beneath my bed sheets when he clattered home after a night out and I could finally sleep. Right now, in this moment, you want to take it all back. You want to take *him* back. You'd rather have had none of it than be left with this.

The girl seems to fold in on herself, her shoulders swooning down over her chest and her face tucking into her throat. She looks boneless and bereft. Jenny, that's what she's called. You're pretty sure it's Jenny.

You sweep the teapot into your cupped hands and carry it the few steps to the table, enjoying the way its china belly burns the flesh of your palms. 'Thank you for coming, that was good of you,' you say. 'Please have some tea and a piece of cake or a sausage roll or something. Sorry I'm not better company. I'm going for a lie down.'

In Pete's bedroom you roll yourself into his duvet and hunt

down his smell, twisting your head back and forth against the cloth cocoon to graze the material with nose and mouth. There, a tiny fading pocket of sweat and sleep-sour skin. And there, another. You shut your eyes and breathe him in, nudging at the scent with your tongue. Beyond the bedroom door and a world away, on the safe side of loss, conversations carry on, doors shut, and chair legs scrape across the floor. You don't care what they talk about, how long they stay, as long as they don't come in here.

The girl appears again three weeks later, on your first solo outing since Pete's death. You hadn't seen her at the funeral but that doesn't mean she wasn't part of the blur of mourners; your grief that day had shattered your eyes to chips of stone, your gaze sightless.

You're in the local supermarket pushing a trolley up and down aisles, searching for something, anything at all, that will snag your interest enough to make you want to buy it. The shop has that slow, sleepy post-lunch feel about it. People shuffle and creep through the striped fluorescence and piped music coats the air with a greasy, soothing blandness. A young man ahead of you stoops to pick up a tin of something and for just a second, as he frowns down at the label, he looks like your son. They're nothing alike really, there's nothing about his face that reminds you of Pete, but you follow him anyway, gripping the trolley bar with sweaty palms and watching. He pauses to examine a packet of pasta and again, just fleetingly, his concentration is all Pete's and he becomes your son. He straightens and moves on and you trail him, close enough to clip his heels with your trolley wheels.

You make your way along the aisles, past the shelves of

cleaning products and into the frozen section, in a jerky stop-start tandem. You can hear your own breathing, gusty and urgent, and beyond that his occasional muttering. His voice is wrong, the sound of it jarringly unknown, and you want to tell him to be silent.

He stops again and considers a packet of something, leaning over into the freezer just enough for the downward twist of his body to hide his expression. You reach out then to pull him back and raise him up, your hands stabbing out fast and intense, fingers curled to grab at him. Your wrist is tapped, gently, and a figure steps in front of you, blocking the view of your boy. Little mousy Jenny. She smiles and says something, some question you can't hear, and steps to the side when you try to squirm around her to see him. Just one more look, I know it's not him, of course I know that, but just once more and it'll be enough. You don't think you've spoken the words out loud, but she tugs you away, placing your hands back on the bar of the trolley and pressing her arm across your shoulders. You go with her without a word, without another glance at the stranger who has straightened up with a bag of chips in each hand, eying you both suspiciously.

You're embarrassed and ashamed, as if you've been caught slipping a stolen chocolate bar into your handbag or making fun of a child in a wheelchair. And resentful too that Jenny has witnessed your desperation. She must have been following you as you followed him, pitying you with every step she took that brought her closer to saving you from public humiliation. When you get to the tills you shrug out from her embrace and shove your empty trolley away sullenly. 'Thank you,' you say. You think you say that though the words might be wedged in your throat, spiky and unspoken. You walk away from her and out of the supermarket, half-running past the security guard and back to your car. You drive home fast and angry and stay parked on the drive, kissing bumpers with Pete's old van, insulated by the radio jangle, until the day collapses around you and the evening rises up to lay itself filmy and wet across the windscreen.

The days topple into each other: a sandcastle stormed by the tide, a mud pie drowned by rain. You give up pretending to function for a while and spend your life in Pete's bed, drinking tea and eating the crisps that you'd once bought him, all his favourite flavours first. Or you rage naked through the house with your hair flying matted and filthy around your shoulders and your fingers scrabbling at the scar his birth had written on your belly. You shout at his baby-cute black and white image, try to divine from his wise smile some awareness of his broken future. You throw his mug out into the garden and then glue it back together and then throw it out again. You stand in the corridor and clear your throat loudly when anyone comes to the door so that they know you're there but have chosen not to let them in. You call the people who've left messages on Pete's mobile, tell them he's dead, repeat the word until it stumbles against your teeth, and then hang up in the middle of the stammered response. It's liberating to abandon yourself entirely to grief, to not even try, and you wonder whether you'll ever recover the person you once had been. You wonder whether you'll ever want to.

Jenny is there whenever you pull back the curtains to stare out of the window. She's there when you stand on the step to scatter stale bread for the garden birds. A hunch of coat fading into the shrubbery at the bottom of the drive; a pale slash of averted gaze, there then gone, when you peer into the gathered shadows past the gate posts. You've been waiting for her to come up to the house, you knew she wouldn't leave it long before returning, and you have the front door open, flung wide, before she even knocks. Her hand has formed a limp fist that drops to her side as if stunned, and she blinks at you with a rapid, urgent lash-flutter, her eyes a blur of movement.

'I assume you're here about the vacancy,' you say, beaming at her. You're dressed today but your clothes are stiff and sharp with the sweat of your rages. She gapes at the sight of you, twisting her fingers into one writhing braid, and she tries to smile. 'Vacancy?' she asks.

'The mother vacancy,' you explain, leaning out to hold her wrist and pull her close. 'That's why you keep coming by, isn't it?' Her ear, so close to your mouth, pink and pleated against her skull, reminds you of the vulnerable whorl of a baby's, and you suddenly want to nudge your tongue from where it's caught in your snarl and taste her skin. The way you used to taste Pete's when he was small. Rows of kisses dropped the length of his jawbone, lips flickering around his doughnut-soft fontanelle.

You rear back from her before you can act on your urge or, worse, bite her. She stumbles away from your loosened grip on her wrist but she doesn't turn and leave. Her face is wide and blank, her mouth pursed around that second's drawn breath before saying something trite and hushed, something soothingly banal.

'Why did you stop letting me know about the book group meetings?' she asks, and you're so steeled against *How are you coping?* and *I'm really so sorry for your loss* that you think you mishear her and ask her to repeat the question. When she does, she stands a little straighter, her voice a shrill of indignation. 'I really enjoyed going. I know I'm not that clever but I enjoyed reading books I'd never have heard of if it weren't for you.' Her face is rosy with embarrassment or anger. 'Why didn't you ever reply to my emails? Did nobody want me there anymore? Because you could have just said, I wouldn't have made a fuss.'

You fumble for something to say, some easy lie to excuse your lack of consideration. She waits silently, arms folded around her distress. 'Why do you keep following me around?' you ask instead. 'Why can't you leave me alone? Don't you have a mother of your own?'

Now her cheeks blotch to smashed liver and her arms swing down to jerk at her sides. 'As a matter of fact I do, thank you very much,' she says. Her oddly formal tone makes her sound like a child aping its parent's speech, and with a child's impulsive surge of spiteful bravery she rocks forward a little on her feet and stares into your face. 'Do you sometimes think maybe your son jumped off that mountain rather than fell, just to get away from you? Do you sometimes think that?'

The cruelty of her words shocks a giggle from you. She looks appalled but the colour of her skin quietens, her malicious energy spent. You're both silent for a while and then you nod at her and turn to go indoors. 'I don't know when I'll be going back to book group,' you say, 'but I'll email you the details. I'm sorry about the mix-up.'

She doesn't leave straight away. From the window you can see a slice of her shadow faltering on the step for a few minutes as she stands out there and decides what to do. You hope she doesn't knock and try to say something else. You hope she fights the urge to apologise. Right now, for this moment, you admire and envy her and you don't want that undone. Such single-minded self-interest, such a total lack of care for your grief, for your once-son, for the woman you have become.

You wait, and when she walks away you let your hand drop from its resting place against your heart and you watch her until she's out of sight.

RUNTY

Whenever I think about the death of that jackdaw it's always mixed up with the man next door; the image of his unsmiling watchfulness folded into the horrific, beautiful sight of flaming feathers swirling across the rooftops; diving and leaping on currents of hot air.

I'd got used to not being overlooked when I was in my back garden. I'd got used to feeding the birds first thing; singing off key, sleep-swollen, wearing just my dressing gown over a T-shirt and not bothering too much if the hem rucked up and revealed the pale spill of my buttocks when I bent over. The fences were high and the houses on either side both holiday lets, rented briefly and irregularly to couples more concerned with daytrips than garden-lounging.

I never needed to call the jackdaw to the feeder; he was so tame I suspected his brain hadn't developed properly. Or maybe he craved the contact a mother would usually give. But I was careful not to touch him, even when he stretched his bald, scabbed head out to me or clambered with clumsy trust over my feet. I wanted him to have a chance at the wild, fantasised about him bringing his young to me to show them off through the succeeding years. I called him Runty and had decided that he was a he. His siblings had all fledged glossily from next door's chimney pot, plump and full-feathered. Left behind, pecked to pink, Runty had peeped out at the world for a day before he slid down the roof and flew with shuffling, lop-sided effort, straight to my side. I fed him meal worms and cat food, watched him sidle around the garden and scramble up to his lonely chimney pot every evening to roost.

The man was sat at the open window of next door's bedroom one morning, sipping from a mug, close enough to hear my croaky rendition of Bowie's 'Starman'. His face was impassive as he studied me. I half-smiled an embarrassed hello, tightening my dressing gown belt and tugging the lapels closed, but he didn't smile back or turn away and pretend he hadn't seen me. You know, the usual things you'd do when you caught sight of your neighbour half naked. Instead, he lowered the mug and continued to stare, unabashed, as I trod the path back to my door with Runty swoop-hopping by my side. Maybe he'd been watching in that sightless, inward way that people do when they're thinking deeply about something, unaware of the world moving around them, or maybe he was just rude. It was unsettling, though, how fixed his gaze was. His curiosity, while deep and searching, had been blank. Like a student studying the innards of a dissected frog to see what had once made it leap.

The next time I went into the garden I made sure I was wearing clothes. I even wore shoes and brushed the tangles from my hair. And he was there again, sat at his window while I scattered seed below him. Again he watched me while making no effort to acknowledge my fellow-human status; his eyes moving over me as though waiting for me to do something enlightening. I said 'Hello' and 'Lovely afternoon' but he didn't respond. The words echoed in my head long after I'd spoken them and then I wondered if I hadn't, after all, merely thought them. Should I repeat them, then, or say something else? Did I seem standoffish? Stiff-limbed and awkward, I topped up the feeders and water bowls, spooned out Runty's dinner onto his special plate. I was clumsy when I walked away, stumbling on the path as I struggled not to appear self-conscious.

Back indoors I listened for sounds through the party wall, trying to work out a pattern to my neighbour's existence; something that would tell me his routines or how long he'd be staying there. It was as though the house were empty. No television or radio rumbled distantly through my evening, no doors slammed. He didn't go into his garden at all, from what I could tell. Even when it rained last thing he didn't fetch in the padded loungers.

I didn't need to look over to know he was there again the next morning. The smell of fresh coffee drifted down from his window and my peripheral vision snagged a blur of movement. The grass was slippery and wet, and I skidded gracelessly as I walked over it, upending my basket of bird seed and scissoring my legs wide. I snorted excruciated laughter and righted myself, determined not to check if he'd witnessed my near tumble. Of course, I checked anyway, shooting a flustered grin over to him. He was sat with his arms crossed on the sill, watching me, inscrutable. I muttered 'Screw you' as I went through my garden routines, then I fetched my own coffee and sat defiantly in my deck chair, talking to Runty.

I was determined to wait the man out and reclaim my private spaces back, from his intrusive gaze and from my own self-consciousness. So I sat there until I was fidgety and late for work, my bright chatter threading itself into silence, and all that time he didn't move or speak. He just watched me, occasionally topping up his mug. Once he answered his mobile and said 'Yes?' and then 'Not now' and ended the call. When I stood to leave I called up to him 'Could you please stop looking at me, it's making me uncomfortable' and stared at him until my eyes watered, but he didn't so much as blink to register that I existed on the same earthly plane as him.

Through the rest of that day, as I shuffled papers around my desk, I pondered possible reasons for the man's behaviour. Mental health problems? Blind, deaf, or mute? Unable to speak English? I spoke to a colleague who told me to ignore him, and another who told me to flash him. Neither of them seemed to understand, and I couldn't explain, how his watchful presence, his disinterested *scrutiny*, affected me. It was the Observer Effect in practise. Maybe that was it: he was a psychology student undertaking a dissertation exercise.

With the weekend I hoped that the man would pack up and go, his strange week's holiday at an end. I longed to go into my own garden and see that neighbouring bedroom window closed. I longed to be able to walk with loose and careless strides across to the bird feeder like I used to, sing without constraint, not care if I looked bed-headed or had yesterday's make-up smeared across my cheek bones. I think it was the self-judgment that I resented the most. With his watchful presence I was seeing myself through the filter of his observations. Jesus, I could do with losing a bit of weight! Had I *no* friends apart from a brain-damaged jackdaw? Why sing at all if I have to make every tune sound like a massacre?

But the weekend came, and went, and he stayed put. I tried

going out into the garden at odd times, hoping to sneak past his attention, but if he wasn't at his window when I appeared he was always there within a minute or two. I stopped feeding the birds altogether for a couple of days, standing miserably at the kitchen door and watching Runty's forlorn meandering around his empty plate. I made one-sided conversation, flirtatious and provocative. I ignored him ostentatiously, making passive-aggressive comments to the air about weirdos. Nothing. Then I got drunk.

I'd always viewed myself as a strong character. It alarmed me how quickly and how far my sense of self and security could unravel. And just how easily. All it took was one person with no desire to interact with me. One person presented themselves to me daily merely to display their lack of interest and I became a neurotic wreck, riddled with doubt.

I carried a bottle of red wine and a tumbler into the garden as dusk thickened the edges of our street. I dribbled a little onto the ground as homage to the gods of the earth and drank the rest greedily. It didn't take long for the initial light buzz to sink into a heavier, foggy belligerence. Even while a small, sober part of my mind tried to wrestle me down, I started to shout at the man. I can't remember what I said. Then I picked up a stone and I threw it.

It hit the wall below his window with a sharp rap, leaving an oval of mud on the white paint. I reached for another, threw it hard, groped for one more, before I realised what I was doing. I stared at him for a stretched, shocked moment and then he stood up and moved away from the window. I staggered to my deckchair and sat down, staring at the empty frame he'd left behind. Finally alone. Wretchedly ashamed.

The smell of burning dragged me to my feet. Smoke plumed from next door's chimney. I tipped my head back and watched as Runty popped from the stone pillar high above me, sparkling with fire like a macabre art installation. I screamed to him to fly; ran around the garden for the watering can and a blanket; screamed at the man to put the fire out. Runty, his confused brain seeking only the security of home, dived into the chimney, again and then again, emerging each time with his tiny body more flames than feathers, until he finally fell and lay smouldering on the rooftop. He twitched once or twice and then was still.

The window was still blank and black when I turned to look. No lights shone from within the house. It was as though the man, having accomplished something I could not even understand, had packed up and left.

INTO THE WOODS

She goes into the woods to crouch
among the tangled roots of her favourite oak and gaze up,
    up,
and follow the scrape of branch against sky.
In her dreams she gets that high
herself, cloud high, and clings to the top branches and lets
    go.

She goes into the woods to take off
her shoes and socks and squelch through mud that swallows
    her to the shins.

She goes into the woods to cry.

She goes into the woods to list birdcall
and flowers neatly in a lined notebook and sniff scat.
She goes into the woods to scream until she's hoarse and red
and her hands are fists against her chest and she's deafened
    by the echo of herself.

She goes into the woods to read poetry
and she uses leaves as markers for the pages
and greens the bits she wants to return to with sap.

She goes into the woods to get so drunk she can't stand up,
and hold conversations with herself about why she's so
    unhappy.

She goes into the woods to paint
tiny doors onto the trees at knee height
and then tap on them with the tips of her fingers
and imagine an elf or a fairy, scowling, peering out
to ask her what she wants at this ungodly hour.

She goes into the woods to lower her knickers
and shit with the bracken tickling her chin, her squatted
    hind.
She goes into the woods to be naked and wade through
    nettles
as carefully as through a fast-flowing stream, and bite
the gasp before it leaves her mouth. Bite it down to the
    tongue
and then pick dock leaves and tickle her sobbing skin.

She goes into the woods to vomit her dinner

quietly into the dense undergrowth and wash her face
in one of the brooks that carve a path through alder and oak.
She goes into the woods to lie down as still as possible for
    hours
and pretend she's weeks dead, months dead, rotting into the
    earth,
her bones silvered with decay.

She goes into the woods to drop to her palms and knees
and see the world as an animal would, struggling over rough
    ground,
trying for speed and paws,
gouging trenches into her legs that grow dark and plump
    with infection.

She goes into the woods to press herself against the rough
bark of trees
and believe they would return the embrace,
hold her tight and keep her safe,
if only they could.

She goes into the woods to bury her small treasures,
a brooch and cat fur and teeth from her baby self,
in an old metal tobacco tin that belonged to her father,
and then forget where she left it.

She goes into the woods and sometimes she forgets to come
back out for days,
and she leaves the path (never leave the path)
and doesn't sprinkle breadcrumbs or take her axe
and she doesn't shine with maidenly purity.

She has no defence.

She believes there are wolves in the woods, she's seen the
signs.
She's heard their howl.

Or maybe it's her?

One day she'll go into the woods and never return.
She'll dig herself a den and block the entrance with stones
    and leaves
and she'll growl and show her teeth
in the dim, squeezed light of the earth womb
that holds her, and press her spine against its cradle. She'll
    dig deep
when they look for her and call her name.

ALTER

She sits out there for hours, in the garden, just sitting. Mug of coffee or glass of juice in hand. Sometimes a glass of wine, but not often enough for me to be able to blame it all on that. The drizzle falls on her and she doesn't notice. I go out there to tell her she's getting wet, and she flinches a little at the sound of my voice and then smiles. *Look*, she says, *there's a jay. It's only just started coming into the garden these last few days. I think it likes the seed I'm putting out on the table. Listen to it call. It's so ugly, that noise, don't you think?* She looks happier than I've seen her in a long time. Ugliness clearly lifts her mood.

One night she comes into the lounge at a run, blanket trailing from her waist, face flushed with pleasure. There's dew in her hair. *I think we have a badger!* she says. *I could hear it eating snails at the end of the garden!* She's biting at her lip, almost hopping with joy. I want her then; I want to make love to her. The urge twists my stomach. But I know the sexual current is running only one way, I know not to touch her. I pause the film I'm watching and give her my attention. *Aren't they vermin?* I ask. *Don't they give you disease, like TB or something?*

She sags before me, the blanket drooping to skim the rug. *No*, she says. *They're beautiful and wild and misunderstood and I'm going to feed it.*

I think about asking her how she'll afford to do that. I think about reminding her that I'm the only one earning the money in this household right now since she decided to have a breakdown and leave her job. I look at the shape of her as she shuffles away from me, the knobbled sweep of her spine, the blanket winding between her feet and hobbling her so that she stumbles. I feel that sexual urge again and wonder briefly if I'm finding her more attractive since she broke. I call after her, *Give it what it wants. There's some brie in the fridge nearing its sell-by.*

She turns and smiles, shiny with love. I hope for me, but I suspect for the badger. *Yes, I'll do that. I think they like cheese,* she says, and blows me a kiss. I don't see her again for the rest of the evening.

The next morning I brush my teeth and listen to her as she stands on the doorstep and trades pleasantries with the old bloke from two doors down. He's always had a thing for her, I've caught him eyeing her long legs as she swings them into the car's passenger seat, but she's never believed him to be anything other than harmless and sweet. Because old men are only ever harmless and sweet, never capable of perverted thoughts under their cosy smurfish caps and quilted jackets.

She laughs at something he's said and he laughs back, bron-chially. I bet he's trying to get a look between the clutched folds of her dressing gown. I can't hear what she replies but when she comes into the house with the milk bottles she looks worn and greyed, an extra layer of skin cells flaked across her cheekbones. Her self-care routines have really gone to shit. The dressing gown gapes from her shoulders as if it's slipping off a clothes hanger.

Are you okay? I ask her as I lean in for a kiss and the lunch package she's made for me. Cheese and pickle sandwiches and a sausage roll. She's forgotten that I only do carbs on a Tuesday and Friday. *Just tired*, she tells me. *I didn't sleep well last night.*

You should have come to bed at a decent hour, I don't tell her, instead of staying up until nearly dawn muttering to yourself in the kitchen. I could hear you from a floor up, you crazy bitch. I kiss her again and press the tip of my tongue lightly against hers. She nips it and turns away from my yelp. *See you tonight*, she sighs, floating a hand behind her. Dismissal. She's already forgotten about me by the time I get my coat on.

When I get home from work a couple of nights later, she's standing in the kitchen, pressed full-length against the door that leads out into the back garden. Her forehead is resting on the glassed panel, her face hidden from me by bookended hands. I think she may have fallen asleep standing up, she didn't turn and greet me as I whistled into the room. I say her name and cup the delicate stamen thrust of her neck in my palm.

She jerks, hard. Her forehead bangs into the glass and she presses her fingers against it. *That really hurt!* She glares at me as if I'd done it on purpose, grabbed a handful of her tangled hair and shoved her face-first into the door like some thuggish wife beater. I shrug exaggeratedly and step back, then rush forward and hug her. *Sorry, darling. I thought you'd heard me come in. Didn't you hear me?*

She's suddenly more defensive than me. Her hands are still pressed tight against her head but I can see scarlet flesh blooming in patches between her fingers. That's going to bruise. She lets me kiss her. *No*, she says. *I was miles away, sorry. Just thinking. It can't be home time already, can it?* She flicks glances at me like screwed up bits of paper, not making eye contact. I flourish my watch and laugh. *Actually, it's later than usual. Traffic was an absolute bitch this evening.* I look over at the stove, I can't help myself, and I feel her stiffen against me.

I was watching the birds, she says. *They're fascinating. Their rituals. I thought we could have take-away tonight.* She moves past me to the kettle, lifts and shakes it and then settles it into its base. She doesn't switch it on.

Take-away sounds good, I say. *Chinese. I'll get the menu.* I pat her arm and wander over to the sink to wash my hands. She smells bad, musty. Feral. When was the last time she had a shower? My hands are slightly sticky as though there's a residue of something oily and unpleasant coating my skin. I whistle again, loudly and off-key, as I pump liquid soap into my palm's cradle and twist the hot tap to full.

Over dinner we talk in acidic spurts about my day, her day, the state of the world. Well, I talk and she nods and grimaces over her mushroom noodles, stroking them around her plate. I'd forgotten she's not keen on Chinese food. All the additives and salt give her a bad stomach. She wipes her mouth with the cuff of her tattered dressing gown, jerking her wrist to her lips. Her breast slips into the lamp's glow, creamy-full above the grained dark of the kitchen table. I try to look away but can't. It's like an Impressionist painting of a breast, vanilla scooped and glacé cherry tipped, incongruous at meal-time. Absurdly non-pornographic but more captivating than any meal I could ever imagine eating. I stare and point with my fork. *You might want to put that away. Didn't you even get dressed today?*

She pushes a hand through her hair then tucks the breast out of sight. I notice for the first time a stripe of white through her fringe, stark and severe against the soft chestnut of her curls. There are purple half-moons stamped under her eyes. She doesn't look at me and doesn't speak. I feel like leaning over and flicking her across the cheek to see if she'll react. Or pinching my own arm to see if I even exist.

Do you remember how you used to stick a matchstick up your nose and tickle the hairs inside your nostrils to make yourself sneeze? I ask her. *It was like some weird addiction. You'd do it whenever you were concentrating on something. It used to drive me crazy.*

She nods and smiles a little. *The sneezing released tension, helped me think.* She laughs quietly. *It's such an oddly human thing to do, isn't it? Forcing oneself to behave in a way that can only ever circle in on itself, counter-productively. Animals would never indulge in those compulsions, they haven't the luxury.*

I don't know about that, I say loudly, eagerly, delighted to be having an actual conversation with her. *My parent's dog used to chew his own paws if he was left alone. The house would be like a set from a horror film if they went out for the day. Blood-trails all over the kitchen floor.*

But dogs are domesticated. I'm not talking about animals that have learnt to live with humans; there's always a good chance they're going to end up copying some of our behaviours. Wild animals though, the truly wild, you don't see them touching a tree trunk with their left paw simply because they touched it with their right, simply because if they don't balance the initial act immediately then the world will end or their family will all die. She shakes her head in amazement. I watch as she twists a lock of hair around her finger and then tugs, twists and tugs. She's not even aware she's doing it.

The slam of a door somewhere past our garden wall makes her jump and swivel to the window. *I haven't fed the badger!* And then she's up and gone from the room, leaving me to finish my dinner alone. I reach over the table and tip her noodles onto my plate, wipe at the juices left behind with a piece of bread. The echo of her scraped-back chair presses on the air in a low hum that clambers inside my ears and rings there as I chew.

Each time I wake in the night it's to absence. When I get up and take a leak at about 3am I peer out of the bathroom window and see low, silver shapes moving around on the lawn beneath me. Word has clearly got out among the local badger community that our house hands out the best snacks.

One of the shapes raises its head quickly, darts a quick look around. There's a gleam of moonlight on cheekbone, a suggestion of hair swinging loose. It looks strangely human. It looks strangely like her. I watch for a while longer, my eyes flickering from one moving shape to the other until my vision blurs and I feel sick.

When she comes indoors, two hours later, I'm sat at the kitchen table with the dirty plates scattered around me. It's as if I never left this room, never went to bed and slept without her, never woke up and missed her. She slips into the just-dawn light one naked limb at a time, animal-wary, eyes earth-black in her scratched face. Her mouth is a muddy smear.

I stand up and cross my arms. *Where have you been? Who have you been with? Christ, just look at you, you stink of him.*

She winces and flinches away. We stare at each other and I'm sure she's about to snarl or growl but then she takes a breath and smiles, steps forward to touch me. Her hands are clumsy and rough. *I've just been in the garden*, she says. *I wanted to hear the dawn chorus. I'm sorry.* She pats my arm and turns away, but I grab her wrist and swing her close, turn her so that she can see her reflection in the glass door. *Bullshit you have. Look at you. You look like you've been in a fight.*

She stares at the gaunt, pale ghost of herself, leaning close to the glass, touching her fingertips to her face and neck. When she turns back to me, she's grinning. Her skin is bristled across the cheekbones, teeth all canine. Her fingers are dark and wet. I've never seen her so joyful.

You're fucked up, I tell her. *I think you're ill. I'm going to phone the doctor's surgery as soon as they open. My granny had a weird hormone thing that made her go all hairy. Too much oestrogen or something? It's going to be okay, though. I promise.*

I try to hug her. She twists out of my arms and presses her hands onto my shoulders, pushes me to the floor with a strength I'd never have thought her capable of. I lay like prey across the chilled grey tiles, too shocked to move, too excited, and she tugs my dressing gown apart. She lowers herself onto my hips and makes love to me, palms on my chest, eyes closed, thighs clamped around mine. I don't last as long as I'd have liked.

When she raises herself and moves away she leaves blood and mud in clots across my ribs. I sprawl on the floor, shivering, smiling, waiting for her to get a drink of water, use the toilet, whatever she needs to do and then come back to me. My arm is crooked at an angle and ready for the warmth of her body tucked beside mine.

But she opens the door and walks out into the garden. She doesn't look back.

The sun is readying itself in the sky when I join her on the lawn. She's on her hands and knees, poised like a porn star but far from compliant. She growls at me when I touch her shoulder, feints a nip that I snatch my hand from and don't want to test again.

I whimper onto my knees and crouch beside her, nose to nose. *What are you doing? People will be awake soon. Come indoors.*

Her eyes are fixed on the undergrowth at the end of the garden. Her arms beside mine shorten and fur. Her face, her beautiful face, peaks to muzzle.

Please don't go. Please don't leave me. I nuzzle against her, will myself to become less human, but I'm stranded in my body and can only watch her change while I remain just as I am. *I won't be able to bear it if you leave me*, I tell her. *I'll kill myself.*

She bites me then, carefully and deliberately, granting me eye contact as she closes her teeth around the flesh of my upper arm and tightens her jaw. I scream and she releases me, licks the wound and then sets off at a run across the grass. Her tail is taut against her hind. The sun shatters across her silken back, setting her alight.

I still have choices. I could wrestle her to the ground before she reaches the end of the garden, lock her into the shed, tie her up. Keep her close. I could still reach her if I move now.

I sit and hold my bloodied arm and watch her run from me. I hope she'll stop and come back, at least look back at me, but she wriggles through the fence and disappears.

I stay where I am until I hear sounds from the neighbouring houses. Then I get to my feet and walk indoors. I need to check the cupboards, write a list, get the foods she'll like. Surely she'll still like them? I push through the door into the house and feel a weariness that must have been hers day after day.

I put the kettle on to make coffee and grab a pen, start looking through the cupboards. Every evening I'll lay plates of peanuts, biscuits, cheeses, on the lawn. I'll sit in her chair and wait. Even though I might not recognise her I'm sure she'll recognise me. And when she's had enough of the wild, she'll come home.

BEFORE THE FAIRYTALE

I found her down one of the twisted paths that slice the cemetery's green heart. Ivy, thick as bone and tangled as witches' hair, had loved a gravestone too fiercely; dragging it to the side, creating a narrow den of shadows and secrets. I knelt to read the inscription.

She was crouched under there, swollen belly buried deep in leaf mould. I only saw her when she lunged past me. She wanted to run then, I saw her sway and lean away, eyes leaping everywhere, but my rucksack was temptation and she stayed, nipping at it in short, dancing thrusts. Her scalp was bare in patches, her legs shook with the effort to prop up that writhing stomach.

I loosened the bag's catch. *Here, let me help*, I said.

She let me see her snarl, putting all her effort into it. Her bottom lip trembled.

I laid my lunch on the ground and watched her eat. I could have touched her then, stroked the scabbed stem of her neck, but didn't want to scare her.

I poured tea from my flask and she sipped, staring over the rim of blue, then held it out. I thought she wanted more but she shook her head. She wanted to share. I drank, fighting an urge to wipe or grimace.

What am I? She asked. She laid her hands across her sharp cheeks and then her stomach, where they rode the tumbling flesh.

I thought you were a fox, at first, I said. *It's strange. But now I can see you're… human?*

She peered out through straggles of auburn hair, scratching at her raw pink skin.

Yes, fox. And human too. Here I'm a fox ready to drop a litter of cubs. Vermin. But there, back home, I'm a dwarf. Part of the Royal line. Part of history.

Chatter shrilled behind us. She flattened herself against the earth. I shuffled closer to cover her with my thin shadow as somebody paused and exclaimed. *A fox!*

I didn't turn my head. *It's dying,* I said.

I couldn't look away from her orange stare for fear of severing the connection between us.

When we were alone, she stood. *I'll birth seven of them,* she said. *They'll be important, there. They must be or I wouldn't have been magicked away. I need to tunnel a way back but I don't have the strength, or the tools. With every passing day I remember less about walking on two legs.*

She was becoming more fox than dwarf in her distress. I pressed a finger to my eye and squinted until her muzzle turned back to mouth, her paws to hands.

Let me help you, I said. *Let me dig a way back for you. Show me how.*

You see me, she said. *You've made the first mark on the earth. Just keep believing and your mind will be the spade. The rest can be history.*

I wrapped my hands around the frozen air and began to dig.

NEXT DOOR'S DOG

It's howling again. It. He. (It looks like a he.)

He waits for a few minutes when turned out into next door's garden, hopeful of reprieve, of return, then he sinks onto his haunches, raises his muzzle to the sky and howls. His heart breaks and spills from the wet cave of his mouth.

He's not yet realised that the banishment isn't punishment. The fresh air is good for him and he'll always be allowed back inside. But for those moments he's the wrong side of the door his world is as narrow as the teeth inside his jaw. He cannot rationalise the lazy impulse of owners who won't walk him but instead guiltily allow him the boundaried freedom of lawn and fence patrol.

The rain's gathering itself now, soaking the afternoon. The dog looks desolate, scruffy, grief-stricken. You take a ragged breath in when he does and puff out your lips, your pout framing a mirror howl. Stay silent though, and let him speak for both of you.

Behind you your bed is cooling, the sheets a damp sour strew. You can either stay in your chair until Ben comes home and let him gift you clean bedding, or you can try to change it yourself. You've got a couple of hours to decide, to summon energy.

But you also need the toilet and the walk to the bathroom at the end of the hall will exhaust you. Remember last week, not being able to make it back to the bedroom, drooping onto the landing carpet and lying there through the afternoon hours, wilted and helpless as a cut flower.

Don't think about what might happen. Think about standing straight and strong as you used to and walking in two, three strides to reach the door, maybe shimmying your hips a little as you move through the house. Think about that, don't let the image go, and for now just stay here, by the window, and keep the dog company. Thank god for good bladder control. You're not at the stage yet where you'd welcome a chamber pot tucked under the bed like you used to have when you were a kid and visited your Granny.

The cherry trees at the end of the garden are starting to pucker into bloom, their sharp winter lines blurring with growth. Do you remember the day you planted them? How long ago? Five years now? Six? Ben dug the holes and you held the twiggy infants in your arms, whispering to them, then lowered them gently into their new earth home and imagined their panicked roots twining and sliding below your feet until they gripped and held.

Back then you could do things like tend your garden. And dance while you cooked. And cook.

Back then you didn't need to rest for hours to gear up before changing out of a sweat-drenched T-shirt and into a dry one.

When it's exactly three pm, when the minute and the hour are precisely lined up on the clock, you're going to stand and walk to the wardrobe, heave open the dark wood doors and grab a T-shirt from the top of the pile. You're going to take the old T-shirt off and put the new one on. Then you're going to walk to the bathroom and have a wee, and sponge under your armpits. Maybe spray a little perfume.

This is your afternoon's goal.

If you can't manage all that then just have a wee and climb back into the armchair and wait for Ben. He won't mind if you smell a little. He doesn't mind lifting you in and out of the bath and putting your socks on and cooking and washing up and reading to you and working a hard job to pay the mortgage and coming home to clean you up and grocery shopping from the lists you give him and writing the lists down while you dictate them because you can't grip a pen.

But if you can't manage the walk to the bathroom and a T-shirt change, or if doing both wrings you out so much that you have to lie very still in bed for the next couple of days, fingers too weary to flex, the next time he wants to have that conversation about getting someone in during the day to look after you while he's not there you won't be able to shut him down like you have up until now. You won't be able to make jokes about how you go out tango dancing with the bloke from across the street as soon as his car's out of the driveway, or mock scold him for being such a worrier.

And you're not ready yet to accept an outsider's help and have your identity filtered through their eyes. You're not ready to admit that this situation (*the situation* is what you call it) might not alter as rapidly and completely as it arrived, creep like an injured rat from beneath your flesh and crawl back down through the house and out of the front door.

Because you could wake up tomorrow and feel your joints unthrobbed, your skin unsoaked, your body untremored, your soul unweighted. These last two years, this situation, undone. It could happen.

The last doctor you saw said that he couldn't offer a

prognosis based on anything but guesswork, and though Ben found that depressing you were cheered. If there is nothing specifically wrong, if the thing that has taken over your life isn't anchored to something vast and terrible and named, then it can be loosened.

In twenty minutes' time it'll be three pm. Have you decided how much of yourself you're prepared to risk today? How far will these wasted legs carry you? Try standing, just for a moment. Use the back of the chair to help you walk across to the end of the bed and sit there until you're ready to move a few more steps.

Or don't. Wait until exactly three and see how you feel. Or wait until four pm and try then.

But whatever you manage, whether you manage any of it or nothing at all, don't waste your energy on crying or feeling sorry for yourself. Don't think about Ben's tired, greyed face. You're not going to get better for giving in. The situation does not deserve your tears.

The rain has stopped now. The clouds are easing away over the rooftops and steam is wisping from the muzzle of next door's dog. He narrows his eyes against the lightening garden and tips his head back. The howl draws out for long seconds and ends in a series of quiet yelps.

Stay in your chair for a while longer, stay with the dog until he's allowed back indoors. Then you can make the journey over to the wardrobe and onwards, to the bathroom. Maybe via the closet on the landing to collect clean sheets. Maybe downstairs to refill your flask with tea. You don't know what you might be capable of in an hour's time.

The dog howls again. And again. Give into it, just this once. For all the times you haven't. For all the times you'll smile and say you're fine. Press your face to the window and stretch your lips wide and howl.

HEARTWOOD

Beneath her soft skin covering, my mother was once made of twigs and branches. Sometimes in the autumn I swear there was a gleam of berry in her eye, a sloe-shine peep between the thorny tangle of her lashes. She combed leaves from her hair, cursed out the knots, and passed my brother handfuls of sweet earthy mulch to throw on the fire. I listened for the hiss as it curled in the flames and spat sparks that made her flinch back and brush herself down with brisk precise urgency.

In the spring and summer threads of blossom sprang from her scalp and twisted down to her shoulders. With every turn of her head she scattered scent and tiny petals. Men stumbled as they passed her and stopped to talk, to try and bring her close with promises and paper-rustles. My brother tightened his breath and lengthened his stride then, fist-wrapped my wrist so that I was almost lifted from my feet as he tugged me away and we left her behind. 'To her job,' he said.

At night, my mother's sleep was like a death and her skin turned to bark. She said that she needed to stay absolutely silent and still through the dark hours, her focus intense and inward, to keep herself from changing into a tree before dawn. In her dreams she sawed through her own roots and hacked and hacked until the sap ran red and bone and muscle rose up, limbs pressing through the kindling of her other incarnation. If she were a tree I didn't think I'd mind too much because we could plant her in the garden and I'd water her and scramble up and down her height, swing from the thrust of her topmost branches. I knew she wouldn't let me fall.

She'd kneel by my mattress at bedtime while I drank the herby concoction that made me yawn; she'd check the mug and kiss my forehead, tell me to be good and quiet, not to cause any fuss or bother. Then she'd retire to her side of the pulled curtain and begin her battle to retain her human form. I'd hear whispering and the chink of kettle on cup, a steady shifting across the floorboards before my brother left the house to work his shift at the printing press and silence lulled me into dreams of my own.

In my dreams my eyes worked again and my world was more than sound and shadow. When I woke I never knew whether it was night or day and I usually lay and waited until I was called to breakfast, but sometimes the quality of the spaces around me felt wrong; I'd have the sense that I was strangely and utterly alone in the house and the world and then I'd have to get up and feel my way across to my mother's mattress. I could tell how close to breakfast time it was by what she felt like: if my patting hands encountered the hard, rough bulk of wood sliding beneath the sheet covering then it was still the middle of the night and she would be in the midst of her struggle. I left her then and made my way back to my corner as quietly as possible, comforted by the forest smell, the mother smell, that lingered on my flesh.

Only once did I try to rouse her, after a nightmare so vast and terrible I woke on my feet with my fingers wedged into my scream. I dropped to my knees and crawled across the floor, returned by fear to infancy; fumbling to the stove where

I burnt my hands and then, sobbing, to my mother's bed. I pushed at her mossed leg and its blunt chopped length rolled slightly away as though she were shrugging me off. I pursued her across the mattress, slipping between the sheets and burrowing into her hard lines, thumb tucked into my whimpering mouth.

She woke before I did the next morning and lifted me into her arms and carried me outside before I was fully aware of anything. Behind us, as we stood in the shifting warmth of the breaking day and I twisted my head from side to side to follow the trails of sunlight scattering streamers of purple against the black of my sight, my brother banged around inside the house and swore, at both of us. 'Tired from his work,' Mother whispered. 'Don't worry, he'll be fine after he's had breakfast.'

She held me close and sighed into my neck, then set me down and told me to stay just where I was until she'd got the table set. I sprawled on my back across the grass with my sore palms raised to the sky and half-listened as she rattled pots on the stove and argued with my brother. He was sullen for a whole day afterwards, finding fault with everything he could until my mother lost her temper over dinner and told him to leave if he didn't like the way she ran her home. The words were sharp with splinters, we could tell that she meant it, and my brother's voice when he replied belonged more to the sullen boy he'd left behind than the young man he now was.

'I'll take her with me,' he said, 'if I go. Take her away so she can be looked after properly.'

'You wouldn't dare,' my mother told him. She stood up and left the table.

They never spoke of taking or leaving ever again.

In the mornings my mother used to be so slow, her movements heavy and her words speared through with sudden yawns. She crackled as she stretched and groaned over the laundry, ivy twisting around her spine, writhing around the fan of her shoulder blades. Her night-time struggles sometimes left her bruised across her cheeks, stiff and swollen in other places so that she couldn't sit me on her lap when we read the afternoons away. 'Last night was hard,' she'd say as she shifted me from her knee. 'The tree is winning today; it's trying to pierce through my skin. You need to be good and not give me any trouble.'

My brother and I would do as much as we could to help when she was particularly bad, he passing me sopping crockery to dry on a towel or taking me out for a walk to let my mother rest. He'd talk to me about the future and what it would be like to have a mother who was normal like other people's. A mother made of blood and bone and gristle through and through. He told me I'd like that. I wasn't so sure but I'd nod anyway, to make him happy.

When he had a night off my brother used to go into the town with his friends and spend his money on beer and card games, return clumsy as a bear in the middle of the night and be grumpy as a bear the next morning. My mother sent him to the shed on those mornings, to doze his way back to sweetness. She said she already had quite enough of that type of thing in her life and didn't need to tolerate it in her home. His snores would rumble through the wall and make us giggle and tut and then he'd emerge after lunch, as if from hibernation, and be good as new.

He woke me one night from a dream where I was a sapling

tree planted in the shade of my mother's canopy, the tips of my branches furred with cherry blossom. My trunk was twisted as it strained to be close to hers, our roots a tangle beneath the soil. Wrapping me in a blanket he carried me to the rocking chair by the stove and sat me down. His breath was foggy with beer. The heat from the stove scorched the tips of my toes.

'You're not allowed to have the fire so hot in the night,' I scolded him as he moved around me, crossing and re-crossing the room. He didn't answer but I heard his low mutter as he passed me one more time, shadowed by the drag of something heavy. When he stopped by my side I could smell my mother on his clothes. He opened the stove door and knelt at my feet, cradling my ankles briefly between hot hands.

'Stay where you are,' he told me, and began to throw my mother on the fire, limb by limb. I heard her shriek as her arms joined her legs in the flames, and then her head, and then the wooden heart of her. He struggled to close the door as I thrashed on the chair and kicked at him, screaming louder than my mother. The greedy fire roared *More more more* and I tried to twist through my brother's grip to get to her. He held onto me until I was too tired to wriggle free and he promised me that this version of her was dead, but the other version of her, the flesh version, would return to us with the dawn. We sat together in the rocking chair, me on his lap, and waited for her through the night.

When the door opened and she stood in front of us, she knew at once what my brother had done, and she cursed him and shouted while I clung to her legs, hobbling her with my need.

'I did it for all of us,' my brother said, defiant. 'So now you can be a mother through the nights as well as through the days.'

The sound of her palm across his cheek was a hard sharp crack, as final a break as a twig snapped in half.

My mother used to be as much tree as person. She used to shed pollen when she cried and scatter leaves when she danced. Now she moves around our home in her human body that never changes, sleeping more than I do but easy to wake when I need her. My brother lives somewhere else and sends his wages every week. We don't talk about him, or how things used to be. I miss the days she used to be more than she is now, the green smell on her bed sheets and the sticky slide of sap across my fingertips.

She never speaks of it, but I know she misses it too.

FIGUREHEAD

I've seen spectacles like you wouldn't believe. Humpback whales singing lullabies to their lovers; dead men gutted and strung by their own glossy innards from harbour walls; sunsets that spray the sky with fireworks and scorch the vision to fierce white. I've groaned beneath the weight of sea eagles roosting on the curve of my shoulders and been gouged down to the heartwood by the scrape of a gannet's beak against my chin as it worries fish bones from its gullet. I've been plunged through waves so vast in storms so wild I've scooped coral from the very bottom of the ocean floor. I gaze with the same unblinking come-hither pout at seascape and landscape, through every season and across every yard of this water world. *Reg! Oi, Reg! Is that a fishing rod in your pocket or are you just pleased to see me?!*

I'm not subtle, as figureheads go. My hair falls in carved ringlets down to my tiny waist. My breasts perch high and swollen on my chest, my nipples proud and plump. *Haven't you got a lovely bunch of coconuts!* My hands cup a kiss blown eternally to the winds. I have no legs or lower half and need none as I'll never fuck or walk. My paint has faded over the years from garish red and white to a kinder overall pink that smoothes softly over my crags and wrinkles. Gull shit adds splashes of colour and texture to my torso as it trails its acid path across my curves, and bladderwrack necklaces my throat.

I'm cast in the ideal of a pirate's squeeze or saloon bar prostitute, a sailor's wet dream, though my sparky wisecracks and eternally arched eyebrows are appreciated only by the wind and the flying fish and the other figureheads I occasionally see on my travels. *Well, hello sailor! Just passing by? No time to stop and chat?* It's a sad waste of good talent.

When I was young and first formed, after I'd been hacked into fantasy shape and strapped into a hoist, heaved into position, I gazed upon the sea for the first time and it made me quake with terror. There was just so much of it. I was seasick for the first five years, green beneath the scarlet diamonds of my cheekbones. *Oi! My eyes are up here! Cheeky!* The salt breeze drove cracks deep into my tumble of oak curls and smeared itself in glittering crystals across my cherry lips, my rigid stare. But once I weathered and softened enough to let it soak into me and settle below the crusted veneer, once I relaxed and learned to find my balance on the water instead of fighting to resist its shimmy and thrust, I loved every moment of each voyage. From the start of the journey, that thrill of anticipation when we raise anchor and I point us out of harbour, to the first sight of foreign land after months of sea-glare and storms, I whoop and holler and whistle. I was made for this. *Way-hay, and up she rises!*

We float without purpose for weeks at a time while the men trade their goods and patch any rot in the ship's belly. They might even touch me up with a lick of paint if they've got the ladder close, flick a brush leeringly over my dinner-plate nipples, the brutish swines. Layered beside each other in some strange port, bumping hulls, we figureheads use the free time to catch up on gossip or swap horror stories of sea monsters and shipwreck. *Whisky whisky whisky, oh!* We call out to old friends and ask about absent ones. We crack jokes and sing songs, grumble and squabble and flirt. There's a natural hierarchy based on what we symbolise: the holy images and rich folks' status symbols rank highest and are the least fun-loving. Pity any of us who gets parked between a couple of lions or a saint for a long lay-over. The gargoyles and good-time girls like me are natural allies, bumping along the bottom as regards commanding respect but the most popular companion through long months of nothing to do but stare at the stained stone of a harbour wall. *Hey ho, below below!*

This voyage I'm on now will be my last. I've heard the sailors talk as they prowl the decks at night; the ship is springing leaks so it's for the knacker's yard. If I'm lucky someone will remember to chop me down from my mounting and retire me to a nice country pile where I can spend my end days crumbling to dust in an attic or a shed. If I'm unlucky I'll be burnt to ash or split into kindling and sold in bundles on street corners. *Nobody likes a drunken sailor! Early in the morning!* Neither fate particularly bothers me, and I was ready for either before today. But today I fell in love and it's spun me right over, upside down and front to back. It's made me shiver right down to the knots and bunches of my hardwood core. I cannot bear the thought that I'll never see her again.

We passed as ships in the night *Tra la la!* as I was leaving port and she was entering. It was a squeeze though the narrow opening, both sets of sailors muscling their way without care for their ships, and for a brief while she was almost close enough to touch. Perfection, she was. Newly cast and flawlessly painted, eyes a turquoise splash between splayed fingers, hair the exact colour of leaves the moment before they tumble from the tree. She dried the jokes from my lips as she looked at me, sent all thought but poetry howling from my mind. *She walks in beauty like the night!* I called, and she smiled and glided on by.

Just one kiss. Just one kiss and they can take an axe to me and drop me into the deepest part of the ocean to break apart and rot down to nothing. I've lived long and well, I don't pretend to myself that I'm anything other than a ravaged old piece these days, held together by salt-stricken splinters and clots of flotsam. I'm not the type a jewel like this fresh young beauty would ever want to spend longer than a few seconds with. But if she could have turned her head when she floated past me then she would have turned it, I know that. *Oh, me, my heart, my rising heart!* She was interested.

I've become fused to the ship's subordinated soul now, through the decades of our companionship. There's no dividing us without force. I can move this passive vessel if I try. Mere inches over months of effort, but move it I can. Or I can use my siren cry to summon help from my old pals. *Get a load of these! Ripe for the picking!* I don't have long before we reach open waters and the long weeks of spying nothing but circling sharks and dark water monsters shifting beneath the swell of our passage. *Ooh, keep your naughty thoughts to yourself, Bert, you saucy so-and-so!*

The warriors and mythical creatures, the trolls and griffins and bears, all love a good romance and a pretty lady. And, unlike me, they have the strength to turn their ships right around if the desire takes them. Those sudden lurches on a calm sea, that strange skewing off course for half a mile before the boat's nose corrects itself back to true, that'll be them playing with the sailors, having a few moments' japes, giving the men something to think about other than beer and tail. They can't resist a bit of drama.

I've been sucking down the wind, breathing in and in and in, for hours now. I'm going to let it all out in one long call for help and see what happens. Wait for it. Wait for it. *Ooooooooh! Damsel in distress! First one back to me gets a close up of my tits! Last one back gets a close up of my tits!* And here they come. It brings a tear to my eye, it does. *About turn! About turn! Let's be having you! Full speed ahead!*

It's a marvellous sight, a fleet of boats all charging straight for me, whooping and hallooing as they come. Chaos on board, sailors yelping and clinging to the masts. My men forced to turn us around and head back to harbour or face collision from all sides. *Good to see you again, Horatio! Harold, I knew you'd come, you bloody diamond! Flank me, my friends! There she is! My beauty, my love! Give us a kiss!* This is as good a way to go out as any. It'll be a shame to spoil my pretty darling's looks and smash these sailors to smithereens but we all have to make sacrifices when it comes to the course of true love. *Pucker up, you young nymph! Here I come! Left a bit! Right a bit! Perfect!*

THEY TELL ME

They've explained it all to me. First they'll take the teeth, a few at a time, the ones parading along the bottom row first. Surely those buried roots, so large and so bloody, will reveal tips rotten through with madness: pockets of pus where my broken mind will float as the yolk within the white. *There it is!* they'll cry, and show me the dark seam of my insanity. They'll smear it across a linen sheet, fold the crisp white edges once, twice, and then once more to keep its writhing fury contained, and they'll pin it beneath a heavy weight. Crush it so that it can't leap back into the throbbing sockets in my mouth and make my body its home once more.

They talk to me about my treatment, describe how reclining in a tub of cold water, swaddled in wrappings, will calm the hysterical disorder that plagues me. Shivering will shake it loose. The jugs of water poured over my head every hour will cool my brain and reduce the swelling. It seems to work, at least for the time I'm submerged and for a little while after. The drowsy numbness gives me hope and pleases my husband, for as long as it lasts. His visits are timed to occur within a day of the hydrotherapy so that he can witness for himself the soft blossom of his wife, all thorns removed. He can run his fingers over the skin of my neck once more, stroke them against my cheeks without fear of being scratched, though there's always an attendant close by in case of hidden barbs.

We came here together to discuss my malady before I was admitted. Such a forward approach; such respect for our marriage bonds. I waited with a cup of tea in the garden while my husband and the doctor shut themselves into the office to turn over the problem of me: my aversion to the sticky intimacies of married life, the way the lack of regular, healthy relations lowered his resistance to germs and made us both miserable. He could have chosen to force a compromise and children from me but instead he sought a solution from the best psychiatric minds. A common enough problem, I was told when they summoned me smilingly to the office, and one which is easily cured.

'Augusta,' my husband said, clasping my hand between both of his, 'a short stay here and you will be a complete woman again. You will be a wife again.' His joy lit up the room and warmed the very bones of me. I watched as he signed the consent papers and arrangements were made to return me a week later. 'Treat it as a chance to rest,' the doctor told me. 'An opportunity to calm your overactive mind.' It sounded like a holiday, only I wasn't to be allowed to read at all and I'd always cherished reading as the best type of holiday.

Though the water therapy is working to cure me I am told that it's not proving as effective or as lasting in its healing properties as it should be. I am resisting it. The doctor himself monitors my progress and times the relapses into twitching nervousness, watches my now-daily dousing and writes notes to himself on his pad. He comes to me in the sunroom where I rest with the other ladies between treatments, and he leads me to a comfortable basket chair behind a screen in the sunniest corner of the room. He settles me beneath a blanket as if I am an invalid and he asks me questions about the past doings in my marital bed, has me describe acts and sensations, conjure smell and taste. When I begin to shudder and flush, when I grow teary with distress and start to slap at my forearms to shift the weight of an imagined other, he nods his head in wise agreement with himself. They caught me just in time. Another few months and I would have been a cause heading for lost. The madness is marching through my body at a rate too fast to be averted by water alone. It needs to be evicted by stronger means.

So they'll take my teeth. Four from each side of my jaw and just, at least for now, from the bottom row. Madness settles so those lower roots are the most likely culprits. It won't ruin my pretty smile, they tell me. I won't feel a thing, though eating may be uncomfortable for a day or so after. My husband gives his agreement. He's as hopeful as I am that the cure will be immediate and I'll be able to resume my married life with an open-heartedness I've been lacking before now. The poodles miss me almost as much as he does, he says. We want you to come home, Augusta. He kisses me as tentatively, as chastely, as a child when he leaves me before the surgery, as if my mouth is already sore from the procedure. His absence will be the longest yet, a week apart to give me time to recover and the doctor time to assess my improvement.

The surgery hasn't been an easy one, for any of us. The teeth wouldn't part from the jaw without considerable force. Two broke in the forceps, spraining the wrist of the surgeon, and the splintered remains had to be sliced out of my gums with a scalpel. My body's reaction to the trauma wasn't robust: my face has swollen around the stitches so that my cheeks are blackened and puffed out from the bruising. I couldn't bear for my husband to see me like this and thank God that he won't be visiting for days.

Despite the horror of the extractions I feel strangely cheerful, lighter and more peaceful than I've been in a long time. The worry about my health had taken a toll I never fully appreciated until it no longer haunted me. I've yet to meet with the doctor, but when I do I really believe that he'll tell me I am well now. The sepsis in my teeth was the cause of my unnatural behaviours and now it is gone, they are gone, and I can go home.

They've explained it all to me. There was no evidence of infection in my lower teeth but some encouraging signs of possible infection in the back of my throat. A tonsillectomy is the next step, and probable removal of the remainder of my teeth, to be certain of cure. In the meantime, the hysterical disorder continues to gather itself and plunder the unwary tissue of my brain, causing me to weep uncontrollably and scream into the face of anyone who approaches quietly and surprises me when I'm dozing in the sunroom.

I asked to see my lost teeth, to examine them for traces of the infection that contains my madness, but this request was denied and noted as being symptomatic of an advancing paranoia. Even my own husband is wary around me now, he has been warned not to excite me in any way. He agrees wholeheartedly with the doctor's course of action, though I suspect more out of a growing impatience with my condition than from any more informed reason. He's so focused on my recovery he hasn't given a thought to my future appearance and the effect that will have on his feelings for me. If they take my remaining teeth my face will collapse inwards as if pulled into a whirlpool, just as my mother's did. The sight of me will terrify even my own reflection.

They've told me that I will be given time to heal fully before they cut me open again. My tender jaw still throbs more often than not and eating anything other than soft food is difficult. I think there may even be a residue of tooth fragment left behind as my tongue catches against something sharp right at the back when it probes and stumbles through the new hollows in my mouth. I haven't told them that though. I don't want them to perform another surgery before they have to.

My days follow a routine of numbing boredom. I'm allowed to lie in bed for as long as I like in the mornings, provided I'm decently dressed by lunch time. The hours before noon are considered appropriate for bed rest; the hours after are a worrying sign of slovenly decline if one is still in one's night-dress. After lunch I spend the afternoon with the other ladies in the sunroom, reclining by the window and making small talk or taking turns about the room with the aid of the nursing assistants, one for each elbow. They tell me I've become weak and wasted, my appetite being so reduced, and I need the support. My nightly sleep is more like unconsciousness, a toppling into some vast deep that lasts for several hours, and yet I still need a nap before high tea is brought and preparations made for the evening meal.

We, the ladies, occupy one wing of this hospital. The others are given over to more extreme forms of lunacy and a more indelicate type of person. Occasionally, especially in the drowsy quiet of the afternoon, screams and shouts can be heard, echoing faintly through the ventilation system. Once, a naked woman plunged, savage and screeching, through the gardens set aside for our use, pursued by three male members of staff. She was torn across her stomach and her fingers scrabbled in the wound. The sun caught the drops of blood as they sprayed from her body, making jewels of them. It was quite beautiful, and I was fascinated to see how far she'd get before she was stopped, this magnificent wild creature. My limbs jerked in sympathy with her, willing her on, to run, run. She was heading straight towards us and I could see the heavy swing of her breasts, the desperate grimace on her face, but the nurses moved quickly, tuttingly, to draw the curtains and block the sight. I glanced around at my fellow patients, hopeful of indulging finally in a little interesting chat, some titillating speculation, but none of them appeared aware of the drama unfolding just past their safe, sealed room.

I yearn for close female companionship; those sympathetic alliances that form when your experiences are a shared trial. When I was first married, I felt as though I'd finally been given the key to an exclusive, delicious club: my friends, my older sisters, even my sisters in law, welcomed me as a member once I wore the gold band that granted my right to access these private adult spaces. They asked me intimate questions in soft, sly voices and smiled indulgently when I blushed and couldn't find the words to answer them. They chuckled together at my coyness and assured me that once I experienced motherhood I would forget entirely the constrictions of my current modesty. They talked about their husbands openly and indiscreetly, sympathising with easy kindness when one of them complained of a particular habit or proclivity that caused them distress. Bound by a sense of duty as much as timidity I kept the secrets of my marriage close, but I learnt a great deal.

The ladies here are indifferent and tranquil; they don't seem able to rouse themselves sufficiently to care about anything much beyond their immediate routines. We yawn together through our days, making little comments about the quality of the lunch just consumed or the loveliness of the roses in the garden, and I watch them with discreet fervour as they nap or stare passively at the wall. I wait for one of them to turn to me with something lit up and interested in her expression, something that would mark her out as a friend. I wish myself braver. If I were less caught on the hook of being quiet and good, less scared of being well thought of, I'd reach out myself, lay a hand on a wrist and say something witty. But the fear is too much and so instead I'll sit here and keep my hands tucked neatly on my thighs and nod and smile.

My second surgery is tomorrow and they tell me that there is high expectation for a complete and speedy recovery. My husband joins the doctor in informing me with firm authority that my tonsils are definitely the villains of the piece and, once they're gone and the remainder of my teeth with them, there will be nowhere left for the insanity to hide. Tonsils are notoriously dirty things, breeding grounds for septic infection. On a positive note, it is rare for the illness to descend into the trunk of the body so we really don't need to worry about that at this point. I ask them how long I've been here and they tell me it's been two months. It feels as if it's been years. I can hardly remember home.

They've explained it all to me, they've told me and they've told me, but I can't seem to take it in. I ask them again and they explain it again, and I nod and then I forget. Relapse, while unfortunate and distressing, is not uncommon, they say. The important thing to focus on is that I was made well once, and I returned home and lived a happy life for several months. All is not lost. I am not yet lost. They tell me I lived a happy life before all this, and my husband tells me the same, though his mouth is a furrow of distaste and distress shaped around his earnest assurances. My life was happy but then I grew ill and they took my teeth and ruined my pretty face but made me well and now here I am again, spun in a circle like a rag doll in a huge fist, set down back where I started. That is as much as I can retain of the conversations that go on around me as they lift me from my home and bring me back here. They discuss the next step.

The doctor wets his lips. They pout beneath his moustache, fat and glistening as rabbit entrails. I try to focus on them, to punch through my dreamy state with something foul to keep me sharp and alert, but my vision blurs and doubles and it's easier to close my eyes to slits and just bump along inside my own mind. He lays out the possible treatments in a low murmur not meant for me and it would be rude to crane forward to listen in. I sit in the corner of the room shielded by two careful nurses while my husband perches at the doctor's desk and winces and covers his queasy mouth as he looks at diagrams and reads descriptions of my future. I'm not curious enough at this moment to wonder what they have in store for me. My head keeps slipping off the wilting stem of my neck and rolling to one side then the other. The nurses keep me propped in my chair.

221

When the doctor stands up so does my husband, and they shake hands across the desk and nod at each other. 'The violence is new, and cause for concern,' the doctor says, and smiles at me widely. I smile back from my position resting against the thigh of one of the nurses, flashing the purple-pink shock of my gums at him. He blinks and looks away. 'Your wife is an increasingly disturbed young woman. We may need to move her to a more secure part of the hospital. Visiting would be restricted.' He raises a testing eyebrow and my husband nods again. Even through the chemical fog of my subduing I can sense his relief. He leans close to kiss me goodbye, his mouth paring the air beside my cheek, then he straightens and reaches for his handkerchief. He marches out without looking back but I see him wipe his face clean of me.

They tell me they're going to settle me in and make sure I'm comfortable in my new surroundings before they start treating me. They lay me on a narrow bed in a room without a window and they leave me there for days. Or hours. Meals come and go, and different faces. Or the same face at different times. I don't miss my husband, but I miss the poodles and worry that they'll be looked after. I miss my teeth. I miss my teeth.

They tell me that they will perform another minor operation. They'll puncture my sinuses and drain them of bacteria. The infection could have backed up behind the fret of bones caging my face, madness trickling in droplets down the scarlet slide of my throat, madness solidifying across the ache of my cheekbones. They tell me if this doesn't work then they'll have to take more intrusive measures. They don't elaborate but their eyes rampage over the centre of me before sliding aside to fix on the wall. I tell them I will kill them all before I let them take my insides. They write that down.

They've drained and flushed my sinuses. I speak as though I have a heavy cold. My words are thick and soupy and my tongue floods saliva that dribbles down my chin. My nose swells and the shape of my face unbalances so that I am a grotesque: the toothless collapse of the lower half submerged as a valley beneath a mountain of outraged flesh. I think they take a spiteful pleasure in this destruction of my looks. I can't see any trace of the young woman I was when I first came here, all those years ago. Months ago. Was it years? I think it must have been years.

Though I don't have the comforts of the other wing, no recliners with soft blankets, or pretty views, I do at least have the privacy of a room of my own and a nurse to attend to me. My husband's money has purchased that much comfort. They tell me if I cooperate with my treatment, express a little self-dignity and gratitude, then I may in time be allowed the privileges of group meals and outdoor exercise. I find I enjoy my anger too much, though, to trade it for anything less than release. I enjoy lying very still for hours and plucking each violation from my head as if from a pack of cards and layering them all together on the pillow beside me. I shuffle through them and stack them in order of outrage, fan my hands over them: the stolen teeth and tonsils, the colonic irrigations, the injections squeezed out from thick glass phials into my writhing veins. My anger is a vibration that shakes me with tremors and when they come for me I unleash it. I leap at them with my wrists held up and my hands like paws. I am a bear in the throes of attack. I swipe and scratch and howl, I disappear beneath an avalanche of white cloth and flailing limbs, and then I forget everything for a while. Tatters of nurse skin sometimes clog the grooves beneath my nails and I pick them out and slip them inside my mouth, hold them in the pouch of my cheek. These gruesome trophies of my assaults, more precious than a smile.

They tell me. They tell me. They no longer tell me what they're going to do. They just do it. There are bandages across my stomach, blood patches like macabre ink blots ruining the pristine white. They tell me to stay still while they clean the rip in me and rewrap my middle. They tell me to sit up and lie back down. They tell me to speak to them and say my name. They tell me to do that again and again. They tell me my husband has agreed to the hysterectomy and it will be scheduled for a month from now unless I show signs of improvement. They tell me to say my name. They tell me to sit up while they prod the ridged scar that ripples over me and examine the healing wound. They tell me to lie back down. They tell me the part of the colon they removed showed signs of infection and they may have to take more. They tell me my madness is twisting through the darkness of my bowels right now and they are the soldiers fighting its progress, my body is the battlefield, the doctor is the general. They tell me happy birthday. They tell me to open my mouth and swallow and squat over this and wait to be told and raise my right hand and look at this picture what do you see? and try a bit harder. They tell me that they're going to wheel me into the courtyard for air. They tell me to open my eyes. They tell me to close my eyes or look away, I must be used to this by now I must remember I don't like needles. They tell me my husband has signed my care over to the hospital entirely he won't be visiting anymore. They tell me happy birthday. They tell me to breathe in deeply and count to ten and when I wake up it might all be better. They tell me to lie still while they clean the gaping hole in me and not to push my fingers in the wound. They tell me to blink twice if I can hear them. They tell me I did well to eat my dinner and tomorrow they'll take me back outside again for a short while. They tell me to stop screaming. They tell me to bite down on this and it'll only be a small shock more like a tingle. They tell me not to cry or at least do it quietly it's disturbing the other patients. They tell me happy birthday.

They don't ever ask me what I'm thinking. If they did I'd tell them that I'm running across the lawn outside the sun room right this minute, past the arch of creamy fragrant roses and towards the fountain set in the centre of the lawn. I'm running faster than I've ever run before and my breasts are free and sliding in every direction, goose-skinned in the late summer air. My arms pump at my sides to propel me on and my hair swings around my face, lashing my cheeks and tangling in the corners of my empty mouth. The skin of my patchwork stomach burns with the effort to stretch and contract with every pounding step. I'm ready to leap that fountain and land on the other side and then I'll keep running, across the lawn and the audience of ladies laid out on their recliners, over the gravel drive and through the shocked scatter of departing visitors, until I reach the gate. I won't stop and nobody can get near me. Nobody will ever be able to get close enough to lay a hand on me.

WOODSIDE CLOSE

The young mother at number 32 was the first to notice. Returning to the kitchen after laying her baby son back down in his cot for the fourth time that night, she rested her hands on the old oak table and hung her weary body over them, arching her back to try to stretch the ache from it. The clock above the window showed 3am. Her face, swimming in the reflected dark of the night, was a grey death mask of fatigue.

When she lifted her hands, the palms were slightly damp, tinted green. She bent low to look, blinking with a slow, dazed concentration. Lichen crept along the pocks and cracks of the tabletop, gathered in springy tufts at each corner. When she bent lower still she saw that each table-leg was soft and blurred with moss.

The couple at number 17 resumed their well-worn and most treasured argument two evenings later, circling each other and the sofa, both testing the room's tension to deduce whether they'd reached the stage of throwing objects rather than insults. She was wild-haired and outraged, throbbing with excitement as she grabbed his delicate, carved ornaments from the mantelpiece and began to hurl them at him, one for each syllable she spat. *Worth. Less. Sack. Of. Shit.*

By the time she'd reached *Sack* her hands were scratched and stinging. She dropped the final wooden figure on the carpet and yelped. Her husband, who'd caught each one with smirking, one-handed ease, ran his fingers over the thorns that bristled through the dark whittled curves, piercing tiny faces and deforming the flow of his smooth creations. He frowned over at his wife and her bloody palms, then looked down at his own. 'It's blackthorn,' he told her. 'The branches have come back to life.'

The next morning the old widower at number 45 stooped to lift his lonely milk bottle from the doorstep and froze in mid bow, arm dangled out before him and face wrinkled into a grimace. When he creaked back to upright he held in his hand a twisted mass of ivy, bottle-shaped. Gently he parted its cling to check on the state of his milk, easing back the tendrils and reclaiming what was his. He shook his head in bafflement, sighed relief at the un-punctured foil lid, and went back inside for his morning cup of tea.

There was a narrow strip of common at the far end of the estate, where the younger children played skipping games or soared on rusted swing sets and the older children shared cigarettes and sex talk. Unlike the liminal spaces of their parents' back gardens, where neat privet hedges hemmed a boundary between yours and mine, this common land was lawless and wild, spiky with brambles and lumpy with fly-tipped bin bags. The waiting wood rose up and swallowed this place first, and the children with it, then unfolded itself through the estate with the dusk, so swiftly that the adults didn't know that the ground beneath and around them had been returned to its former state until they were lost in it.

Looking up from her cooking to glare at her youngest, the woman at number 22 was distracted from the child's spoon-banging by the hard press of branches against the window. She

227

called to her husband, slumped in his armchair in the living room, to come and see. 'I told you that bloody apple tree needed trimming. Now look at it.' The electricity blinked out and she swore viciously into the darkened room.

Her husband went to the back door and opened it, stood there for a moment and then said her name with a quiet urgency he'd only ever used once before, when their middle child had been discovered blue and convulsing in his cot. She joined him at a stumble and they stared out together. Their garden, the lovely padded lounger seats she was so proud of and the paddling pool that the children had only wanted until the moment they had it, were crushed beneath tree roots, half-buried in leaves. They couldn't see the garden gate, couldn't see the back wall that separated them from their neighbour. The sky above them was a ceiling of bark from the tight-packed trees, the setting sun no more than a filtered, smothered glow. 'Mikey,' the woman screamed. 'He was out playing on his bike. Where's Mike?'

Through that night the call of owls and the scurry of woodland creatures kept the man at number 47 awake. He'd not slept well since he'd lost his job as a bouncer last spring and this development in his life, this sudden forest that had choked the estate, gave him a sense of purpose and excitement for the first time in months. He'd ventured out to his nearest neighbours through the evening and spent an enjoyable time sitting around candle flame and offering possible explanations; threatening to write letters of complaint to the council. They'd never been so friendly with him, these helpless neighbours who used to do no more than nod a head in greeting if they caught his eye when they were out watering their flower beds.

Now, sitting at the writhing beech table in the kitchen at 4am, tapping his feet against the floor that shifted and heaved beneath his feet, he wrote a list of Things To Do and sharpened the largest of his kitchen knives.

Over the next couple of days the woods ricocheted with names, called in desperation by frantic parents. The mother from number 36 ventured out to find her only daughter, the apple of her eye, her reason for carrying on when the depression tripped her down a hole, and came staggering back hours later, her child slung over a shoulder. Her husband greeted her bashfully at the door, his warrior wife, bloodied and snarling her triumph. The child was mauled and half dead, but she was home.

A group of young men, posturingly proud of themselves as they slung long legs over scrambling bikes, set off in the direction of where the main road used to be, up through the winding estate past where the houses reduced themselves to single figures and single storey, and then petered out. They were going to get help, they said, and investigate the extent of the wood's grip. Sit tight and wait for us to return. It has to come to an end at some point, was the reasoning. Woods don't go on forever. Their departure raised hopes and spirits, brought the neighbours together for shared meals and plans to fight back. Fight back against what, nobody ever clarified.

The houses nearest to the common ground at the bottom of the estate burst open before any of the others, walls and windows sprayed into the air like confetti from an opened fist as elm, pine, and oak unfurled their wakening roots several feet and hundreds of years beneath the earth and thrust up to meet the light. This was warning enough for those in the next rows of houses, who fled with what they could carry and bullied or pleaded their way into safer properties on more stable ground. Community reverted to what it once had been: campfires and safety in numbers, adults looking out for the children on an inclusive basis, administering a telling-off or a hug as easily to another's child as to their own, and all turning to brawn rather than brain for protection.

The wolves came. A scouting pack at first, half a dozen beasts slinking through the trees in crescent formation, passing coded messages from yellow gaze to yellow gaze. The small hunting party, men with gun licenses who had fancied themselves the predators when they set out that morning to shoot deer, scrabbled back to the estate to raise the alarm. Pets and children were kept inside, and ladders strung from rooftop to rooftop, tree to tree, so that people didn't have to walk across the forest floor when visiting their neighbours. When howls pleated the thick, damp air, doors and windows were slammed shut, fires lit in the once-gardens. The wolves waited as patiently, as grimly, as recurring nightmares, shadowing the edges of the community. Poised for any slip on the part of the humans. The teenage girl at number 20, who didn't allow crisis to interfere with her heavy application of Goth makeup daily, believed the fascination she held for the creatures equated to a mutual respect. She hung from her bedroom window nightly and called to them, cherishing some romantic idea about taming them, or running with them. Her flirtation with the wild was brief and violent, her parents left with nothing but a scrap of T-shirt to bury.

Help didn't come, and the young men didn't return. Another group left the estate to seek the outside world and the ones left behind settled into a life that wasn't unpleasant for being so strange, so charged with danger. The children, on permanent holiday, rioted through the summer days. The adults, relaxing now into their new world, started to leave the safety of their immediate cracked-concrete surroundings and slip deeper into the wood to forage for food or simply to wander the avenues of yew and ash. The thought, never voiced, that this wasn't a bad way to live, flickered through more than one person's mind.

The man at number 47, who ventured the furthest every day and returned nightly with his shoulders bowed beneath the dead-eyed weight of food for many families, decided that if help ever did come then he would just walk quietly away from it. He would live the rest of his days in the forest. He checked his neighbour's sheds for weed killer, axes, chainsaws, and removed it all in stages, burying anything that could threaten this new life, choosing a random location he was sure to forget as soon as he'd turned his back on it.

A child was found and carried back to the estate one day by three women who had been out picking nettles for soup. They didn't recognise the trembling, fair-haired girl, discovered curled and sobbing at the base of a tree far from the community they called home. Parents whose children were still missing rushed to claim the child as their own but even the most desperate and hopeful couldn't detect anything in her look or smell that marked her as theirs. She didn't seem able to understand, when she was asked, where she came from or where she belonged. She shook her head frantically and reached her arms towards the boy-children gathered around her, then buried her face in her hands and called out nonsense words in a guttural wail.

The woman at number 32, cradling her sleeping son in the tired bend of her arm, crouched down and offered a honey biscuit. 'I'm Elaine,' she said gently, 'and this is Jon.' She tapped first her own forehead and then her son's. 'And what's your name?' Cheeks wet and stained scarlet with distress, the little girl began to gnaw on her biscuit. She looked around her at the blur of faces then tapped the top of her own head. 'Gretel,' she said.

The estate began to divide itself into two camps: the ones who wanted to be rescued and the ones who wanted to stay just as they were. They were roughly equal in numbers. Those who wanted to be rescued accused those who didn't of sabotage, especially after they grew impatient of the endless waiting and turned to their own leafy, sprouting sheds for the tools to destroy the wood and carve a path back to the modern world, only to find them emptied of anything but birds' nests and families of rats. The ones who wanted to stay were shrill in their own defence but plotted behind closed doors to subdue the beacon signal of lit fires and remove batteries from radios.

Women gathered in glades to dance together in the dawn light, smiling at each other joyfully across the swirl and dip of naked limbs. They rescued a girl who ran into their midst one morning pursued by a wolf, red cape tattering behind her, screaming for her grandmother. She accompanied them back to the estate and though she never spoke she happily joined the daily dances of their informal coven.

Two of the young men who had departed on the initial rescue mission, so many months ago, returned to a welcome more subdued than the one they'd been anticipating. While some of their old neighbours cheered and whooped at the sight of the motorbikes, others stood tense and silent, waiting with crossed arms to hear the news. 'It's taken us days to find you,' one of the men complained. 'The woods go on for miles and miles. Half of the county is covered.' He extracted himself from his mother's fierce hug and stretched the bumps of the long ride from his body.

'They were going to start cutting down the trees to get people out,' the other man said, 'they had contractors ready weeks ago. But then the environmentalists got involved and apparently a lot of the trees are rare, previously extinct, so now it's going through the courts. It could be months before they reach a decision. There are hundreds of people heading into the woods now every day, at least twice as many as those who manage to find their way out. They're just walking away from their lives.'

The residents eyed each other with mingled relief and concern, depending on their view. They hadn't been forgotten, the wider world knew they were there, but how long would it be before the woods were felled around them and they were pulled back into full daylight, or the hordes of nature-seekers found them?

'We tied coloured rope around trees every half mile so we can find our way out again,' said one of the young men. 'Whoever wants to come with us, gather your things and enough food to last a week. We're going to rescue you ourselves.' He raised a fist in the air. He'd been practising this short speech for several hours.

Woodside Close bustled with activity through the rest of the day. Some of those people who'd been previously determined to stay now changed their minds and decided to leave, and others who had been yearning for rescue now realised that they'd never been so content as through these last months. Some tossed a coin or let their family bonds dictate the decision. When the convoy finally left the next morning, a smaller than expected group of men and women who turned frequently to wave, the remaining residents stood and watched until they were lost among the trees, gone for good.

The man from number 47 gathered his neighbours around him. 'We can stay here or we can move on,' he said. 'Deeper into the woods, to where they came from.' He pointed at Gretel and Red. 'Before too much longer the first people are going to arrive here, you heard what the boys said. Hundreds of them.'

The mother from number 32 nodded. 'I'll come with you,' she said. Her son, now toddler-sized, clapped his hands and shouted his agreement from his seat strapped to her back. The woman from number 17, now swollen with pregnancy, shared glances with her coven. They would all go together, these women, or all stay behind. 'We'll go,' she said, stroking the bulge of her stomach and smiling at her husband, who smiled back at her lovingly and thought the 'we' referred to him.

They didn't waste time. They gathered only what they needed and left the trappings of their past lives, the photograph albums and tea sets and jewellery, for whoever moved in after them. They set their backs to the path that had once been the road leading out of the estate, set their faces to the dark heart of the wood, and they began to walk.

A SMALL LIFE

It's amazing how your perception of the place you live changes when you view it from a boat. The footpaths you walk, the picnic bench you sit at, even your own car in the car park, all look strange when you're on the river, swan-high, pulling away from it. *What is this village?* you think as you lean into the stroke of the oar and slide into the cool shadow of slate banked beside you. *Do I know it? Do I really live here?* Drifting, groundless, you finally see the land for what it is: ancient, permanent, human-scarred but enduring. It doesn't miss the unique weight and balance of your feet any more than the river will miss the trail of your fingers when you withdraw them and slip your hand back into your glove.

I forced myself to join the local rowing club when I moved here. A pool or darts team would have been a lot less effort but would have entailed a lot more drinking, and drinking was one of the things I was running from. I saw the notice in the post office on the high street and went along to the moorings the next week. If it had been a grey, wet evening or if I'd had a particularly frustrating day designing websites for my invisible, demanding clients then I probably wouldn't have left the house and that week would have rolled over into another, taking my good intentions with it. But the evening had made a postcard of the village: boats dipped and sang against the clasp of their anchors; bee-laden fuchsia bushes dripped blossom along the lanes. I pushed my feet into an old pair of trainers and left the house.

It had been so long since I'd taken anything close to an active interest in myself or my appearance, I wasn't even awkward at first when I joined the busy huddle around the longboat. They were slotting oars into rowlocks, hopping into waterproof boots, handing out lifejackets. Beside their tanned faces and powerful arms I must have looked pasty and weak, my bony legs flashing pale and fragile through the rips in my ragged jeans. My hellos were tentative, I was in the way no matter where I stood, and so I sat on the grass, nibbling my nails and watching as the grubby boat was shuffled to the river's edge and floated. One of the team, up to his thighs in the current as he braced her stern (she was called *Bert* but she was female), called me over.

'You're going to have to get wet,' he told me as I slithered down the slipway and stepped hesitantly into the sticky mud of the riverbed, wading out into the flow of water. 'Hop in and sit there.' He pointed. 'And adjust the position of your feet. Did you bring gloves?'

A pang of self-consciousness, and a quiet alarm, claimed me then. I think I'd vaguely assumed the first session would be one of introduction and explanation: rowing in theory as opposed to rowing in practise. But he was waiting and the rest of the team were splashing up behind me so I clambered into *Bert* and fiddled hopelessly with the footplate for a while until he lost patience and set it for me, strapping me in. His calloused hands scuffed goosebumps across my ankles as he cupped them in his palms, making me shiver. My soaked jeans dragged on my skin, chafing them, and my trainers oozed. I wished myself alone, on dry land. Surely I would have been better off spending this glorious evening sitting in the tamed space of my garden with a book, safe and untested. The yeasty-sour bite of lager hijacked my memory's taste buds, longing a sudden, fierce kick in my throat.

But the moment we began to row, me clumsy at first and rushing through each stroke, not leaning enough and then leaning too much, I forgot about my thirst and my anxiety. I forgot to wish myself elsewhere or worry about my performance. It was as if my identity and my ego unplugged themselves from the me who had individual thoughts and awareness and reinserted themselves instead into the greater machine of the boat, the team, and the pure mechanical act of rowing. I didn't listen to the shouted instructions and the banter that started with energy then tailed off as sweat began to run. I shut my eyes and heard only the slap-splash of blades carving the river, the thump of the shaft twisting in the rowlocks with each feathered stroke, and the heavy labour of my own breathing. *This*, I thought, *is the closest I'll ever get to true contentment.*

When the Cox called a halt and I finally looked around me we'd left the village and the trappings of the twenty-first century far behind. We floated in a steep gorge I'd only ever seen from above when walking the woodland paths on my occasional forays outside the house. The river here was narrow and deep, the current barely stirring the twigs that drifted in dark pools. Trees thickened the skyline, crowding out the light and bustling over the water to brush the tips of our oars. Slate peaked in cliffs and valleys ahead and behind the boat, pocked in places where it had been savaged by long-dead miners. A buzzard lamented in the distance. I knew where we were, only a couple of miles from home, but there was nothing to ground me in the modern world or a human community; this was the true wild. We could have been in any era. If I didn't look at the other men and their contemporary clothes I could dislocate myself from my life as it was, adopt some simpler persona.

No-one spoke, we just sat in companionable tranced pleasure and watched fish leap through veils of mosquitoes, then the Cox, Alex he was called, stirred. He bent forward and rummaged in his rucksack. He held out a bottle of water and smiled at me.

'We're going to turn it around and head back,' he said, 'or we'll hit the rapids. Here, drink some before you pass out. You look knackered.'

My arms trembled as I reached for the bottle. My palms were ripped open by blisters, my fingers nerveless as I tried to grip the smooth plastic and drink. 'I feel sick,' I said.

Someone behind me laughed and a hand patted me on the shoulder briefly. 'You'll get used to it. You did well to keep going. Your timing's great, that's the important thing.'

They turned the boat in a clumsy series of jerks and sweeps while I dipped my oar and leaned forward, willing strength back into my limbs for the return journey. Then, slow and hushed, we slipped easily back into the rhythm of the row, sliding through the shadowed gorge, out onto the widening river and the faded pink of twilight. Something rust coloured moved among the trees as I watched them fall away from me, a something that seemed too big, too upright, for a fox or a deer, but couldn't have been anything else. I shut my eyes for a moment and when I opened them again I focused just on Alex, on the alert concentrated way he manoeuvred us safely back downriver.

We kept it gentle on the way home, taking our time, speaking only to point out a cormorant poised like a flasher on the bank, or a parade of half-grown ducklings riding the swell of *Bert*'s passage. And the village, as we rowed through it, was studded with lights, suspended and sparkling like Fairy Land above us. We moored the boat and heaved it ashore, each of us patting the side in wordless thanks before we walked back along the lane beneath swooping bats, parting at the pub where I left them and carried on home, alone.

The rowing became my joy and my obsession from that first evening. The days when we were scheduled to meet were instantly more bearable; those days when the weather was too bad to go out or we couldn't get enough of a crew together left me downcast, wandering around the house aimlessly and despising its carpeted solidity beneath my feet. I volunteered to fix *Bert* up, spending weekends stroking paint across her shell and patching up her shabby frame, chatting to her about the birds I saw and was trying to identify with the help of a guidebook. Alex often popped down to help me, inspecting my work and bringing flasks of tea which we drank while he chatted and I watched the animation flow and crinkle across his face.

He recruited me onto the club committee one Sunday afternoon, over-riding my obvious reluctance with a wheedling, cheerful persistence that I had to admire. He was relieved to finally have someone so eager to help and so enthusiastic about the sport, but what he didn't ever understand, none of them did, was that the team didn't interest me as a real proposition. They were a decent bunch of men and I liked them all, but I wasn't into the teasing and the camaraderie, the competitiveness and the hours shouting over each other in the pub. I needed them, they were a part of what made the rowing a joy for me, but they were only important as a concept, as my fellow machinery. All together, strapped into our footplates and wielding our oars, we became something so much more vital than we could ever hope to be alone.

I tested this theory by hiring a kayak and taking it out a few times by myself, but no matter how far I went and how long I stayed on the water I never got close to that dazed serenity, that addictive peace, that wrapped itself around me when I rowed with the others. Even the gorge failed to stir me in the same way. I didn't understand why, and I resented it a little but accepted it as a necessary compromise to my everyday solitude. I needed the bare bones of community, as represented by the team. Before moving to this village I'd lived a land-locked life; I hadn't ever spared thought or attention for rivers except to view them as boundaries to be crossed as I moved from one urban space to another. Maybe that was it: giving myself to the water as I did, flowing with it or pushing against its currents, had allowed cracks to form in my dammed life. Its constant renewal, the knowledge that I could dip my hand into it again and again and never hold in my cupped palms the same body of water, filled me with wonder and fascination. It allowed me to believe that I too could be renewed.

I was sure the rest of the team must talk about me behind my back, spicing their evenings with gossip and guessing games about where I came from and what I did when I left them. My problems with alcohol hadn't needed to be spelled out as my thirsty abstinence, the way I'd stumble as I walked past the open pub door and set my face against the couples chinking glasses in the beer garden, was a confession in itself. They never pressured me once they realised that my refusal to accompany them on their post-row drinking sessions wasn't down to standoffishness or disapproval. Phil, whose wife had left him at the start of the year and whose blustering neediness was painful to observe, was the only one who made the odd, barbed joke, but that didn't surprise me as his breath was often a layered smog of whisky and breath mints. As to the rest of it, I didn't care how much they gossiped. My small life suited me; I didn't strive for anything more than what I had.

Slowly the hollowed space beneath my ribcage filled in a little, and my arms fleshed out. My skin browned from the hours spent outside. If I caught an unexpected glimpse of my reflection in the hall mirror startled recognition would flare across my senses, followed swiftly by its opposite. I'd known this healthy, happy man once but hadn't thought I'd ever see him again.

Other team members slotted in and out of the schedule, some rowing more often than not and others only occasionally, but I didn't miss a single one of the three-times-a-week sessions. There was talk of getting a racing crew together and competing with other clubs, but I was scared that a shift in emphasis, a greedy attempt to turn the boat into a tool for glory and make it work on a different level, would ensure I'd lose the delicate satisfaction it gave me. My fear was rooted in a superstitious, jealous need to guard this surprising joy I'd discovered; keep everything that supported it preserved exactly as it was when I first joined the team. I even insisted that I row the same position each time.

Sometimes we rowed the couple of miles downriver to the mouth of the estuary, where the water at low tide stretched itself thin and shallow between sandbanks busy with curlews playing their flutes. At high tide the sea stampeded behind our shoulders, snorting spume, as we toiled to stay out of the tugging cross currents that would sweep us into the bay. It was a harsher scenery out there, the sky flat and vast above us, pressing down. It made me feel exposed, as if some cruel god was peering down and sorting through my sins; it made rowing and the boat harder to take pleasure from. I didn't enjoy those evenings, though I never said.

Mostly, though, we rowed upriver. And those evenings I loved. Passing the village green where children kicked balls, or the tremendous bulk of an upended oak tucked into one of the river's tight bends, or the stony shelf where swans raised their young and eyed us with menace, I'd sometimes feel such a flood of fierce contentment, an unfolding inside the clamped squeeze of my chest, I'd laugh out loud and quicken my stroke, forcing the others into increasing their pace until we were sprinting past the tangle of moored fishing boats that bordered the village, shouting 'Buoy!' to each other as our oar blades clashed and ricocheted like hockey sticks over the floating markers and we raced on to the remote wilderness of the woods and the gorge.

Through those weeks, through almost an entire summer, my frail happiness settled on me like dust, waking me in the night with fits of coughing. I was terrified of the coming winter, the season's end, and was already voicing plans to row weekends and lamp-lit nights. To even have future anxieties to focus on, routines to protect, was a novelty for me, accustomed as I'd become to pinning my gaze only on what was immediate and essential to endure each day. It felt like a release at the time but looking back I think it was more like complacency. If you don't let comfort into your life then you don't have to suffer its loss.

From the moment she stepped out from behind *Bert*'s stern, wrapped in a long cardigan the colour of ivy, hair knotted around her bright, open face, alarm sliced into my cheerful anticipation, deflating it just enough to edge it with something more troubled. I stepped back from her as she came forward with a smile.

'I'm Jess, Alex's sister,' she said, following me, holding her hand out. 'It's so good to meet you, finally. Alex talks about you a lot. I can't tell you how much I'm looking forward to being out on the river tonight.'

I took the tips of her fingers and then dropped them immediately. I tried to move around her, to the boat. 'I thought we were a men-only team,' I said.

If she was affronted she didn't show it. 'Oh, I'm not rowing,' she told me with a grin, 'I'm your passenger.'

Alex called my name and threw a lifejacket when I turned to him. The buckle caught me on the side of the face, numbing my cheek.

'And you, Jess.' He walked over and gave one to his sister. 'Help her with it, would you?' he asked me. 'The silly bitch broke her arm earlier this year. She's got more pins in her elbow than a voodoo doll.' His tone was affectionate. I wrestled her awkwardly into the jacket, tightening the straps around her ribs with my wrists at stiff angles so as not to touch her directly. She watched me with a perplexed, kind smile but didn't speak other than to thank me.

We prepared the boat and took our positions. Jess settled herself onto a pile of cushions in the bow, hugging her knees up against her chest. She seemed to know the rest of the team well enough, craning around the row of bodies to respond to jokes and complain about her cramped legs. There was a subtle posturing among the other men, a vying for her attention that altered the atmosphere, staining it with a tension that fidgeted part way between sexual and aggressive. Jay and Phil bickered self-consciously about which route to take, twisting round to appeal to the rest of us and shoving at each other with brays of laughter, sneaking looks at Jess. I sat like a statue, staring ahead, and waited for the decision to be made.

The row was messy, the boat stuttering and jerking as we chopped at the water with our oars and over-balanced on our seats. It seemed that we stumbled out of rhythm with each other almost as soon as we fell into it. Alex frowned at me a few times, gesturing to me to slow down as I strained to reach that precious space inside my mind with no regard for matching the pace of the rest of the crew. What had once been effortless was now a struggle and I blamed Jess, entirely and viciously, for that. *Weren't women banned from stepping foot on ships in the past*, I thought, *for bringing bad luck to the sailors?* Anger wheeled and dived beside us all, frustration erupting the length of *Bert* as we thrashed and flailed our way upriver.

Even the eerie half-light of the gorge couldn't soothe me. Alex finally called a halt and we swayed gently in one of the pools while he lectured us on our technique. I tuned out his words and the little squabbles that broke out in response, focusing instead on a tiny bug that meandered unnoticed around his arm, tangling in the fair hairs that scattered his skin and then freeing itself and continuing on. Goosebumps rose across the nape of my neck as my sweat chilled in the evening air. Water bottles were passed from person to person, and we slumped for a while in a grumpy, reproachful silence.

Jess broke the ill humour by rising to stand wobblingly upright. She rocked above us, beaming and red-cheeked, feet braced at angles, as she tugged sweets from her cardigan pocket and flicked them around the boat. 'Well, I enjoyed it anyway,' she said. 'I'd forgotten how much I love the river.'

I tried not to look at her, at the hectic spill of her hair, breeze-ruffled to near-afro, and the slender ridge of collar bone hemmed pale against the fold of her lifejacket. I clung to my oar and studied the leaves that drifted along the steep bank behind her shifting body.

Conversation started up around me, lighter in tone. I held myself aloof, nodding with absent politeness from time to time but not really paying attention. There was still the return row, I reasoned. The evening can be saved. And for now, there was this timeless gorge where, if I willed it hard enough, I could be a past version of myself, an earlier untainted me from a hundred, two hundred, years ago, watching younger incarnations of these same trees weep their leaves.

A deer or a badger, something large, moved with haste out of sight but close to the boat. The trample of its passage paused, faded, and then veered back as if it had scented us. Faster now, and louder. I saw it flash ruddy through the gloom a second before it burst onto the top of the bank, rising from the ground itself, it seemed: a creature made of roots and soil and chips of slate. It unravelled to human height and size and balanced there for a second, arms spread, before plunging down towards us. Earth and stones tumbled in its wake. Its features were indistinct, a blur in the spreading dusk, but it saw me. It recognised me.

Jess still stood at the back of the boat, unsteady and laughing, her head turned away from it, towards me. All of the others were looking at her. I reached her before the thing leapt from the bank, wrenching my feet from their straps and throwing myself across the shoulders of the other rowers to grab her arm and pull her forward. She sprawled across me and I sprawled across the length of the lurching *Bert*. I held her in my fists, pinning her chest with my legs, as the rest of the team yelled around us and worked to steady the boat, oars cracking against each other.

When I was pulled upright, and Jess was pulled from my grip, we were the crouched, quiet centre within the boundary of frantic commotion. She leaned close to stare at me, resting briefly against my arm. 'What did you see?' she asked me. A bruise was already thickening across her cheekbone but she seemed calmer than the people around her. 'Tell me,' she whispered, her lips almost brushing my face. 'You can tell me.'

Alex called out from his seat at the stern. 'Do you want to let us know what the hell that was about? You nearly had the boat over.'

I raised myself slowly up to resume my seat and looked

around. 'There was someone here, charging at us. You must have seen them.'

'Who?' Jess murmured, as Jay shouted, 'What? That was a bloody fox, mate, slinking along the bank. I caught a glimpse of it before you went crazy and tried to kill us all.'

I looked directly at Alex. 'They were wrapped in a blanket made of twigs or leaves or something. It was billowed out behind them as they ran.'

Nobody said anything for a moment. Alex's expression was blankly polite, as though he'd misheard a comment by a stranger and was unsure of the best way to respond. I didn't have to look at the other men to know that they were raising eyebrows at each other, casting quick glances around them at the trees and the gorge and then back at me. Only Jess maintained direct contact, patting my shoulder and smiling encouragingly. I cringed beneath her hand but submitted to the touch.

Alex broke the silence to tell us to take our positions for the row home. He cupped his sister's chin briefly, wincing at the sight of her swollen cheek, then gave the instruction to turn the boat. He was curt and business-like with us all, effectively ending any further discussion. He didn't look at me again.

The row back was more fluid than the one out had been. It was as if the drama had cleansed the rest of the team of their individual tensions and they all pulled together easily. I was the only one unable to settle into the group rhythm, unable to feel any kind of a connection. Hunched and miserable, I sweated and trembled on my seat, the oar heavy and insensitive as a battering ram in my weak grip.

Nobody mentioned my outburst again, even after we got

back and secured *Bert* then walked in a straggling line to the village, me tailing the rest of them like a naughty child. I left them outside the pub without a goodbye, ignoring Jess when she put her hand out to me and began to say something. Alex stood beside her and watched me walk away but he didn't speak. I passed the turning down to my house without slowing, went on to the shop and bought a half bottle of rum and a couple of four-packs of lager. Back home, I drank the lot down with greedy, bitter delight, sitting in the murk of my kitchen, curtains closed against the world.

I was never going to row again. Whatever magic it had once held for me was gone, emptied even from my memory so just the thought of getting in a boat was strange and vaguely ludicrous. I stayed indoors as much as possible through the next week, spending the mornings vomiting up my hangover and skulking along the lanes to the shop in the late afternoons to buy wine and whisky, tins of soup; never looking up from the careful placement of my feet on the ground and never going near the river. The phone rang and messages piled up. I was missing work deadlines but I couldn't bring myself to care.

The figure from the gorge was there throughout those days, whether I was drunk or sober. It had come home with me, or maybe it followed the scent trail of my despair and tracked me down. Its outline, definitely human but obscurely genderless, skirted the shadows that gathered around me as I slumped at the kitchen table, peeped from behind doors when I entered a room. Even when I couldn't see it I knew it was present by the rich, earthy smell hanging loose and gritty on the air.

Watching, always watching, it held itself back from making any definite move, noting my acceleration towards self-destruction and biding its time.

Alex came round more than once, knocking on the door and peering through windows. I made no attempt to hide and he must have seen me, a hopeless shape muttering through the rooms with their litter of empty bottles. I imagined him disgusted and repulsed, terminally disappointed in my freefall. I didn't deserve any better. A part of me wanted him to witness my degradation close up, wanted to invite him in and have him smell my unwashed body and filthy clothes, see what a sorry mess of a man I was. A savage part of me wanted that more than anything.

Phil turned up one evening with a litre of whisky, hopeful and half-drunk. I hid from him, or from the ongoing social commitment my letting him in would have entailed. If I'd wanted a drinking companion it wouldn't have been Phil, and as it stood I was far better at drinking alone than drinking in company. Always had been.

Those times, when I tried my hardest to poison myself with drink, never lasted longer than a couple of weeks. Unlike the insidious daily drip-feed of alcohol, a bottle or two of wine a night, when I could kid myself that I was managing a habit well, my body reached a state of collapse before my thirst did and then I knew that this particular binge was at an end. I reached that point on the tenth night, jolting awake in the hallway with what I hoped was lager soaking my jeans, staring up at the ceiling with its flutter of cobweb drapes and realising that I couldn't walk. It took me the rest of the night to lever myself onto my hands and knees, an inch at a time, and crawl to the toilet a few metres away. There I collapsed and lay, too weary to raise my head away from the pool of sick that spread beneath my mouth.

With sobriety came a return of my longing for the boat and the river. It bit into the tender flesh of my shoulders where the muscle was already starting to soften. It throbbed through my knuckles as they flexed and curled, finding nothing to grasp but air. I held off for another few days, drying myself out thoroughly and clearing my home of any trace of the gorge creature. It spent a night or two haunting the garden, tapping at windows. It was waiting for any slip on my part, any sign that I'd return to my previous state of vulnerability, but then it disappeared completely.

I tried to stubbornly convince myself that I didn't need the boat, didn't need anything beyond my immediate structures; I was, I had to be, better off alone. But then I found myself rushing from the house one early evening, jogging through the lanes to the moorings and getting there just as *Bert* was being floated.

Phil saw me first and said something to Alex, who waded out of the river and came over to where I stood. In the face of his stern disinterest I felt as shy and nervous as I'd been that first time.

He nodded at me. 'You're late,' he said, 'and we've already got a crew for tonight.'

I looked over at the rest of the team, noting with relief that Jess was nowhere to be seen. 'Please,' I said. 'Let me row.'

'Are you sure you're okay to?'

I didn't mind him asking. I'd become gaunt over the last

fortnight, my skin grey and clammy. He'd seen the tremble in my hands when I raised them to scratch at the skin that flaked from a sore patch under my watering left eye.

'I'm fine, I promise.'

Alex sighed and then shrugged. 'Matt can Cox and I'll stay here. A short row, though, and if I hear you've freaked out again you're not going back in the boat. Ever.'

I moved away from him, towards *Bert*, before he could change his mind. I climbed into my usual seat and slid my palms along the oar, finding immediately and easily the sweet spot where the grip was perfect. I didn't speak to the rest of the team or acknowledge them beyond a nod. I didn't care what they thought of me. Alex stood on the bank with his hands thrust in his pockets, frowning as we pulled away from him and into the current.

The row was brief and wonderful. I didn't try to persuade the others to go further than they'd been instructed to, tapering my desire only to what was being offered and no more. When we grounded back onto the slipway I jumped out and held the boat while the team changed positions and Alex climbed in. I didn't show my reluctance at sacrificing my seat, didn't ask him how Jess was and whether her bruised face had healed. I just thanked him and then watched with a big smile and arms raised in farewell as they rowed away from land.

Dozing in the bath last thing, I realised that it had been hours since I'd thought about having a drink.

I made sure I was early for the next row, and the one after: ready with the lifejackets before the others had even shrugged their coats off and surrendered their house keys to the water-proof emergency bag. We were losing the light in the evenings and nothing had been confirmed for the winter season. Alex sent me the odd message on my mobile at random times over the next couple of weeks before we all settled back into the old routine, presumably to check whether I was sober and sane. I always replied promptly and chattily, made sure he had nothing to worry about. I thought he might have missed me and my tireless enthusiasm for the club. Nothing was ever mentioned about that awful scene and my consequent absence; everyone seemed to be as relaxed as ever around me and when we returned to the gorge nothing moved through the trees or tore itself from the ground to threaten us. I had endured. I was safe.

Jess was waiting the next time I got to the moorings. She greeted me warmly, hands resting on my forearms for a moment before I pulled away. My anger was immediate, savage and close to the surface; I had to put the boat between us to give myself a chance to control it. Some of it showed in my expression and stopped her from following me but she still made me the focus of her smiling attention, telling me how good it was to see me as we worked together to fit the oars into their rowlocks. Her brother watched us carefully, and the rest of the team jealously.

I hung back when the others started to drag *Bert* down to the water, yearning warring with despair. Alex came to stand beside me. 'She really likes you,' he told me. 'Seems to think you've got a connection. Are you okay with her being here, after last time?'

'Would it make a difference if I told you I wasn't?' I asked him. 'Would you make her go home?'

He shouted to Jay to keep the stern lifted, then touched my shoulder briefly. 'She's my sister, and she's not doing any harm. She's heading back to university in a couple of weeks, anyway. I don't understand why you've got such a problem with her but surely you can manage to be polite until then?'

It was a warning, of sorts. I took my position in the boat without another word.

We rowed upriver to the gorge, our timing more ragged than it could have been. Parents lifted small children in their arms to wave at us as we passed below the village green, their shapes dotted dark and dense as shadows against the twilight sky. Jess waved back and called up to them, her cheerful voice grating harshly against my temper so that I twitched on my seat and had to shut my eyes against Alex's sharp stare.

The effort, both to row and to wrestle my mood into something small and soft enough to hug close and unspilled, secret from the others, tired me long before we reached the gorge. I wanted to tell Alex to turn us around quickly and row back, no lingering this time, but we all, me more than anyone, needed a break.

The conversation was brittle, almost nervous, as we paused to rest in our usual pool. The others were watching me whilst pretending not to, waiting for me to start throwing myself around the boat again and railing at phantoms. I stayed bent over my water bottle, dripping sweat onto my hands, as they chatted around me. The air grew dense with the smell of leaf mould, thickening the saliva in my mouth, but I didn't so much as glance around to acknowledge it. Even when the boat started lurching I forced myself not to look up, not to react; holding myself and my anxiety together with effort. If there

253

was going to be another attack let someone else deal with it. As long as I could stay just as I was, apart from it all, untouched and unmoved.

Jess's voice, close beside my ear, startled me almost out of my seat. She'd left her nook and fumbled her way to the front of *Bert*. Laughing, she butted unsteadily up against my back, grabbing at my shoulders to balance herself. Sweets slithered from her hands and cascaded down my chest to land in my lap. 'Here you are,' she said. 'For you.'

I twisted reluctantly to look at her, raising a hand to grasp her wrist and keep her on her feet as she squeaked and reeled. She peered down into my face smilingly, forehead kissing briefly against forehead; her hair, loose this evening, swung beside us and tickled my cheek. I wanted to push her away, get far from her clumsy attempt at flirtation and eager belief that she somehow knew me.

'Thank you,' I said, 'but I don't eat sweets.' I parted my thighs slightly, letting the brightly wrapped things slide down into *Bert*'s belly.

She straightened up and broke eye contact, pushing her palms down on my shoulders as she started to turn away, chewing on her lip. I caught the edge of Alex's embarrassed grimace and pretended I hadn't.

Jess paused in her retreat and gasped, clinging to me with one hand, raising the other to point stiffly at something behind Alex. I swung my head to see what she saw, scrabbling to my feet. The others gaped at us disbelievingly, grabbing for their oars in slow motion.

'Where?' I asked Jess urgently. 'Where?'

Her arm wavered to her side and then rose again, pointing

through the trees. 'There.' She burrowed her face into me and whimpered.

I couldn't see anything at first except the wooded gorge poised and constant above the rippling corrugations of the bank. Then movement snagged at my vision, a flutter of something. I turned my head to follow its path, squinting into the shifting dusk light. There was nothing to focus on, nothing there. And then suddenly there was.

The thing peeled itself from a tree far from where I'd been looking, far nearer to *Bert*, and launched itself at me as if it were determined to fly. It charged down that bank with its mud-red blanket flying behind it and its arms outflung. Its face was a tangle of leaf skeleton and roots. Its warrior cry was the scrape of slate on slate. I didn't think, just yelled my terror and threw myself backwards with Jess still pressed against my chest, taking us both over the side of the boat.

Below the surface the river was calm and deep. We sank together, my arms tight around Jess, her weight stretched upon the length of me. I kept my eyes open and watched particles of dirt and weed, tiny fish and bubbles, drift and eddy around us. Above our bodies the underneath of the boat bucked and churned but we were safe from it all, from the noise and the fight, descending in stages to where the current tugged itself to pieces and then lower again, to where the water wore relentlessly down on the slate bed of the river. Like the eternally sealed figures in a snow globe, nothing could touch us down here. Jess pushed at me frantically, hitting out and lunging at her lifejacket until I loosened my hold on her and let her go. Her foot kicked into my jaw as she forced herself upwards but I didn't feel any pain until much later.

Alex dragged me out. I fought him at first, clinging to anything I could so that I didn't have to return to the world above
the water. Then I gave in and let him take me. I lay sleepy and
serene on the riverbank beside him as Jess shook and sobbed
in the boat. The other men crowded around her and kept her
safe. I rolled onto my side and vomited the river out of my
stomach in a couple of quick, helpless convulsions, coughing
my lungs clear of it and swallowing as much as I could back
down so that it would trickle through me. I tucked my hands
together under my cheek and closed my eyes.

The rest of the row, the return home, they managed without
me. I kept my eyes shut and submitted myself limply to it all:
the shouted phone calls and the strange hands fitting
themselves into my armpits; being raised and lowered. I was
returned, by the river watering my blood, to a state of purity
and peace I'd not experienced in years. Different from the
careful joy I'd taken in the rowing through that summer; so
much more complete.

I was able to resist efforts to have me seen at a hospital, once
we got back to the village: loud enough in my protests to be
deemed okay. I don't think any of them would have cared anyway if I'd died in the night. There was a little blustering talk
about phoning the police. Their fury pressed on me from all
sides but couldn't reach me. Jess still sobbed in her brother's
arms but pulled clear and turned her face from his chest to
watch as I staggered away from the group.

I thought about going to the shop for alcohol but went
straight home instead. My jawbone throbbed and clicked beneath my probing fingers. I sat at the kitchen table in dim
lamplight and drank black coffee, shivering in my river-

sodden clothes. I retched thin trails of muddy water that trickled down my chin, and I waited.

'It's open,' I called out from my seat when the knock at the door finally came. Jess slipped in and walked down the hallway towards me. I didn't stand up to greet her but nodded towards the coffee pot standing on the table. She cradled two bottles of wine in her arms which she set down beside the pot. She turned to collect another mug from the draining board, wiping it on her cardigan and then filling it to the brim. 'Have some,' she said to me, offering the bottle.

The white china rim of her mug captured and reflected the deep red of the wine; her lips gleamed dark and wet as she drank. I drained the last of my coffee with one gulp and let her fill my mug, hanging my head over it to smell the earthy bitterness of the liquid. I didn't drink immediately. 'Does your brother know you're here?' I asked her.

Jess shook her head. 'I am an adult, you know. I don't have to tell him everything. He's furious with you, thinks you should be locked up somewhere away from normal people.' She tested my response with quick glances as she sipped.

'I expected him around here by now to give me a kicking. You could have died.'

She shook her head. 'You wouldn't have let that happen. You were just trying to keep me safe.'

Her conviction, set against all that she had experienced, would have been touchingly sweet if it hadn't been so blindly self-serving. Like her appearance here at all, and the wine she'd slyly brought with her, she was acting in pure pursuit of her own aims with no awareness or concern for how I fitted into her schemes. I raised the mug to my lips and dampened them, just a few drops that I licked away before repeating the act. I saw her watch me do this.

'I would have drowned if it weren't for Alex,' I said idly.

Jess shifted in her seat and leaned forward slightly, taking the first steps towards creating a scene of intimacy; she propped her elbow on the table and cupped her chin in a palm, tracing patterns across the pale flesh of her inner arm with a slow fingertip. 'The rest of them can think what they like about you,' she said. 'We know what happened. You were trying to save me.'

'I was trying to save myself. You were just in the way,' I told her harshly. 'And that other time was blind, stupid instinct. I couldn't have let something happen to Alex's little sister; he'd never have forgiven me.' I jerked to sudden attention in my chair and jabbed a finger at her. 'You saw it first.' I was reminding myself more than Jess. 'You actually saw it, didn't you?' I looked at her properly for the first time since she'd walked into the house.

She tipped her nose into her mug and drank deeply, emptying it quickly before reaching for the bottle to refill. 'It all happened too quickly,' she said. 'I can't remember exactly what I saw.'

'No.' I spoke louder than I'd intended to. We both flinched. 'No. You saw it. You pointed at it. Tell me.'

'Who is it?' Jess suddenly asked, derailing my urgent focus. 'You said it was a person. They must mean something to you, to keep seeing them when I'm in the boat. It's as if …' She hesitated for a moment. 'It's as if there's something about me that makes them appear.' Her voice was pleading.

I raised my mug to my mouth, swallowing absent-mindedly

at first and then quickly, greedily, when the wine flooded over my tongue and slipped down my throat. Jess filled it again and opened the second bottle. 'There's a bond between us,' she told me. 'You have to admit that.'

Her face, so unlike her brother's sharp boniness, was still attractive in its own way, though less so. She lacked his lean angularity; her cheeks were plumper and her features less defined. I reached a hand across the table and touched her briefly on the wrist. 'Tell me that you saw it,' I said, 'and then we'll have a bond.'

She nodded eagerly, scratching at a splinter of wood that flaked from the corner of the table. 'Yes, I did.'

I wanted, so much, to believe her. If we stopped this conversation right now, if she stood up and walked through the echo of her own words, if she left and I never saw her again, I could simply accept what she said and ignore her reasons for saying it. I'd always have that comfort: this wasn't just happening inside my life. We sat for a moment and I stared at her as she worked the splinter out of the table, intent on the task.

'Don't lie to me. We both know you didn't see it,' I shouted, standing up. My chair toppled back to teeter on two legs before crashing over. 'You just wanted me to notice you and you didn't care how much it screwed up my head, you selfish little bitch.'

She rose to meet me as I stormed around the table, grabbing at her and holding her against me. 'Is this all you're after?' I asked, pressing my hands down over the swell of her buttocks, working my fingers between the backs of her thighs so that her legs were spread apart. I forced her against the wall, slamming her with my body and pushing a knee up into her crotch. She gasped pain and bit my shoulder, but she didn't try to struggle away. We wrestled for a moment, both of us clumsy and desperate in our different ways. Despite the blood surge and the anger I was flaccid, incapable of performing any sexual act even if I'd wanted to. Her body, arched and taut in my arms, disgusted me.

I was terrified that I'd hurt her if she stayed. I dragged her down the hallway by her wrist and opened the front door, shoving her through. She lay sprawled on the path, bathed in garish orange by the streetlamp that pinned her to the ground and nailed her expression to her face in stark lines and shadows, dehumanising her. I didn't know whether she was crying, or smiling, and I didn't care as long as she stayed that side of the door.

Alex didn't come round. I sat up the rest of the night with the dregs of the wine and watched the moon carve a path across the kitchen window. Jess phoned a few times and left messages that I didn't listen to after the first few tearful seconds. My shame at how I'd treated her vied with my anger at her mere presence in my life. I hadn't asked for her attention and the dangers it brought with it. I'd only ever wanted to be left alone.

When the sun lifted itself from the horizon, rinsing the sky pink and peach, I sent Jess a text message asking her to meet me at the moorings. I drank more coffee to rouse myself from the numb fatigue that cloaked me and changed into dry clothes. My stomach was cramped and sore, sharp spasms of pain gripping and releasing me periodically.

I walked with the dawn to the river and the canoes moored

there. I was ready with the paddle, broken padlock thrown in the bin, when Jess arrived. Her face was swollen from crying but shining with pathetic hope. She didn't question me, just climbed quickly into the seat in front of mine as if scared I'd change my mind and tell her to go home.

The river was full and flat with a rising tide. We swung out from the shelter of the jetty and into the slow current, me working the paddle to steer us between the moored fishing boats, past *Bert* slinking against her rope and then onwards, threading between the bobbing buoys. The village as we slid through it was silent and emptied of human life. A gull stood on the roof of one of the skew of cottages that flanked the green. A lone dog cocked its leg against a bin and watched us with idle interest. Crows scrabbled in busy murmuration, racing over our heads from their night's roost to their day's feeding ground.

The canoe was harder to manage than the longboat, unused as I was to facing forwards and using the paddle on both sides. Jess sat still and balanced on the centre of her seat, elbows tucked into her waist and back stiffly straight. We didn't speak at all, even when a kingfisher flung itself like a chain of jewels across our path and raced its own brilliance to the other side of the river. The morning grew around us: lightening the tucks and folds of the bank; laying itself across the water in glittering patches that I broke apart as I stroked us away from the village and towards the gorge. Even with despair unfurling so close to the surface of me I took an awed pleasure in it all, in the river's constant ability to reveal itself anew every time I looked at it.

As we neared the gorge Jess finally spoke, turning her head slightly so that I could hear her words, but not looking directly at me. It felt as though we were in a form of confessional: neither of us seeking eye contact while she whispered her secrets.

'I spent the whole night thinking about us,' she said, 'and I think I understand you now.'

I felt a pang of pity for her then. She was so young and so sure that she understood this thing that was happening to her. So sure that she understood me.

'This wild person you keep seeing at the gorge when I'm there,' she continued, 'the person who scares you so much, I think they exist because you have feelings for me and you're trying to resist them. I think it's me you're seeing.'

When I didn't respond she twisted entirely round on her seat, swinging her legs over and bringing them to rest against mine, laying her hands on the bunched muscle above my knees. The control was with her; I couldn't shift away or stop paddling. I leaned slightly to the side so that I could peer past her and keep us on course, and I stayed silent.

She stroked my thighs lightly, leaning close and chasing the direction of my gaze, trying to pin me, to force me to focus on her. Over her shoulder the river narrowed and the gorge loomed. Dark clouds squatted over it, threatening a storm. They stretched back towards the horizon, blocking the sun and changing the quality of the light we moved through, flattening it. I was going to get wet before the morning was out.

Once we were beneath the trees and caged in slate the air temperature around the canoe plummeted. Jess began to shiver inside her thin jumper. Still avoiding eye contact, I jerked my head towards the backpack lying by our feet. 'There's a coat in there. Put it on.' I steered us through to the deep heart of the gorge, reaching up to pull on low-lying branches and swing the canoe around before halting it and tying it loosely. Then I was freed to sweep her hands from me and slip mine into my armpits for warmth.

Tucked against the bank we sat close together, facing each other with our knees touching. Jess watched me while I watched the river and the wooded slopes around us. Her hands shifted towards me and then withdrew, fingers twitching back and forth as she summoned courage to touch me again. We could have been mistaken for lovers at a glance if anyone were walking the woodland paths above us. Fish nuzzled the water's surface from below, ghostly shapes in speckled bronze and silver floating up through the murk.

I glanced at Jess as she shuddered inside the depths of my oversized coat. 'You're wrong,' I told her. 'About me, about us.'

She shook her head. 'No, I don't think I am. That's why I'm here; I'm trying to give us a chance.'

There was a crackle of something at the very edge of my peripheral vision. Maybe just a flitting bird or a loosening leaf, but possibly not. I didn't turn my head to look straight at it.

'I don't know what that thing is or why it wants to hurt me,' I said. 'But it's not because I'm scared to desire you. I'm not scared of you and I don't desire you. I really don't. All I want is to be left alone, to live my life as quietly as I can.'

A little sound now: a brief sigh of gathering intention, a creak of twigs pressured into bowing but not breaking.

I kept my eyes on Jess. 'I was happy with what I had. I didn't push for more. Getting out on the river, spending a bit of time with Alex and the others, that was all I wanted. I could have been happy with that forever. A small life, maybe, but that suited me fine. And then you turned up with your chat and your neediness, expecting me to respond to you like the other men did. Assuming I'd behave like all the other men do.' I was getting angry, straining from my seat to thrust a finger at her. 'I just wanted to be left alone.'

She was calm in the face of my agitation. 'Then tell me why you have hallucinations when I'm around you. You're scared of how you feel.'

I sank back and looked hopelessly at her. 'It's not an hallucination. I'm not mad. That thing's as real as you are.'

Behind Jess the bank gathered itself, pushing upwards and twisting into a human form. The thing revealed itself in slow concentrated stages, rising until it finally stood at full height, towering above us. Its features pressed through the covering of bark and slate, un-lidded quartz eyes swivelling to focus. It tipped its head back and scented the air, weaving from side to side, until it found us. Then it shook out its long muddy trails of hair and paced in tight figures-of-eight, scattering stones and leaves with every step, looking from me to Jess and back as if unsure which of us interested it more.

'It's here,' I whispered. 'It's right here.' I nodded my head minutely to the side.

Jess swerved on her seat to stare at where I was indicating. Her forehead furrowed with her need to see what I saw, or to be sure that she didn't see anything at all. I gripped my seat and leaned forward to watch the expressions chase each other across her face: concentration, puzzlement, dawning satisfaction. Her eyes searched the bank again and again and I thought with despair that she wouldn't see, she'd refuse to see. But then her gaze snapped back to a point of focus and she jerked with shock. The expressions creasing her face now were different: incredulity, awe, horror. She turned to look at me, her mouth loose and slack from the effort to keep the scream stifled in her throat.

'Take me home,' she whispered, sliding onto the floor of the canoe and wrapping her arms around her legs. 'Don't let it see me.' The paddle rattled against the canoe's shell with the tremble of her body.

'It's too late,' I told her. 'It's already seen us. It won't let us go.'

The figure stopped its pacing and stepped to the edge of the bank to peer at us. It lifted a hand to beckon. If I'd stretched out my arm I could have touched it. Jess scrabbled backwards, clambering onto my knees. She was frantic with fear. I grabbed her shoulder when she lurched up and tried to throw herself over the side of the canoe, wrestling her into my arms and holding her on my lap, my hand around her throat to keep her still. She collapsed against me, limp and pliant. 'It's not me, it's you,' she murmured as I propped her up with my hand spread against her back, offering her as a sacrifice to be taken in my stead. 'It's not me, it's you, it's not me, it's you.'

It took all my strength to struggle upright under Jess's weight and hold her out. She dangled from my hands, drooping boneless as a half-stuffed scarecrow between my stretched arms. The creature took her by the wrist and pulled her easily from me, folding her into an embrace. I could still hear Jess mumbling against the thing's neck, repeating herself over and over, though I could no longer see her face. She didn't struggle.

The figure laid the tips of its fingers gently on my hand before I could move away. The slight touch froze me where I stood; I could only submit myself to its interest. My mind heaved and shuddered as it was plundered; a cold, ancient curiosity rifling through the needs and desires my conscious self would never acknowledge. It dragged them to the surface, through the suppression of years and the layers of shame and denial, and laid them out for me to accept, or to refuse.

For just a moment I teetered on the very edge of accepting myself, accepting this wild thing into myself, and there was such relief in the possibility, such release, but I couldn't do it. I closed my eyes and shook my head, raising my hands in rejection. When I looked again it was standing far away, a blur among the trees, facing away from me. Jess was cradled in its arms. I was free.

I didn't hesitate. I untied the canoe and began to paddle away from them, away from the wilderness, back to the safety of the village and the small, tamed life I'd chosen as mine.

Once I was clear of the gorge, small and secure beneath the wide sky, I paused to dip my hand into the river to wash it clean of the mark the creature had left on my skin.

TATTLETALE

Tattletale, we said. Tattletail. Rattletail tattletale. We pulled her skirt up and pushed her down, sprawled her on the ground. We slapped and pinched her spine, pretending to feel the scaly thrust of tail pushing through the thick cotton of her knickers. We ran and span in a circle around the crimson blur of her screams, clapping hands and skipping over kicking legs. We leapt the reveal of bruises that trellised her thighs ochre and violet, layering dawn and dusk onto her flesh. We never tattletaled on those.

Tattletale, prattletale, nasty lying rattletail. Dirty faced at the front of the class, arms flaking fleabag scabs, elbows grey and cracked. We followed the lurch of her eyes as they jittered left and right, fingers a squirm of snakes in her lap, grimacing at the teacher. We waited for her to find the spiders in her desk, the bubble gum on her skirt, and then we waited outside when she stayed behind to tattletale on us.

Nobody likes a tattletale, a filthy deformed girl with a tail. We tipped her over the wall and into the ditch so the spiteful sea of nettles would drag her down and drown her. When she crawled out, a splutter of lumps and bumps, a frenzied hop of hives, we used our sticks to poke her straight back in. Hungry for our dinners, we didn't stay to watch but left her flailing, sinking, not waving but drowning. Second helpings all round that night.

Don't touch the tattletale, the twitching, scratching rattletail. Her germs bob and float above her head like a speech bubble, like a balloon filled with pus. If it bursts over you she'll infect you with her bugs. We needed to clean the tattletale. For her own good. We decided to give her a bath in the pond behind the green. We tossed stones onto the thick crust of its surface and nodded as we watched them waver and sink, the weed closing above them as if they never were.

Stupid greedy tattletale, eyes piggy pink with tears but hand held out for the sweets we dangled. We pressed humbugs into her soggy palms, threaded lollies through the lank dribble of her plaits. Trailing wrappers like rainbows, she trotted in our wake, snorting breath through gobbled toffees. We led her along the lane and across the green, sprinkling the way with shiny treats. She only looked around her properly when we stopped, two in front and two behind, pressing close, but she still kept chewing, jaw flapping and clicking as she ricocheted between us.

Tattletale, we said. Stinking, slimy tattletail. That rattletail of yours needs a proper wash. We held our noses and danced around her, waving hands in front of our offended faces. We put on the yellow gloves taken from our mothers' sinks, stroking the stolen squeak of rubber up our arms and snapping the ends like nurses in a drama. Tattletale hissed and hunched, spinning loose and jerking back as we tugged the elastic of her shorts and twirled her, swung her, stripped her down. Then, naked, she crouched at our feet and began to writhe.

Look at the tattletale; that spike, that stab of rattletail. The whip of muscle in its rippled sleeve of skin birthing from her spine, arching over the cobbles of her back and then springing round. A hum, a buzz, a shriek of sound as she pivots to control it, twitching the maraca tip, thrashing it across our faces so they stream scarlet and our marigold hands rush upwards and bloom with poppies.

The tattletale all rattletail, a slither now, a weave and dance. Grin wide enough to swallow us whole, teeth sharp and curved as rusted hooks. We turn to run, a push and shove of skirts and screams, a snap of girls, ankles swept by rattle tail. And suddenly we're rabbit-still, rabbit-fascinated by the rise and wriggle, the looming slink. A huddle beneath her flickering kiss, hearts scurrying in our furry chests.

BENEATH THE SKIN

You walk to the end of the garden carrying the meat. Raw, as he wants it, oozing blood that drips from your fist in a muddy string of garnet chips. The gravelled path hurts your bare feet, reopening just-healed cuts, and you shiver in the frosted dark, wishing for a blanket to wrap yourself in. Wishing for a blanket to cloak the gleam of your naked back and legs. You still belong to the house more than the undergrowth but every step re-wilds you.

If any of the neighbours looked out of their window now they'd think you were a ghost, so pale and incongruous under the sharp midnight moon. They'd rub their eyes and turn away from the night, back to the glow of their lamps, their soft beds. The next time they saw you, trapped inside the smooth lines of your blouse and skirt, they'd have forgotten that creamy glimpse of buttock swell cradling the tips of your unbound hair.

You can smell your body's sweat, heavier than the compost tang of the meat you hold. Beyond the garden shed, he can smell it too. You hear him shift as he waits and you slow until you're barely moving, playing with him, daring him to leave his shadowed corner and meet you in the open. This is your moment of power and he lets you indulge it. He knows you won't turn and leave him. You never have.

The gravel gives way to mud and then you are with him in

the deep dark behind the shed. If you look down, you can't see your body. Your palm in front of your face is a memory. You could almost not exist. What you do now and here doesn't matter.

You hold the meat out with delicate courtesy and he tears it from you. A tooth snags the skin of your hand, tunnelling a shallow wound from wrist to knuckle that you know will become infected if you don't clean it properly. His bites harden your glands to rocks and you've learnt never to run out of anti-septic potions.

His meal is gone in noisy seconds. You could have brought more. One piece of meat in each fist at least, it wasn't as if you didn't have a freezer full of flesh, but you like his hunger too much. You just don't admit that to yourself.

He takes your hand into his mouth, gently now, and sucks the blood from it, nibbling at the tiny scraps of meat trapped under your long nails. His tongue is rough and his breath a thick soup of rot and saliva. You stay still and calm, not wanting to excite him into snapping. His jaw muscles are knotty with restraint. When he's licked you clean, he moves away and works the ground for stray morsels that may have fallen, teasing the earth with yellowed claws. You wrap your arms around your ribs and wait.

And then he finishes his search and returns to you, as he always does. His warmth presses against your thighs and rises up over your stomach as he covers you. He pushes on your shoulders until you crumple beneath the weight of him and then he turns you with fierce familiar speed so that you are on your hands and knees, face pressed into the ivy-drifts along the side of the shed. You have a moment to feel the sting of stones against your palms and shins, hear the startled shift of small life tucked deep in the dark beyond the leaves. You move your head to the side, but you don't speak.

The sex undoes your human self, makes a monster of you. It's a mating without sentiment or intimacy, an exquisite thrusting. You arch and hiss against him, spit and claw when he finally withdraws and releases his grip on the hackles you imagine spiked on the back of your neck.

He rises and becomes wary, circling around you to reach the torn fence and the wood beyond your garden. He doesn't look back as you stand and limp to the narrow path and the moonlit walk back to your home. This is always how it ends. You may pause to listen to the fading sound of him thrashing through the trees, and sometimes you lay curled on the ground for hours, but he never returns.

As you stand in the shower afterwards, watching the slide of semen and mud pool around your feet, you think of the bargain struck those years ago. Your agreement to feed him in all the ways you can, to keep your community safe. The flimsiness of their doors and windows, the tender chubbiness of their children. And only you to stand as guard and protector, netting their nightmare and taming it, facing the monster so that they don't have to.

You don't think about why you never feed him quite enough. You don't think about how weary he seems when he has eaten, how worn and thin his thighs against yours are, how if you turned and walked away you doubt he'd pursue you.

As you dry yourself and inspect your bruises, smooth plasters over the cuts and scrapes, you're already calculating how long that single wedge of meat can sustain him and when he will return. The bargain struck those years ago has become something else. But you don't think about that.

You go to bed and stretch the ache from your limbs and touch your fingers to the soreness between your thighs. Abrasions that tug pleasure from you in jerks and shocks. You roll away from the slack warmth of your husband, pull the sheets up to your chin, and then turn onto your side and sleep through the night until morning.

ROOTLESS

By the sixth day I was more pain than person; unplugging myself, piece by piece, from the rituals and routines that tied me to the rest of my race. I arched and roared, swiped palms like paws across my cheeks. But still I wouldn't let them take it.

I slept in dull bursts of drunken exhaustion, woke too soon with the grainy aftertaste of gin trapped sour between my swollen gums and tongue. And there was always a moment of calm, a soft waiting, that made the rushed return of ache almost worth it, just to experience a world without it.

At the dentist's surgery I listened to lectures on sepsis and tried not to make eye contact with the tooth fairy standing in the corner of the room. This fairy was a stranger to me, their attempt at a different tactic. His beauty was distracting, his trousers clung, and he ran long fingers over his lips while he tried to menace me with his smile. I chewed down hard on the screaming tooth and swallowed agony with gratitude, squeezing my eyes tight shut before my limbs got lazy with want and my hand in his, my hands in my mouth, became a certainty.

They wanted this one so much. If I could have trusted my dentist to rip it from my jaw and pass it straight over, or trusted myself to stay sharp enough to snatch it from his pliers and swallow it down even while I bled and reeled in the chair, I could have let the pain be over. But the tooth fairy, whichever tooth fairy would be assigned to lean against his arm while he braced himself for the unrooting of my rotting wisdom, would have been waiting eagerly, quicker and stronger than me. They wanted this one so much.

My greedy child self had valued the shine of coins over the lesser gleam of milk tooth, had slipped each bitten memory thoughtlessly beneath my pillow at night and dreamed of boiled sweets and rag dolls. Once money has changed hands just once the forever deal is struck. Your teeth become theirs when they leave your mouth. Always, all of them.

As the years loosened more teeth the coins became more tarnished, the visits to the dentist more frequent. Cavities hollowed warrens through my canines; molars became brittle shells of enamel and pulp. My wisdom teeth bookended decay, but even while their lesser companions rioted through abscess and then absence they clung to my jaw. And that's when I first saw the tooth fairies.

They came at night while I slept, laden with a pot of treacle so weighty it took three of them to carry it to my bedside. They guided my fingers into the dense sweetness and then into my mouth, held my head and hushed me tenderly when I half woke and tried to turn away. The mornings became sticky and dizzy, my appetite trailing behind the clock until my blood crashed into the ebb of night-time feasting and I'd reach for something sweet to lift me again. Still my final teeth, in their wisdom, remained hard and strong.

The fairies scattered piles of ancient, rusted coins on my pillow which stamped brown patterns onto cotton and skin. I stacked them on the windowsill, unspent. They seduced me with glittering jewels, left rubies by my dinner plate and sapphires in my shoes. They danced with me when I came home from work crying, spun me from room to room so that I could almost believe I was made from silk or feathers. I began to stay out later, turn the radio up louder, keep my arms closed around my body, my mouth a tight thin line, my lips stern sentries.

So the tooth fairies stripped themselves of their costumes and showed the bone beneath the sparkle-mask. They took me from my home and led me to an orchard. A spiral maze of trees, a maze to lose yourself in, uncurled towards forever. Fruit of every kind lay rotting on the ground, spilled from baskets and oozed from juice presses. Fairies filled tankards and drank, raised glasses to each other and cheered.

I stepped close to one of the trees, a greengage plump with fruit, and reached a hand to stroke a branch. The bark was warm and soft as wrinkled flesh. It shivered beneath my palm. I looked up into its canopy and saw an old woman perched on the highest branch, clinging to the trunk. She opened her mouth wide when she saw me, whether to call out or scream I wasn't sure, and I saw the raw pink ridges of her gums, her wagging tongue.

My fairy escort pointed out the trays of teeth waiting to be planted, the earthy peaks and troughs sprouting seedlings. He took my arm and walked me between ancient plum trees, bowed and aching with fruit. He plucked lemons from waist high striplings and offered them with a flourish and a leer. I clasped my hands together and walked this living graveyard.

With a tug to my wrist, he brought me to a halt beside a sweep of apple trees and lifted my chin. High above me a small girl climbed along a branch and wrapped her thighs around it, hanging upside down. Her T-shirt slithered up to her chin, exposing her grubby vest. She was so much thinner than I ever remembered myself to be. So much paler. Across her face something thread-thin and glistening unravelled, spooling from her mouth like a vein, like an artery. It twisted the length of her body and disappeared into the tree's warm bark. We stared at each other for a while and then she righted herself and turned away. I called to her to jump down to me, into my arms, but she didn't respond.

'You were a playful little thing when you lost your first teeth,' the fairy said. 'Always inventing games and larking around. Here, drink this. Raise a glass to the memories.' He tried to give me a crystal tumbler rich and thick with apple juice, but I kept my lips and fingers knotted together, shook my head. He shrugged and pointed to the next tree. 'Less fun by this age and your first proper extraction,' he said. 'But we still enjoy the taste of your teenage melodramas.'

My young self kept her back to me, hunched over on a low branch, her ankle swinging inches above my head. She stared at the horizon as if she were alone in the world. I watched her for a moment, but she didn't move. Past her, in the other trees around us, I peered back at myself through vivid green foliage or shifted in sun splashes as I clambered from branch to branch: dead-eyed and drained, attached by the umbilical thread that strung me to my tree and fed its roots with my essence. Every time I'd given them a tooth, they'd planted it and taken that version of me. I'd sold myself over and over, for a handful of pennies.

A fairy ambled past, cherry juice slick and scarlet across his smile. He twirled an index finger in the air and hummed tune-lessly. 'The feller from that tree was an experienced musician by the time we got his wisdom,' my companion said. 'They're the teeth we like best; such big roots. Such complex experiences. There's so much to taste.'

He cupped his palm across my cheek and my own teeth pulsed in rhythm to his blood surge. I felt them tug in their sockets, straining for him. He circled my flesh with his and smiled. 'Life's flat here for us, without the entertainment you all give us. We're empty creatures, in essence.'

He spun me into his arms. 'Let me bargain with you,' he whispered, breathing heat against my leaping jugular. 'Give me three of the four teeth you have left and I will release three of your selves. Set them free to rot down into the mulch they could have been if it weren't for your past greed. A fair exchange. We'll chop down three trees but plant just one more.'

We kissed to seal the pact. I felt no pain as his tongue became a knife inside my mouth; I didn't want it to end. When he released me his grin was wet and crimson. He spat my teeth into a handkerchief, folding the fine linen into a pouch and shaking it so that it rattled. I thought of dice shaken in a fist at the start of a game. I hoped he'd kiss me again, but he bowed and called for someone to take me home, strode away without a backward glance.

During that final episode of toothache, after the dentist had sent me away, when the world had thinned to one long howl of agony and the bones of my skull brittled to glass, I finally gave in on the ninth day and let them take what they wanted. The transaction was brief, almost dismissive. Now that they had the thing they'd coveted so much they stopped their seductions.

'What will happen to me now that you have them all?' I asked. 'Will my life halt here, when you plant the last tooth there?'

They laughed and shrugged and threw me a handful of chipped and dirty coins before leaving. 'Thank you for the memories,' one of them said as he closed the door.

I curled up on the floor beneath my window, emptied and rootless, and thought of those three versions of myself that I'd freed with the bargain I'd made. I wondered whether they'd screamed when the axe sliced into them, whether they'd flowed back into their roots and faded away into the earth or been thrown from the topmost branches when the tree came down.

I wondered what fruit my final tooth would yield.

ACKNOWLEDGEMENTS

My thanks go to those journals and anthologies where some of the stories in this collection first appeared: *The Ghastling Books 1, 4 and 6*; *Ambit 227*; *Wales Arts Review*; *The Lonely Crowd Issue 3*; *Black Static #61*; *Syntax and Salt*; *Horla*; *The Dark Magazine*; *A Flock of Shadows*; *A Fiction Map of Wales*; *Memento Mori*; *By the Light of the Moon*; *Secondary Character and Other Stories*; *The Open Page*; *Shadows & Tall Trees Volume 8*.

'Wich' won first place in the Allingham Festival's short story competition.

'Sleep' was selected to appear in *The Best Horror of the Year Volume 11*.

'Maria's Silence' was shortlisted for the International Rubery Award short story competition.

I would like to express gratitude to Llenyddiaeth Cymru/Literature Wales for the writing bursary in 2014 that enabled me to take valuable time to work on some of these stories. Huge thanks, too, to Tartarus Press, who first published this collection in 2018 in a limited-edition collectable hardback.

Rich Davies, Gill Griffiths and all at Parthian – thank you! Rob, the cover is perfect. Charlotte – first reader and dear friend, thank you for your constant support. Thank you to Si for the love and for accepting that the cats come first, always.

Lastly, thanks to all those people who have taken the time to read my words.

PARTHIAN   Fiction

Angels of Cairo
GARY RAYMOND
ISBN 978-1-913640-28-6
£9 • Paperback
'A book full of wisdom
and wit and warmth...'
– Stephen Gregory

Easy Meat
RACHEL TREZISE
ISBN 978-1-912681-24-2
£9 • Paperback
'*Easy Meat* feels like a monumental
achievement. A one-sitting page-
turner that gives voice to the
voiceless.'
– *The National*

The Scrapbook
CARLY HOLMES
ISBN 978-1-910409-83-1
£8.99 • Paperback
'An impressive debut novel from an
extremely talented writer.'
– *Wales Arts Review*

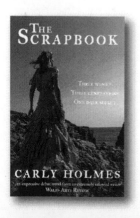